BROOD OF VIPERS

MAGGIE CLAIRE

World Castle Publishing, LLC
Pensacola, Florida
Copyright © Maggie Claire 2021
Paperback ISBN: 9781955086165
eBook ISBN: 9781955086172
First Edition World Castle Publishing, LLC, May 18, 2021
http://www.worldcastlepublishing.com
Licensing Notes
Cover: Karen Fuller
Editor: Maxine Bringenberg

This book is dedicated to Diane Smith. Thank you
for always supporting my work.
You are greatly missed.

PRELUDE
(From Pack of Wolves)

"On your feet," the frigid as a snowstorm voice of the Déchets' guard demands as he rattles the lock of a grimy cell deep in the palace's dungeons. "You have a visitor."

A lithe form shifts in the darkness, a mass of frizzy dark hair covering her face. "Who seeks me now after all this time?"

"You could have spent your days by my side had you chosen to share your memories with me," a muffled voice replies as Alaric wipes his nose with a perfumed handkerchief to ward off the pungent odor of human waste and death. "I feel no sympathy for you, Helena."

"Majesty." The woman scorns the word, her piercing eyes glaring at the regal intruder. "Have you come for that again? My answer is unchanged."

"You always were the most stubborn girl I had ever seen. But no, I have come to make a deal with you instead." The king steps into the cell, ignoring the squelching of his shoes as he crosses into the dirt and muck. "A chance at freedom, at life outside this dungeon. After all this time, I am sure you miss the sunlight." He stays a safe distance from the woman, just out of her arm's reach as he continues. "Don't you miss the feel of the fresh air on your face? Don't you long to use your Windwalker abilities once more?"

"What's the catch?" Helena mutters as her fingers inch along the stone floor, desperately seeking a sharp knife. Even a rusty piece of the horrid iron bars would work—it would burn her skin to touch it, but pain would be worth it if she could jab out the king's eye. No anguish could be worse than anything she's already endured.

"I'll send you and one of my guards over the Devil's Spine. My border guards report that a Windwalker was seen deep in these enemy lands using enough power to be witnessed for many miles. Yet no one of that strength has gone missing from Déchets in a long time."

"Why me?" Helena asks, trying not to let the snarl of hatred loose in her throat.

"You know the land, the people, and their ways. And it will give you a chance to prove your usefulness once more. Fail, and you die. Refuse to go, and you'll die slowly. The choice is up to you."

With immense effort and a curse as her stiffened limbs break free from their long underuse, Helena crawls up to stand by the cell door. Her body shows its bones under a thin coating of scarred skin, barely more than a walking skeleton. "You give me no choice, Highness; I will obey."

CHAPTER 1

"Oh, Helena. There is always a choice to be made. You should know that better than anyone," Alaric chuckles as he guides the prisoner's frail body out of the cell, his fingers hooked around her thin shoulders as she slinks toward freedom. He grips her tightly to remind her that he can drag her right back into that hellish cell if he chooses, discarding her like the trash he considers her to be. "And aren't you the least bit curious? Another rogue Windwalker living in secret in that horrible land. Don't you wonder if it is someone you might know? Someone from your past?" He leans close to her ear, brushing her oily, matted hair out of the way so she can feel his breath against her skin. "Think of it! Freedom, using your powers again, sating your curiosity about this traitor…it's all within your grasp. Help me find the Windwalker, Helena."

"I'm not surprised at all, Alaric. Surely I wasn't the only one who grew bored of living under your rule," Helena retorts, wincing and wheezing as the king's elbow slams into her ribs. The blow feels like it loosened her vertebrae, causing them to shift and grind against each other as she doubles over to catch her breath. When she can speak once more, Helena hisses with hysterical laughter, "Really not the best way to get me to help you, Alaric."

"Stupid girl," Alaric snarls into her ear, dragging her back toward the cell. "I can rescind my offer of freedom just as easily as it was given. There are plenty of other wastrels in this place that would kill for the chance to see the sunlight again!" Alaric pauses in front of the cell opposite the one Helena has called home for the last fifteen years. He shoves her hard against the bars, uncaring as her skin sizzles where it touches the metal. "Feel that?" he taunts, lifting one hand to catch her thin arm, pressing its entire length up against the iron.

"Let me go!" Helena shrieks, struggling against the king's hold. "I'm burning! Stop it!"

"You were always so strong," Alaric whispers, leaning forward to sniff the air around her arm, relishing the scent of scorched flesh. "All that magic inside you yearns to be used, Helena." Grimy fingers from the cell's occupants brush and claw at her skin, pawing at her frail body through the bars. Gleaming, wicked eyes rake their stares over her skin, murmuring and whispering their dark promises and demands.

"Get off me!" Helena growls, cringing away from the unwanted touches, turning her hateful, wild gaze on the king.

"Maybe I'll throw you into this cell for a change of scenery. What do you think, boys?" Alaric announces, and immediately the prisoners holler and praise their glorious, merciful king. "What do you say, Helena? Is that what you want?"

Helena groans in defeat, dropping her head as she whispers, "No, Your Highness." As much as she may hate this man, the alternative offered by him is a far worse fate. "I would be pleased to accept your offer of freedom, Your Highness." Each word burns like bile on her tongue.

It cannot be this simple, Helena warns herself, turning a skeptical glance toward Alaric as he pulls her out of the clutches of the prisoners. He says nothing else as he urges her to move, her knees buckling under the weight of her fears. *After all these years, there's got to be more to his plan than just sending me over to Cassè as a spy. He must be desperate; that's the only reason he would come for me.* That thought brings a tiny, rebellious smile to her lips.

Howls of screaming prisoners assault them as they leave,

mostly insults aimed at the king. Helena lowers her head as she moves toward the exit, forcing herself to keep her eyes away from the cells. A shiver dances over her shoulders as she steps between the guards that line this part of the prison's walls. *The worst prisoners are kept here, close to the exit,* she recalls, wincing as a burly guard on her right bangs his sword through the cell closest to him, slicing at the occupant to shut his mouth.

It had taken Helena a couple of years to figure out why Alaric put the worst offenders in this part of the prison. *Why not house them deep in the depths of this place, where no light or fresh air can be found?* With nothing more important to do, she'd spent the greater part of her days trying to understand the king's reasoning, to no avail. It wasn't until one of the prisoners from the first cells was drug down into the heart of the prison and housed beside her that everything made sense.

She never knew that young man's name. By the time the guards had plopped him into the cell, he was screaming and groaning unintelligibly. "What's going on?" she demanded, risking the guards' wrath as the prisoner's haunting cries burrowed into her mind. "What's wrong with him?"

"Gouged out his own eyes. Couldn't stand to face another day glimpsing freedom, knowing he'd never stand unshackled in fresh air again," the guard replied grimly, shaking his head as he sighed. "The king's ordered no treatment to be given to him. Might be days, might be weeks, but eventually, he will die. Going to be a long, horrible thing to endure until it's done, Helena." The guard had the wherewithal to look guilty and shaken by the experience, his face the color of a birch tree's bark.

Freedom. The word rang in the air like the peal of a bell. *The worst criminals are close to the exit, where they are constantly reminded of the lives they could be living. Fresh food on the guards' plates, fine ale and camaraderie, cool breezes when the doors open… yes, that would be a constant, terrible way to torture the minds and hearts of us all.* Helena looked around her darkened cell with a fleeting sense of gratitude. *At least here in this gross, unlit hole, I can allow myself to forget the things I'm missing. I can let the darkness swallow me and make me a forgotten memory in the lives of those I once loved. Not that there is anyone out there on either side of the Devil's Spine who cares anyway.*

It had taken the young man eight days to succumb to his injuries, and by the last day, Helena's nerves were raw from the sounds of his retching and incoherent, fever-driven outbursts. Eight long days for the stink of rot and infection to permeate the cells. Helena's nose wrinkles at the memory. *I can still smell his death.* Her fingers drift up toward her shaggy mane, rubbing the oily strands before bringing them close to her nose. *I don't know if I'll ever be able to remove that awful odor from his demise. It stains me even now, four years later.*

As Helena and Alaric make the last turn toward the outer doors of the prison, Helena notices a small circle of four other offenders waiting for their approach. Each one of the prisoners is still bound, the shadow of a guard towering behind them. Before Helena can ask any questions, Alaric wordlessly shoves her into the circle's remaining empty space. A palace guard immediately falls in line at her back.

"A minor detail I neglected to mention, dear Helena, is that your freedom is not a guarantee." Alaric drawls, a cruel smile upturning his lips as what little color is left in her cheeks slowly drains away. Sauntering around the circle of captives, Alaric's face beams as he announces, "You are five of the most notorious traitors of Déchets. Normally you would rot in my cells until your bones crumbled to dust. However, I am a gracious, merciful king. And I am offering you a chance to earn your freedom by tracking down an unknown Windwalker that will take your ranks in my prisons." Murmurs arise from the other four prisoners; whoever pulled them from their cells must not have shared the king's plan. Alaric shifts, changing the direction of his path as he continues his explanation. "However, before I let you go, you must prove yourself to be worthy of such a gift. You will be given a week to heal and train with your guards. Then you will run the tunnel."

Outraged cries ricochet off the close walls at the mention

of Déchets most infamous, mysterious torture. No one who runs the tunnel has ever lived long enough to speak of what horrors it holds. None who have attempted it have ever survived. Fear dances along Helena's nerves, and she tries to disguise the quiver of her lip by yawning as though she is bored. "How does running the tunnel accomplish anything?" Her words sound shrill to her ears, her voice raspy from years of silence. "Are you so devoid of sport that you've come here to handpick us for death? Is this your strange way of ensuring our speedy execution?"

Alaric's iron gauntlet cracks hard against Helena's mouth, causing blood to burst from her bottom lip. She stumbles back into the guard behind her. She finds no comfort against his hard chest. Instead, the guard shoves her back into her place in the circle. The king continues laying out his expectations, never stopping to answer her question. "Whoever completes the tunnel proves themselves to be strong enough to be my emissary into Cassé. You track down and bring that traitor to me, and you earn your freedom. Simple as that."

Whimpers break out among the four other criminals, some in delight and others in terror. Alaric's eyes flash with excitement, certain he's baited the trap well enough that they will comply. After all, who could resist the potential reward of their freedom? Alaric's satisfied smile reminds Helena of a fat housecat toying with five scrawny mice, more interested in killing the frightened rodents for cruel amusement rather than food.

Helena takes a moment to examine each of the other prisoners, sizing up her competition while she stands close to them. The first is a burly, broad shouldered man named Bryn. He wears a gross, dirty patch over his left eye, but his shoulders are still broad and muscular. It appears he's kept up with his workout routine, finding ways to maintain his strength even from the depths of his cell. She faintly recalls Bryn's transgressions against the court—the destruction of a local tavern that was a favorite among the guards. It was the guards' retaliation to take one of his eyes. Helena had never understood why Bryn had earned a long stay in the prisons for such a thing, but his time on the inside had not managed to break his defiant spirit. Bryn stares hatefully at Alaric, harsh unspoken curses screaming from his hateful gaze.

The second, a young girl, looks like she can barely stand up straight, her mousy brown hair draping over her face. Whatever her crime, it must have been after Helena had earned her cell. *She looks to be barely fifteen!* Helena's gut clenches at the thought of a child locked away in this place. *What could she possibly have done to deserve this fate?* The girl peeks through the curtain of her hair, her burnished caramel eyes landing squarely on Helena's outraged face. She seems to shrink into herself under Helena's scrutiny, and Helena forces herself to inspect the rest of the prisoners, hoping to ease the girl's fear.

The third is a notorious thief by the name of Ellis. Helena remembers him well; she'd watched his trial and sentencing, marveling at his flippant, borderline defiant personality. He'd been caught sneaking out of a princess's chambers with her tiara when he was only seven years old. He smiled all through his trial, and he practically skipped toward the prison guards, waving and blowing kisses in the air to all who watched him disappear. Looking at him now, Helena estimates his age to be around eighteen. His rail thin body and tired eyes are the only signs of prison life. Catching Helena's eye, he smiles and winks, proving his spirit remains unbroken.

The last is another child, barely thirteen years old and hardly fit for such a task. His voice wavers as he addresses the king. "But no one's ever survived the tunnel, Your Majesty. So how can one of us do it?"

Helena holds her breath, awed by the child's bravery. She might be crazy enough to endure the punishments for speaking out of turn, but she had not expected a boy to follow suit. Watching Alaric's eyes cut in the direction of the boy, Helena wishes she could grab the child and shield him. *He shouldn't be in a place like this! What could the boy have done that was so wrong?* Her hands rattle the chains around her wrists as she instinctively reaches for him. But when her feet lurch forward, the guard behind her drags his hands across her waist, securing her in place before she can offer aid to the child.

"Well, just because nobody's done it before doesn't mean you can't survive the tunnel! And I'd say that whichever one of you can accomplish it will prove to be worthy, wouldn't you?" the king responds as he kicks the boy's knees out from under him. He moans as they crack against the tiles, tears pouring from his pain widened eyes. "And if the tunnel kills you — well, that frees up a cell for another traitor, doesn't it? Now, speak out of turn again, and I will not let the healers work on you. Think you'll survive the tunnel without their aid?" He ignores the boy's shudders as he addresses the group once more. "The guard behind you is your trainer. They will oversee your healing and progress until next we meet." The sharp strikes of Alaric's boots clatter on the stones as he strides to the exit. "Oh, and Helena, I chose your guard especially because I know you and he have such a good history. Enjoy your reunion, however short it may be." He laughs to himself as the steel outer door screeches on its hinges.

Helena waits while the other prisoners and guards disperse to the infirmaries and kitchens. She can barely force her breath from her lungs as she listens to the sounds around her. *Surely Alaric wouldn't be that cruel?* Even as she thinks the question, she scolds herself for being naïve. *What am I saying? That bastard thrives on twisting needles of guilt, regret, and agony into the hearts of his victims. He practically lives on suffering more than other food and drink.*

"Turn around," a heartbreakingly familiar voice commands as calloused fingers brush her elbow.

A flood of memories spring to life as Helena flinches from the innocent touch. *I am going to die,* she declares to herself, facing the man who had once been the center of her world. *He loved me so much, and I betrayed him. And the way I left him behind…. If the tunnel doesn't kill me, seven days with Ithel certainly will.* Helena shuffles in place, unable to raise her head and meet the guard's eye. Her heart thrashes wildly in its ribbed cage, the force so strong it causes her shoulders to quake. "I am so sorry, Ithel. I never —"

"Save your apologies," Ithel growls as his fists clench at his sides. "We have seven days to get you ready before the tunnel." He guides Helena toward a hidden exit on the left side of the stone walls, completely enshrouded in shadows. A mirthless chuckle erupts from Ithel when Helena stubbornly keeps her eyes focused on his shoes. "If we survive this week, then we will talk about the past."

"What do you mean if *we* survive?" Helena's eyes snap up to inspect Ithel's furious expression, flinching as she notices all the subtle changes from their years apart — a small scar over his upper lip and a longer, wicked counterpart through one eyebrow. His icy eyes are now haloed by sun wrinkles, giving his already angry countenance a cold, assessing squint. He keeps his hair closely cropped to his scalp now, but Helena remembers how it used to fall to his shoulders, catching the sunlight in its auburn waves. And his mouth, which used to be constantly on the verge of a smile, now bears deep frown and worry lines.

If Ithel notices her scrutiny, he does not react as he answers her question, confirming Helena's deepest fears. "If our prisoner dies, so does his or her guard. I think it was the king's way of keeping the guards invested in his plan." He jerks Helena through a side corridor to the closest infirmary, his rough hands like sandpaper on her fragile skin. "Everything has turned into some sick form of entertainment for the king and his court. People kill each other in the streets out of greed and sport. Death and meaningless destruction are a daily part of our lives. That's what has become of Déchets while you have been languishing in the dungeons, Helena," Ithel barks as he shoves her toward the open arms of the awaiting medics. "Now do what they tell you. You look like hell."

The bright lights nearly blind Helena as tentative fingers

brush the open, unhealed wounds that crisscross around her wrists and ankles. The medics crowd around her, whispering to each other as their insistent fingers poke and prod her flesh. *I feel like a side show of the circus rather than a prison patient.* The snide thought keeps Helena from hyperventilating at the proximity of so many new faces after years of isolation. *Step back,* she longs to command as another medic's dark eyes loom on her left. *I crave space and open air. Just let me have a moment's peace!*

"Helena," they all suddenly whisper at the same time, addressing her as though they speak with one voice. "Use our strengths to heal yourself." They force their energies into her, assaulting her body even as they speed her recovery. By keeping their mental connections one-sided, Helena has no choice but to obey and endure their ministrations. The naming bonds are an invasion that Helena has always abhorred. Some of the medics grow faint and drop to the floor as the process continues, and more step out of the shadows to replace them.

It feels like hours before the barrage of energy stops pulsing over Helena's body. Now her skin bears thin scars and fading, yellowed bruises, her hair no longer filled with lice and crawling bugs. Her eyes hold no brightness from fever and infection. Even her figure has filled out to healthier proportions, and for the first time in years, her stomach churns in preparation of food. For so long, she has been so numb to hunger that the sounds from her growling stomach are threatening to her ears. She catches her reflection in a mirror, running her fingers along her full lips once more. No signs of dehydration, no flaky, cracked skin. The alterations are so striking that it brings fresh tears to Helena's eyes.

Ithel waits in the corner of the room, his cool eyes never missing any detail even as he appears bored by the scene. "Food over here," he announces with a yawn, dropping his gaze to his bowl immediately after he finishes speaking.

Helena crouches over the nearest nurse, her hand brushing hair from her cold forehead. "She's dead!" Staring at the other medics, she wails, "They all are dead! But why? Why would they do this? Why didn't they stop sending me their energies before they drained themselves dry?" Helena's skin grows clammy, her stomach lurching as it floods with guilt. *They killed themselves for me! They are dead because of me!*

"They were slaves, Helena, not doctors and nurses. Part of the king's rule has been reinstituting slavery. He keeps slaves to serve in his house, and he has his magicians spell them to give up their life forces when he commands it." Ithel slides a bowl of something warm and steaming toward her, not bothering to look and see if she takes it. "They knew they were going to die, Helena. Don't feel guilty. You couldn't have stopped it even if you'd known."

Helena's hands quiver as she holds the bowl, now repulsed by her need to eat. "I'm sorry for them. Truly."

"Just eat, Helena," Ithel demands gruffly, turning his cold, furious stare on her until Helena's hand slinks toward a spoon.

Helena barely takes a sip of the stew and immediately regrets it. The lukewarm, oily liquid tastes like ash when she finally swallows. Choking, Helena waves off her guard's assistance, tears streaming down her cheeks. "I...I didn't ask for this, Ithel. And I don't think I can eat anything right now." *Not so soon after witnessing all this death and destruction.*

"Don't let their deaths stop you from gathering your strength," Ithel admonishes, tossing a crusty of bread at her elbow. "Finish this bowl, then get another helping of soup and at least two more pieces of bread. You're going to need it." When Helena hesitates, Ithel growls, "Or do I need to force your mouth open and pour that soup down your throat myself?"

Reluctantly, Helena picks up her spoon once more. "What were their names?" she whispers as she eats, unable to savor her first real meal in years. The bread feels like putty in her mouth, and when Helena swallows, she fears it will spackle her throat shut. Gasping, she reaches for a glass of water, wishing instead that she could wash away the deaths that stain her memory. *I wonder if I went back to my cell if I just shut myself back into that darkness and contented myself with the idea of rotting away down there — would Alaric allow it? Or would he kill me? Would he come after Ithel?* It is the thought of causing Ithel any more pain than she already had that stops Helena's feet from scurrying back toward the dungeons.

"I have no idea what their names were, Helena," Ithel mutters as he chews, stirring his soup and avoiding her gaze.

"Liar," Helena challenges, her hands shaking as shock finally begins to wear off. Her mind still cannot register that her skin is no longer aching from dryness or splitting and oozing in an effort to provide its own moisture and relief. "Tell me their names, Ithel; I know that you know them. You always took time to learn people's names, even among the low-born. It was the first thing I loved about you."

A cup slams onto the table, making Helena's mouth go dry. "Let's not pretend you ever gave a damn about me. Not after everything you did." Ithel picks up their bowls, carrying them to a wash basin and ignoring the fact that Helena still has her spoon. "Rest here on one of the cots. No one will disturb you. There are extra robes in the cabinets so you can change clothes. I will find you later this afternoon to begin training. Do not leave this room under any circumstances."

"What about them?" Helena points to where the bodies should be, but only a huge pile of sand remains. "Well, can I at least go out to the balcony?"

Ithel doesn't turn around as he calls back. "No. Stay indoors and in this infirmary. If you leave, I will know, and I will immediately throw you back into the prison myself. I don't care what the king would do to me, so don't think you can browbeat me into submission. Do not test me, Helena. Much has changed during your prison stay. Including me."

Only once Ithel is gone does Helena chance a wistful glance outside. The palace is still as lavish as she remembers, a stunning marble creation etched into the side of a mountain. A shining city on the hill; an unparalleled gem of Déchets. The market towns bustle with activity as people buy and sell things they do not even need. So very different from Cassé, where people starve and struggle on a daily basis.

Helena's stomach grows heavy with her meal. *How can I face these next seven days?* Ithel, her former lover, the man she'd betrayed so many years ago. Then the tunnel. *How can I hope to survive? And if by bittersweet mercy I do win this challenge, how can I return to Cassé? How can I face all those people I failed?* Her mind races with hopeless possibilities even as her body begins to fall into an exhausted sleep.

***

"They are selling our people to Déchets as slaves?" I shriek as Fox, Cyrus, and the rest of my former house relay the horrors of their encampment with Wolf to me, Enomena, and Drake. We'd all shared our true names, but I still felt comfortable using the house names with Bittern, Grouse, and Goldeneye. It gave me some sense of normalcy in this chaos, a reference point to ground my mind. *Hard to believe I might ever look back on the House of Vultures and be anything but repulsed by it,* I murmur to Siri through our bond, but she does not respond.

"I got the impression that this is a regular agreement he's made with the border guards." Cyrus's voice breaks in as he adds another log to our campfire. The embers sizzle as they sink into the sand outside the Pith caverns. We had quickly returned to their safety after escaping Wolf's claws at the House of Piranhas. Traveling day and night, we made it back to the Pith in less than two weeks, stopping only when we found nameless unchosen. The Ddraigs searched through the people quickly, hoping to find their Cadogans. So far, at least half of the Ddraigs who fly with us still have not found their warriors.

I lean heavily against Siri's warm scales, seeking comfort in her proximity while the other Ddraigs curl up around their Cadogans in my company. The eyes of the crimson Ddraig are ever watchful on my right, and I try to ignore his unspoken threat. *We have far more important matters to attend to besides Ekard's impending mutiny,* Siri agrees, snorting in derision as she stares down Drake's Ddraig.

Ekard opens his wide maw, glowing embers of flame roiling to life in his jaws. It is a mildly veiled threat, a reminder of his intentions that is only stopped when Drake intervenes. "Enough, Ekard," he mumbles, but to my mind, the tone of his words is really saying, "Not today."

"No doubt they have some established trade agreements in place with Déchets. So, how do we stop them before another slave shipment is made?" I wonder, turning our focus back to Wolf's tyranny and traitorous actions. "I don't want any more of our people being sold off like chattel."

"But the enemy here is not a 'they' or 'them,' Iris; it's just my brother. Cane is the only one responsible for this atrocity," Cyrus snarls, turning an accusing glare at me. "And you put him in power, filling his head with all these fanciful ideas. He plays at becoming king because of you."

I cringe under the weight of his words, knowing they are true. *I have to clean up this mess. Take Wolf out of power before he even has a chance to complete the goal I set before him.* "We'll make this right," I mutter softly, but my feeble words crumble like brittle bones until even I do not believe we can find a solution to the problems I've created.

"How many Cadogans did he sell to Déchets, do you think?" Bittern wonders, her fiery temper rising to color her words with hateful rage. The sight of her unmasked face covered in henna-like Dadeni lines still unnerves me. It gives her a wild, savage appearance that is only intensified by the resentment that never leaves her expression. "That man of yours is a menace, Iris. Can you bear it if we kill him?"

"He's not her man!" Cyrus barks, a hand reaching toward his sword. "He's a monster, and Iris would never choose him." Cyrus steps in front of me, his eyes growing wild. "Especially not now. Right, Iris?"

"Well, you aren't my man either. So stop fighting my battles for me," I growl, standing up to challenge Cyrus's outburst, wrapping my fingers around his thin shoulder. But though my words are harsh, my touch is gentle. When Cyrus whirls around to face me, the ghosts I see swirling in his eyes confirm my suspicions: his mind fights against an enemy that no longer exists. *Can he perceive reality from the horrors of the past? Does he know he quarrels with Bittern and not the monsters that still plague his dreams?*

I can hear Siri's huff of disappointment rumble behind me, warm smoke curling around my limbs. *Cyrus may not be your man yet, Iris, but he will be one day.* Siri's constant reminders of her bond with Suryc—and the inevitable end result of my coupling with Cyrus—only rankle my nerves. My opinion of Cyrus has drastically changed over these last few months: he's not the sadistic asshole I once believed him to be. But I still cannot reconcile myself to the fate that Siri and Suryc have chosen for me.

Cyrus trembles under my touch, glaring at me as he prepares to argue his point. I can feel the tension in his bones like a coiled-up serpent ready to strike at its prey. *Me,* I shiver at the thought. *He's ready to attack me.* Cyrus's voice is a soft, deceptively calm growl. "Are you saying that after everything you've seen, after everything he's put you through, you would still choose Cane? How can you be so stupid, Iris?!"

"Enough of this!" Fox interrupts the furious retort building on my tongue, Cyrus's mouth hanging open as his hands begin to shake. "Your bickering solves nothing! And Bittern, we cannot dwell on the slaves already sold that might have belonged with the Ddraigs. There's nothing to be done to save them now that they are in Déchets."

"They're probably already dead." My head and heart ache with the memories of my last days at the House of Piranhas. *Cane was acting like a madman. I doomed him by sending him on this mission to become the first king of Cassè. And I genuinely thought it was the right thing to do. What kind of monster does all of this make me?* I have no answer as I expel a long sigh, closing my eyes in defeat. "I still can't believe—"

"He's a menace, Iris! You saw what he did to me! No

amount of wishing could possibly blot out his sins!" Cyrus bellows, his hands lashing out to clasp my throat.

"Cyrus!" I whimper, my fingers clutching at his hands, desperately trying to break into his vicelike grip. "Please!" The word is hoarse as a dull, burning ache blossoms to life in my chest. Tears turn my eyes glassy, blurring the sight of his furious, feral expression. "Cyrus," I plead one final time, forcing my body to stop fighting against his. Rather than claw at his hands, I run my fingers down his wrists in calming, circular patterns, willing him to see that I am not his enemy.

A second before I fear my world will black out, Cyrus's eyes clear. He drops his hold over me, and I fall hard into the sand, choking and coughing on the clean air now scorching through my bruised throat. Cyrus stares at his own hands a moment as if he cannot believe he almost choked the life out of my body. Then, before I can stop him, he runs over to the cavern's mouth, dropping into the waiting darkness with an uneasy grace.

"Are you okay?" Fox demands, his assessing eye carefully running over the bruises now purpling the skin under my chin.

"I wasn't going to say anything about Wolf," I croak, rubbing the tender spots just under my jaw, the accusing eyes of my peers boring holes into me. "I was going to say that I cannot believe we have made it this far without more losses than we've already taken." None of the others seem convinced by my words, and even Siri looks suspiciously at me. It's unnerving, and I feel my body tense under their scrutiny, my shoulders creeping up toward my ears.

"You saw only a portion of what he endured," Grouse pipes up, shifting her body to be closer to Goldeneye for comfort. "It was awful, Iris. I...I still hear his screams in my dreams. I don't think I'll ever stop hearing those tortured sounds."

"Did he tell you about the shape-shifting creature that Wolf bartered for with the border guards? Or that he was forced to travel in a coffin?" Bittern's voice is hollow as she recalls her days in Wolf's caravan. "He won't talk about what Wolf did with that monstrosity, but I know it changed him, Iris. Wolf broke some part of his spirit that we can't seem to repair."

My eyes are wet with tears, my breath lodging in my throat as I whisper, "He's never said a word to me about it." Still, I'd seen the damage through Siri and her connection to Suryc. I'd witnessed firsthand tortures Wolf inflicted on his brother, how his Vibría monster had stolen my face and used my mouth to fill Cyrus's mind with poison. How he'd watched me die over and over again and then witnessed me rising up in my death only to torture him further still. And I'd heard the gut-wrenching whimpers and moans of Cyrus's terrorized mind splintering. As Siri had shown me everything Suryc allowed her to know, I'd endured it all as if it was happening to me. "I don't know what to do to help him cope," I admit in a soft voice, wiping stray tears off my cheeks as they fall.

Why would he come to you for help at all, Iris? Why would he share anything so personal with you? What have you done to deserve his confidence? Siri challenges before slamming a wall between us through our mental bonds. My mind clouds with images of the sky while Siri broods and probably plots against me. I hate that she can shut me out so easily. Is she shutting me out because of our quarrels? Or is something else going on, some strange plan that I'm not allowed to see because she doesn't have faith in me?

I saved him, didn't I? Isn't that proof that I'm trustworthy? I long to scream, yet deep down, I know that is a weak response. The fact that I was the one who sent him back to his brother still plagues me with guilt.

"I should have done something to stop it," Fox confesses, staring into the flames as though they hold some unseen cure to ease his conscience.

"We should have tried to stand up to Wolf more," Grouse whispers, Bittern and Goldeneye bobbing their heads in silent agreement. "Though it might have cost our lives, we should have fought that bastard anyway. Or at the very least, we should have taken Cyrus and run away."

"We all were at fault for Cyrus's sufferings." My voice breaks as the weight of my sorrow drops heavily on my shoulders. "I failed him more than any of you."

"Fox, you did what was right in the end, standing against Wolf for the damned souls left to his mercy. The fact that you joined our ranks, prepared to die with us, says a lot about your character," Goldeneye exclaims, patting Fox's shoulder in comfort. "And Iris, I don't think Cyrus holds anyone but his brother responsible for the things he's suffered. He's struggling now, but he will remember the real culprit in time."

While I don't believe that's true—at least not in reference to me—I take some measure of false comfort from the hopeful condolence. We sit in silence for a few heartbeats, staring into the fire or up to the night sky, searching for truths or secrets that might solve our problems. "What are we going to do?" Grouse wonders forlornly, Goldeneye easing his hand into hers. She turns a small, sweet smile in his direction, and I watch Goldeneye's face light up in response.

Those two have been thick as thieves for as long as I can remember. I don't know why I never saw them as a couple before now. Watching them, it's as obvious as a rainbow against a storm cloud, and I find myself grateful that they are not Cadogans. It would've broken their hearts to have to split up because their Ddraigs had coupled with other mates.

Enomena leans over, sensing my deepening brood, and declares, "You envy their happiness, don't you?"

"No. I envy their freedom," I reply before I unwind my long legs and rise from the fireside. "Grouse, right now we're going to sleep," I announce, pushing all thoughts of Ddraigs and their idiotic coupling rules from my thoughts. "Tomorrow, Cyrus and I are going to teach the newcomers what little we know about being Cadogans. We are going to keep practicing and connecting with our Ddraigs. When it is time, we will meet our enemies on the battlefield, and we will fight for our rights to live free without the rule of Déchets or Wolf or anyone else."

Before any of them can respond, I scuff my shoe in the sand, dousing the fire to make my point.

Grouse and Goldeneye move off together, disappearing with the fire's smoky fingers. Bittern leans against her Ddraig, Nepsa, and prepares to bed down right where she sits. Enomena brushes my arm in silent consolation before sauntering over to Anemone and taking to the skies for a quick evening patrol.

"Anything to add, Drake?" I grit my teeth, desperately trying to fight against the rage that simmers in my heart every time I confront this man and his scarlet Ddraig. Whatever our problems, they stem from a place far deeper than our unorthodox meetings. It is a clash of personalities, an instinctual battle of wills and alpha controlling natures. No matter how hard I try to conceal my dislike, I cannot find the will to be cordial or understanding.

"I'm not your enemy," Drake reminds me in a flat voice. I suspect he doesn't even believe these words himself anymore. And judging by the way Ekard snorts and glares at me, I know not to trust him when he pretends to nod his hulking head in agreement.

"Just…for the sake of all the other Ddraigs and Cadogans, let's try to get along," I demand, clenching my jaw when I realize I can barely follow my own advice. "You and Ekard continue to keep the nomads in line, and I'll work with the rest. If we can at least appear to be united, we can keep the peace. Then, when the great battle that is coming has passed, we can figure out how to survive in whatever world is left over."

Drake's eyes glitter in the darkness, eerily like his Ddraig's as he hisses, "Just you worry about following your own plans, Iris. As long as you don't make a move against me, you will have my loyalty. But the minute you double-cross me, I'll let Ekard challenge Siri. And who do you really think will win that war?" He backs away from my place by the fireside, Ekard's teeth gleaming as his Cadogan's threat dissipates into the air.

I sulk to the edge of the cavern, watching the skies as

the evening chill overtakes the deserted lands. It is so very easy to fall into a proverbial pit of despair, ruminating on all the failures and bad judgments I have made in my half-hearted attempts to be a leader. Every poor choice I've made parades through my mind, accusing me, judging me, and illuminating all of my weaknesses. My arms prickle with goosebumps, and instantly, I regret my hasty choice to put out the fire. "Acting without thinking," I reproach myself, chafing my arms with my hands to warm them up. "That is probably my greatest flaw."

"I rather think your biggest problem is that you trust too easily," Cyrus whispers, stalking out of the shadows beside me. He removes his dark over-shirt, dropping it lightly onto my shoulders as he eases down to sit almost close enough that our arms touch. The wildfire of memories in his eyes has dulled. Rational thought replaces the fear and rage that surged through his blood earlier. "And when you trust someone, you give them your complete loyalty. Even long after they have failed to deserve such a gift."

I sigh as warmth envelops me, sliding my arms into the sleeves. "I never said I had just one problem area," I retort, hating the fact that my words are true.

"That could be said for us all," Cyrus muses, staring off into the stars overhead.

"Not for you," I rasp, the humility in my admission making my heart feel small in my chest. With nothing left to say, I curl further into his shirt, inadvertently inhaling the scent off his clothes. *He smells like the forest after a rainstorm, the way the air is filled with spicy aromas from the trees.* There is a sense of peace for me in this smell. The forest has always been my safe haven, my refuge from the chaos, brutality, and danger that came with living in a major house. *Is that what Cyrus is becoming for me now? A place of shelter, a kindred spirit to safeguard my secrets?* The very idea makes my body quiver.

"I'm sorry I got so upset," Cyrus whispers, and I can hear the tremor in his tone like he's barely holding onto a tiny tether that keeps his sanity anchored to his body. Those ghosts that haunt his mind will not be laid to rest easily. And that knowledge breaks a piece of my heart that I hadn't even realized belonged to Cyrus.

"I...I'm sorry for everything you endured at the hands of your brother. I never meant for any of it to happen." I hear his breathing hitch at my admission of guilt and remorse.

Cyrus nods his head, the tension easing from his shoulders a little as he quips, "And you're wrong, you know. I have three major flaws." He coerces a lighter tone into his words; I think it is an attempt at friendly banter. It is a small victory, a chink in the icy wall that has been a permanent fixture between us since we left the House of Piranhas.

And the soft smile that springs to life on my lips is not at all forced. "Oh yeah? What are they?" I inquire, genuinely curious to hear him explain his own personality.

"I don't assert myself like I should. If I had, Warbler would be alive, Creeper would never have been in the House, Falcon would never have had as much control as she did, and you would never have hated me." Cyrus doesn't bat an eye as he continues, never once stumbling over his words. "Second, I hate my brother to the point that I want to kill him slowly. I want him to endure every horrible thing he did to me seven times over." He takes a quivering breath before he whispers, "And lastly...you."

"Me?" I startle, jerking my chin so I can watch Cyrus's face for more clarification into his meaning.

"Yes, you. You are my biggest flaw. Everything I think and do ties back to you. 'Will Iris like this? Will Iris agree or disagree with this thought?' I ask myself at least a hundred times a day what you would say or do in my place. You'll be the death of me." Cyrus coughs, a hand grasping his chest where the tubes had been. Despite our mental connection and Suryc's powers to speed healing, these wounds are still tender. It's like they are actively avoiding the Ddraig's magic, clinging to Cyrus's skin as a physical reminder of his brother's sins.

"Why haven't you talked to me about everything Wolf

did to you?" I question, my heart heavy because I know that turning the conversation to this topic will kill these fleeting moments of peace between us. "Why did I have to hear it from our Ddraigs, from Bittern and Grouse and—"

Cyrus's body stiffens beside me, his breath releasing in a hiss. "They told you about—"

"The girls mentioned the shapeshifter and travelling in a coffin," I finish, a lump growing in my throat. "Siri showed me bits of Suryc's memories, so I gleaned a much better picture of the tortures you've faced from them. How did you endure it, Cyrus?"

"I asked them all to keep quiet about everything. I just want to forget it ever happened!" Cyrus's hands ball into fists, then he huffs and drops his head. "Don't trouble yourself over those things, Iris. I survived. That's all that really matters in the end. The pain was manageable most of the time. I mean, I've been around you most of my life, so I've already had practice in dealing with difficult people." Cyrus grins at his barb, but the haunted look never leaves his eyes. I can see the shiver in his muscles, and I can feel the quaking rustle of his breath. "The Vibría monster was different. It...made me question reality. I lost track sometimes of what was an illusion and what was truth. That was the worst part of it all, I think."

My body turns without my conscious thought, my hands resting on either side of Cyrus's cheeks as I exclaim, "Cyrus, if I had known how bad it was going to be—"

"I...I do not blame you." Cyrus smirks at my amazed expression, quickly adding, "Oh, don't get me wrong, I did hate you a little during the lucid moments when I was enduring it all. And I truly believed that maybe you intended for Wolf to hurt me. I even suspected that this was all part of a plan you and my brother had concocted. But now that it is over...," Cyrus brushes his fingers over one of my wrists, forcing my hand to stay in place on his cheek as he whispers, "I see that you never intended me harm. And in the end, it all worked out for the best. All the Cadogans we found at the House of Piranhas would have been lost if you had not come there searching for me. Many lives were saved by the way the events unfolded."

"I wish I could be as forgiving of myself as you are to me," I admit, swallowing against the sob trying to claw its way out of my throat. "All I see is that I caused you unimaginable pain. I don't think I can ever apologize enough."

Cyrus stares at the spot where his hand wraps around my wrist, his fingers tracing the Dadeni lines that glitter on my skin. He raises his eyes to mine, giving me a small, intimate smile. My cheeks blush under his close inspection. "Iris, I'm going to ask you something, and I don't want you to get upset. I want you to know that I'm thinking of a time way off in the future, nothing immediate."

"Go on," I shiver, already suspecting what he wishes to know.

"Do you think there will ever be a day when you will want me? I mean, I know what the Ddraigs say about our future and that it's inevitable for us. But if circumstances were different...do you think you could ever have chosen to love me of your own accord?" Cyrus looks away, staring at the horizon as he finishes this speech, waiting patiently for my answer. "I'm not pushing for anything romantic between us, Iris. I just want to know where I stand in your eyes."

Where you compare against your brother, I almost accuse, biting my tongue to keep the words from breaking the tentative trust that's built between us tonight. My heartstrings snarl at his words. It is a tooth grinding, bone jarring sensation, as though I've just heard a discordant note played in the middle of an otherwise perfect song. Thoughts jumble in my mind, mixed emotions and past regrets boiling up to the surface as I consider the conundrum sitting beside me.

"I...I feel so many different things toward you that I'm not really sure how to answer you," I begin, hating the way I see his shoulders droop. "In the House of Vultures, all I saw in you was weakness. I thought of you as a tyrant, and I loathed you every time I thought of you. Then, after Warbler...." My words die off as the face of my old friend floats back into my mind. "I hated you as much as I hated myself for what happened to her. But I saw something different in you the night of the wake when you spoke so kindly of her. It was a softer side that I didn't think you could possibly have in your personality. It made me question whether I had judged you too harshly. And then our world was upended by the Ddraigs. I became so conflicted, especially after everything was revealed by the Carreglas. You aren't weak at all; in fact, you're probably the strongest man I've ever met. You were a lifeline to me when I was just a child, staring out my window. And you've been an invisible, unsung hero that has protected me ever since."

"My Child of the Moon," Cyrus interrupts, one hand brushing my ivory hair. "Now a woman of starlight and cosmic fire." Cyrus's fingers trail down to my shoulder, toying with the ends of my hair as he listens to my speech.

Speaking so much of my heart makes me feel vulnerable. Yet, I force myself to continue because I owe Cyrus my honesty. *I owe him everything,* I admit to myself, as the memories of our childhood rush back to me. My voice continues to pour out my feelings, and I do not shrink from the words, even as they lay my soul bare. "When the Carreglas showed me your grief on the rooftop that night after I'd killed Creeper, I realized you were playing a part, hiding your true feelings under the mask of leadership. You secretly loathed Creeper and Falcon. You hid behind your well-crafted lies. I saw my own reflection in you. And I knew you were doing it all to keep me alive."

"To be fair, I acted that part for the rest of our housemates as well," Cyrus mumbles, and I think my admissions are making him a little uncomfortable too. "I had many lives to protect in the House of Vultures — they needed a tough, strong leader. It's such a relief to be free of that place."

Though he doesn't say it, I suspect Cyrus feels unworthy of compliments or high praise. *He sees himself as a monster because of the choices he made to save me.* "You played the role of a villain, Cyrus. It doesn't mean you are one," I exclaim softly, my fingers wiping away small tears that slip down his cheeks.

Then Cyrus's hands travel up to cup my face as he sighs, "You were always my first priority. You always have been, Iris."

"When I discovered Cane had been the one to scar your face, I felt so much heartache and pity that I could hardly breathe. And that your father had tried to kill you because he didn't think he could save you — how did you survive the chest wound?"

"I had an ally," Cyrus answers cryptically. I wait for an explanation, but no more words are dispensed on the subject. "Do you pity me still, Iris?"

"Yes, I do, Cyrus," I confess as I remember the day I found him in the tent after Cane had so cruelly tortured him. "I'm afraid a part of my heart will always be broken over everything you endured because of me." *You think of yourself as a monster, but the reality is that it's me!* I almost shout, the truth of my words creating an insatiable, hollow void in my chest. *I'm the poison in your veins, Cyrus. You called me your flaw, but really, I'm your worst enemy. Don't you see that? All of your pain and suffering would never have happened if you hadn't attached yourself to me!*

Cyrus's body becomes unnaturally still beside me, his hands carefully lifting away from my skin. I immediately miss their warmth, and it's an effort to keep my face from leaning closer to him, seeking his touch once more. "Hatred, loathing, confusion, pity, guilt, and heartbreak. Not exactly a strong chance for love to grow in the midst of all that, is there?" I can hear the sorrow he carries in the way his voice wobbles.

How could you still want love from me? I wonder, surprised that he can regard me with any measure of tenderness. Rather than ask the question aloud, I simply lean my head onto his shoulder, scooting closer so I can drape my legs across his lap. His arm wraps around my waist, securing me to his chest as though it is a natural response to my closeness. My eyes overflow with unspent tears that soak into his shirt, and I feel his own drip down onto my hair. I do not know how long we sit there, clinging to each other's broken heart in the grieving darkness. Yet, in this moment, I know I would not choose to be with anyone else.

***

"I've dispatched two patrols to search for signs of nameless unchosen in the area. Any that are found will be immediately sold to your border guard contact, Matthias. The rest of the men are waiting for your orders. Where are we going next?" Jackal stands ramrod straight as he gives his report to Wolf, who reclines behind a ramshackle desk in the House of Piranhas.

"Everything's so clean here," Wolf muses, staring at the whitewashed walls that seem to be permeated with the crisp, fresh scent of the salty ocean air. "It's like the entire house resets at night. A new day, a new life, a clean slate. Not unlike this one here, huh?" Wolf murmurs, jutting his chin toward Lynx's baby. Her strapping young son slumbers against Wolf's shoulder, healthy and strong after such a long, difficult labor. His chubby little fingers curl in the fur on Wolf's mask, and he coos softly like a little dove with every exhaled breath. *Little Dove.* Wolf repeats the nickname in his mind, his frown deepening. *That won't do at all!* "He needs a mighty predator's name," Wolf declares, shutting away all thoughts of birds and their connection to the House of Vultures. "I wonder what he will choose for himself when he is of age to take a mask."

The juxtaposition of battle worn leader and fragile, sleeping newborn unnerves Jackal's normally unflappable resolve. "Sir? Do I send the men to track and destroy the Ddraigs? Or do you have another destination in mind?"

Wolf raises a finger to his lips, freezing when the child moves. He sighs with relief when the babe does not cry out. "This one's kept the whole house awake since his birth," Wolf whispers to Jackal, a strangely wild look crossing his eyes. "He likes me, though. I'm sure he always will, unlike some fickle-minded woman." A sharp, aching pain lances through his temples, reminding him of the naming bond that still holds sway in his thoughts. *How do I break free of her?* He wonders with a frustrated growl, pulsing starbursts of light erupting in his vision. *How do I remove this hold she has over my mind?*

"Sir? The Ddraigs?" Jackal insists gently, watching Wolf's hands tighten around the baby's back, as though he fears someone now comes to try and take the child by force. The claws on Wolf's fingers dig into the newborn's tender skin without bringing blood. Jackal holds his breath, silently hoping his leader does not screw up and hurt the baby. Despite his loyalty, Jackal cannot help but wonder if recent events have caused his leader to finally lose his mind. Wolf's erratic, thoughtless behavior and constant obsession over his brother and Iris only fuel Jackal's suspicions. "What should I tell the men—?"

"Send half the soldiers after the bitch and her new lover," Wolf growls, standing up and hurrying over to a makeshift bed of folded animal skins. He roughly sets the newborn onto the pile, not even flinching when the child hiccups awake. "Lynx! He's hungry again!" Wolf calls out as the child cries for his mother. Wolf wraps his clawed fingers into his hair, and when he pulls them free, clumps of tangles rip away from his scalp. "Tell the men to find my brother and the traitor, but do not engage them. Instead, report back to me. I intend to play the spy like she has managed to do in my camp! Then, when I find the best means of ripping all that she loves from her grasp, I will seize the moment in cold, calculated clarity."

Jackal nods once just to prove that he's heard his leader's commands, backing out of the room just to keep out of trouble. Wolf twitches by the window, his claws biting into the frame, permanently marring the whitewashed wood.

"Wren! Get in here!" Wolf demands, shouting to be heard over the child's wails. He cuts his eyes over to the baby's wide-eyed, open mouthed grimace. *So tiny and innocent,* Wolf realizes, leaning over to pat the child's head softly. *So easily hurt.* "I'll take care of you, little one, even when all the rest turn their backs on you." *Just do not leave me,* Wolf amends in his mind, stroking the soft, auburn curls that already dust the child's scalp.

"You wanted me?" Wren exclaims, examining Wolf's bright eyes with a gnawing sense of worry in his stomach. "Something wrong with the boy?" Eyeing the sniffling child, Wren quickly assesses him for any bloody or open wounds. Seeing none, Wren hides his sigh of relief and asks, "What can I do for you, Wolf?"

"I want you to help me create a plan to catch the traitor and her Ddraigs," Wolf declares, turning to face the purported master of disguises of the House of Vultures. "*She* told me how you tricked her when she was trying to help the child from Déchets. You were able to get past her defenses in ways I cannot. You know her better than anyone else, I suspect. So how can I trick her into coming back to me?" Wolf stresses the vehemence of his conviction by pounding his fist on the desk. "What is her greatest weakness? How can I exploit it? And most importantly, how can I make it seem like the choice to return to me is her own, not some forced reaction to stave off an attack from me?"

"I will consider it and get back to you," Wren defers diplomatically, carefully putting his hand on Wolf's shoulder. "Right now, let me help you upstairs. You look exhausted, and I think it would be in your best interest to rest. Jackal and I will keep things running smoothly until you wake."

"Fine, fine," Wolf mutters as he follows Wren's wishes. He stumbles up the staircase to the room he's claimed as his bedchamber. Wren watches him slump down onto the bed, not even bothering to remove his dirty boots. "What's wrong with me?" Wolf mumbles, yanking the covers off the empty side of the bed, cocooning himself into the soft linen until only his mask can be seen.

"Well, I think part of it has to do with Lynx's child. He's kept you awake for the last few nights," Wren explains with a sigh as he carefully uncovers Wolf's boots and unties the laces.

"Then kill it, Wren," Wolf demands, his speech slurring as a wave of nausea overpowers his stomach.

"I'll...take care of it," Wren assures without giving away any sign of disgust. Yet the very thought of killing a child brings bile up into his throat. After dropping Wolf's boots beside a dresser, he adds, "I think the other part has to do with Iri—"

"Don't say her name!" Wolf howls, covering his ears with his clawed fingers. He digs into his skin until tiny scratches appear on his scalp and cheeks.

"I'm sorry, Wolf," Wren murmurs, genuine pity flooding his heart as he watches Wolf suffer. "The mental connection you share with her through the naming bond is—"

"Going to tear me apart from the inside out," Wolf interjects as another bone-jarring pain rattles his skull. "It was getting bad before she came into camp and proved herself to be a whore by betraying me. But seeing her stilled the ache. Now our new separation has caused it to begin anew."

"Why doesn't she seem fazed by it?" Wren wonders as he watches Wolf's quaking fingers wipe across his mouth. "Iris spoke and acted so lucidly when she was here."

"It must be her wretched Ddraig," Wolf growls, his claw-tipped fingers biting into the silky sheets. "I bet her precious beast has a means of blocking the naming connection, shielding her from any of the unpleasant side effects." Wolf sighs, sinking lower into the bed.

"Okay, so how do we help you?" Wren questions as he paces around the bed, but Wolf has already slipped into a fitful sleep. Wordlessly Wren stalks out of the room, gliding down the stairs without making them creak even once. He slips into the kitchens, intent on finding Lynx.

"Something I can do for you?" Lynx snaps from her seat at the table, and Wren feels his face flush as he notices her nursing her child.

"Wolf's going crazy, and he's told me to kill your son. Says he's making too much noise at night," Wren explains, deciding that the best means of getting any cooperation out of this irritable young mother is to simply be direct.

"I didn't want this child," Lynx declares, a haunted, half-crazed gleam brightening her eyes as she stares at her son's little hands. "He was not...made by my choice. And I thought when he was born, I would want to kill him myself. I fully expected to hand him to a nursemaid and demand she find him a new mother. But I was wrong. Instead, when I heard him cry out after that horrible labor I endured, all I wanted was to protect him. Love snuck up on me; somehow, it found a way to grow and overpower the hate I feared would be the only emotion I'd ever felt again." Lynx carefully grabs for a knife on the table, holding it out in Wren's direction. "So, if you try and touch him, you will die. And if by some miracle you do manage to hurt my son, I will make sure your death is agonizing and slow." Though her words are quiet enough to not disturb the baby, Wren fully believes Lynx is capable of making good on her threats.

Wren raises his hands to show his compliance. "I have no intention of following Wolf's orders! Despite my unscrupulous reputation, I do have some standards. Killing children has never been something I could stomach. Actually, I want to help you, but I need to know where your loyalties lie."

"With him," Lynx answers immediately, dropping her gaze to her son. "I'll do whatever it takes to keep him alive."

"Even if that means running to Iris and the Ddraigs?" Wren whispers as a fear douses his veins like icy water. The plans taking shape in his mind thrill and terrify him. He's never had any reason to involve anyone else in his exploits before. Yet circumstances have changed; Lynx and her son need an ally, and Wren could use a scapegoat to his advantage. *Accuse Lynx of desertion and spying for Iris, and Wolf will never suspect that I am actually the traitor. He'll focus his hatred on Lynx. He's already got a bad taste in his mouth from a woman, so it will be easy to persuade him that this woman is just as bad as Iris. He'll gain some measure of trust towards me, and I'll secure my place in his pack...until the time is right.*

"If it keeps my son safe, I'll do it. I mean, I owed Wolf a great debt for killing the monster that gave me my son, but that debt only goes so far," Lynx replies as emotionlessly as if she were discussing the weather.

"Then slip out tonight, and get as far from this place as you can. I suspect that the Ddraigs will return to a location they know. Go to the Pith," Wren urges, his hands reaching for bits of dried meat and day-old bread for Lynx to carry on her journey. "Give a message to Mynah for me. Tell her I have joined Wolf's pack, and I will get her any information I think valuable."

"You mean to stay and act as a spy? Why not come with me?" Lynx demands, securing her child in a sling over her shoulder. With her free hands, she ties the food into a cloth that can be slipped into a sack on her back.

"I think I'll be useful here. If I can find out what Wolf means to do, maybe I can get word to Iris so she can thwart his plans. You just be careful, Lynx. Jackal's men are scouring for nameless unchosen. Do you have a bigger knife than that little kitchen cutter?" Wren inquires as he watches her stow the tiny blade into the top of her boot.

Lynx scoffs at his query, ripping a nasty looking serrated blade from a holster hidden in the folds of her skirt. At least as long as her forearm and shaped like a long canine tooth, this thick steel's sharp edge gleams hungrily in the light. "After I endured Lion's attentions, I never left home without this baby. If I run into trouble, I'll be able to get myself out."

"Okay. Get whatever else you think you need, and be ready to run at dusk," Wren reminds her, leaving her to her preparations.

Despite all his years as a clever, cunning spy, never once did Wren notice Jackal's shadow at the window, a silent observer to their plans.

CHAPTER 2

Sweat drips off Helena's chin as she dangles precariously from the highest ramparts of the castle walls. "I can't do it," she screams, one hand slipping off the polished marble, her chipped fingernails scraping for anything to cling to as she slips. "I'm going to fall!"

"You made it this far," Ithel reminds her, his voice as impassive as his next command. "Climb the rest of the way, Helena. Or don't...it's up to you, really."

Her arms muscles twitch and clench, unused to exerting this much effort after all her years of idleness in the palace prison. Helena's feet swing, toes searching for a foothold along the smooth, sculpted wall. "It's no use, Ithel! I'm not going to make it!" Helena pants as her fingers begin to go numb.

"Then you fall, and you use your Windwalker magic to soften the blow," Ithel suggests, leaning over the ledge to smile at Helena's outraged face.

"You haven't let me test my Windwalker abilities!" she shrieks, wishing she could punch that smirk off his face. "Who knows if I can still use Windwalker magic at all?!"

"Then I guess you die, and I'll be straight behind you in death," Ithel drones on, never moving from his perch as he waits for Helena to finish her climb. "If that doesn't sound pleasant to you, Helena, then I suggest you move your —"

A groan pours from Helena's mouth as her left foot

finally feels a slight chink in the marble. Wedging her toes into the crevice, she gives a final push with her legs. Helena elbows her way up over the rampart's last ledge, sprawling on the sun-warmed stone of the infirmary's patio. She closes her eyes and lets the sweat evaporate from her clothes. Huge blisters ooze on her feet from the friction created by climbing up slick marble. Scrapes and bruises mar her ghostly pale flesh with their vivid colors. A hysterical, laugh-like sob erupts from her lips as tears slip down her face and pool on the stones under her head.

"See there? You made it just fine," Ithel murmurs, smirking as he paces around her prostrate form.

"You are such a bastard!" she cries, sucking air into her over exerted lungs. Her hair splays out around her head, and she can feel a breeze rushing over her midriff as her shirt flaps over her stomach. Still, the marble at her back fills her with a sense of safety, and she is too tired to move even her aching fingers.

Ithel saunters away and crouches in the shade of a nearby statuesque angel, twirling a knife in his hand. "That's as may be. But you made it without relying on your Windwalker abilities to save you. And you didn't fall. I call that progress."

"Yes, I survived, but barely!" Helena huffs, dizziness overtaking her as she attempts to sit up. "I hardly think my performance was worth bragging about."

"Barely alive still counts, so quit complaining." Ithel jerks himself away from the angel, leaning over Helena's body to examine the blood stains trailing down her arms. "Show me your hands," he instructs, carefully inspecting her wounds even as he ignores her vulgar gesture. "And your feet?" Ithel dodges her foot as she kicks, catching her ankle and wrenching it up toward his face.

"Easy!" Helena wails as her overworked muscles scream at the mistreatment. Her knee quivers as the tendons holding her kneecap in place threaten to snap in their fatigue. "Please! Let go."

Ithel hardly seems to notice her pain as he exclaims,

"Not bad for a first try! These wounds will form hard calluses. Soft hands and feet would not keep you alive in this challenge anyway. Keep going like this, and you might make it through the tunnel successfully after all." He drops her foot like it's a weight too heavy to be carried.

"What's in the tunnel?" Helena asks with a moan as she finally sits up, her spine creaking as a wave of nausea and shock overtakes her. *I could have died just now! If I'd let go, I'm sure I would have.* The cold reality washes over her nerves as bile rises in her throat. "How am I supposed to survive if I don't know what I am fighting? No one ever talks about what's actually in the tunnel."

"That's because no one knows. Those that have attempted the challenge have never survived long enough to spill its secrets," Ithel admits as he hoists her off the ground, dropping his hold on her tiny waist as soon as her feet are stable. "The few people out there who were there when the tunnel was constructed are not allowed to speak of its secrets. They are spelled into silence; revealing the contents of the tunnel is a death sentence for them. So, we must prepare you for everything imaginable."

"Why not just float out using my powers?" Helena suggests hopefully as she moves into the shadows along the wall, wincing as her blisters squish on the marble. Cursing the pain, she struggles to walk, waving off a couple of doctors who attempt to treat her wounds. "I'll be fine. Don't use your energies on me," Helena mutters as guilt pangs rise in her stomach. The faces of the slaves who'd already saved her life float through her thoughts, slowly shifting into piles of sand just like their bodies had done. *How many more must die for me? How much more can I endure before I go mad?*

"Make all this death mean something, Helena, and it will be worth their sacrifices," Ithel whispers gently, backing away from her side. Not to be deterred, the medical team swarms around her, slipping into her mind and forcing her body to heal despite her wishes.

Relief brings fresh tears to Helena's eyes when none of these people die. Though they appear to be extremely fatigued and ashen faced, all of them are able to walk away from her side. "Thank you," she croaks as they go to rest in the infirmary, wordlessly slipping into the sick beds that line the walls. Sighing, Helena turns to Ithel and whispers, "How did you know I was thinking about the ones that sacrificed for me?"

"I recognize that sadness in your eyes. As to using your Windwalker abilities, I suspect you will not be able to compel the magic once you're in the tunnel. You will have to rely on your own strength and wits to survive." Ithel smirks as he retorts, "Though from what I know about you, your wits won't help you much."

Helena's arms are too weak and jelly-like in their movements to strike Ithel for his insolence. Choosing to ignore the jibe, she asks, "Well, climbing I can do, so now what?" Helena stretches her muscles, the feel of her healthy skin a delight under her fingertips. For so long, she's been nothing more than a waif of the Déchets' prison. Stroking her smooth, shiny hair, Helena savors the sensations of being clean, well-fed, and hale once more.

Ithel's mouth forms a thin line as he holds his knife toward her chest. "Believe it or not, that climb was an easy one. But what if Alaric has your hands broken or your feet burdened with heavy chains around your ankles? What if you are stabbed or shot with an iron arrow, so the wound does not stop bleeding? What if you are given a hallucinogen? No, Helena, you are not even done with climbing." He lunges over her before she can react, his blade sliding easily through her palms and the pads of her fingertips. While she stares at him in stunned silence, Ithel shoves her to the ground. Sitting on her legs, he makes quick work of her feet with his knife, slicing each one at least five times below the now hardened calluses and the fleshy parts of her toes. "Now, go back down to the ground floor and do this again, Helena. And I want you up here even faster!"

"You son of a—"

"Let's see if your Windwalker magic still works, too," Ithel interrupts as he drops her over the side of the rampart.

Helena cries out, her body flipping in a freefall state as panic overwhelms her senses. Seconds pass like hours as she tries to slow her breathing, to grab hold of any thread of magic in her veins. "Please!" she wails, searching for any means of slowing her fall.

We thought you'd left us, a tiny voice whispers in her head, a tinkling bell that almost gets lost in the rush of the wind. Then, a familiar, tingling sensation begins as magic sizzles to life in her veins once more, like a lid has been ripped away from an overfilled jar. Power ripples around Helena's body, slowing her speed until she floats toward the earth like an autumn leaf gracefully descending from its branch. When her feet hit the ground safely, Helena shouts a stream of curses and obscenities up to the snickering guard at the top of the ramparts.

"Flattery, Helena, gets you nowhere!" Ithel calls back, desperately trying to tamp down the relief billowing through his heart as her irate voice filters up to him on the breeze. "Keep it up, and I'll become even more diabolical. You'll thank me if you survive. Now get back up here without your powers!"

"I hate you!" Helena shouts back, pure rage urging her to climb. Her bloody fingerprints stain the side of the palace, but she does not feel anything but fury. "I am going to kill you!" she rasps, using the ever-growing rage to fuel her ascent.

"I will welcome my demise with open arms," Ithel answers softly as he wipes his bloody blade on his pants. "After this week ends, I will probably be a friend of Death anyway." The thought of watching Helena die in the tunnel plagues Ithel's mind. He imagines her dying a thousand different ways, and in these fevered dreams, he sees his own final moments too. "You don't realize it, but I really am trying to help you," Ithel confesses in a whisper that fades away on the wind long before it ever can reach Helena's ears. "You don't know how much I love you still. Even after you betrayed me. Even after you left me to rot in this hellhole. Even after you chose someone else. I love you still, Helena. And I will do whatever it takes to make sure you survive."

***

"You sent for me?" Wren questions as he steps through the doorway into the pristine kitchens of the House of Piranhas. Someone had been busy this afternoon, and a pot of fish stew simmers on the stove, the pleasant aromas assaulting Wren's nose. However, despite its tantalizing scent, Wren cannot focus on food. The sun had fallen from the sky hours ago, and with each passing breath, Wren worries over Lynx and her son. *Did they make it past the guards? Are they safe out there alone? What if they encounter hostile nameless unchosen? Can they find their way to the Pith from here without a guide?*

"Yes, Wren. I believe we have some business to discuss." Wolf points to the chair beside him at the long driftwood table, his voice as cold as the first winter snow. "I was hoping we could talk strategy and set up some rules for handling misguided allegiance."

He knows, Wren suspects, immediately reevaluating his strategy. Unease stiffens Wren's legs, yet he disguises his fear easily. He saunters over to the chair and drops into a relaxed position, forcing his arms to remain uncrossed. Everyone always believed Wren had otherworldly powers of deception. Wren smiles easily at the memory, using the emotion to make him appear approachable. *It's all a matter of body language,* he laughs to himself. *A lie's words are only half the deception; I've got to play the part. Keep my eyes and ears open for anything I can use to downplay Wolf's suspicions.*

"What's got you smiling?" Wolf barks, inspecting Wren's expression closely.

"I was just imagining my old House mates' faces if they could see us together, discussing plans like old friends." *Partial truth to hide the lie.* Wren smiles wider when he sees Wolf nod, convinced by Wren's explanation enough to stop asking about it. Wren uses the advantage to open the dialogue, intending to appear innocent. "You mentioned earlier that you wanted a way to trap Iris." *Sometimes I even frighten myself with this act.* Wren suppresses a shudder as he speaks of hurting the girl. While he'd go through the motions stoically, the idea of attacking anyone from his former house fills his heart with dread. "Are you wanting to kill her or just drive her back here to your arms?"

"Actually, I'm more interested in your strategy right now, Wren," Wolf replies, pointing to the door. Jackal stands with his arms crossed, and between his feet lies a limp, distinctly female body. Wren's blood turns to ice as Wolf continues. "My commander informs me that you instructed Lynx to return to the Ddraigs. He overhead your plans to let her take her son and leave the House, reuniting with the traitors to my rule." Wolf lifts his gaze until his eyes bore into Wren in a challenge. "Jackal made it sound like you even know where they will be hiding. Have you been keeping secrets from me?"

Don't panic, Wren assures himself, shaking his head and releasing the air pent up in his lungs as a plan takes shape. "Jackal! You bloody fool!" Wren uses his fear to spur him into acting furious. He stalks over to the wide-eyed commander and punches him hard enough to crack his mask. "How could you be so stupid?"

"I...I don't understand," Jackal stutters, one hand rubbing his jaw. "What are you talking about?"

"It was meant to be a trap!" Wren huffs, turning so that Wolf can witness one of Wren's finest performances. His voice does not falter as he skillfully crafts his lie. "I mean, doesn't it seem strange that Iris and the rest of the glorified thieves would leave one woman behind?"

"You're thinking she's already a spy for the Ddraigs?" Wolf fills in the blanks, lowering his eyes to the shivering woman. "A mother and child would be unlikely—"

"Exactly," Wren interrupts, spinning the words to fit his agenda. "No one would suspect a new mother. We'd all fall into the trap, believing that Lynx would not endanger her child. No one would question her loyalty, and Lynx would be free to report on our whereabouts." Wren stares at the cowering woman, forcing his eyes to clench in cold, detached assessment.

"But how would she relay messages to the Ddraigs?" Jackal questions, his hands open at his side as he watches Wren pace. "How can you be so sure you are right?"

"I don't know I'm right at all," Wren snaps, pausing for effect while he gathers his thoughts. "Unless the Ddraigs have allied with the nameless unchosen. I mean, we all know the nomads range far and wide across Cassé. What's to stop them from sharing information on their travels?"

Jackal nods as comprehension dawns across his features, believing the plausibility of the lie instantly. Wolf sits still, his expression impassive. "So, what do you suggest we do then, Wren?"

Facing Jackal, Wren ignores the terror rattling his spine and demands, "What did you do with her child?"

As soon as the words leave his mouth, Wren hears the gurgling of the newborn at his feet. Peering down, he sees the babe bundled in a shawl, held tight in his mother's arms. Bending down, he eases his arms around the boy.

"No! Don't you dare take my son!" Lynx screams, jerking and writhing as she clutches for her child. "You rat bastard! I trusted you! I thought you were trying to help me!"

"Your boy will be safe," Wren assures, genuinely hoping his words are truth as he adds the necessary threat to keep Wolf from growing suspicious, "As long as you cooperate with us." *Please keep your mouth shut.* Wren prays she will understand how he's desperately trying to play both sides and keep her and her son alive at the same time.

"You mean to use him as a bargaining chip," Wolf smirks to himself, a new level of respect and wariness creeping into his mind. "I'm impressed, Wren. You're as heartless as your reputation claims, aren't you?"

Wren ignores the leader, letting his cruel persona lift long enough to catch the frightened woman's attention. The change in his demeanor gives her pause, hope filling her eyes as she waits for Wren to assist her. Leaning close to Lynx's ear as he reaches for her son once more, he whispers, "Say nothing." When he stands tall with her son in his arms, he allows himself to act once more. "I believe they both can be useful, Wolf. Iris will want her spy unharmed, and you will have two lives to trade for her secrets. And if we keep the boy alive, then we will have someone to hold over Lynx, making sure she stays in line."

Wolf nods once, and it takes all the strength in Wren's abdominal muscles not to shout and praise every forgotten god of the land.

"Jackal! Set up patrols with the rest of the army. I want all nameless unchosen in the proximity to be captured, questioned thoroughly, and executed for aiding and abetting the Ddraig rebels."

"At once, Wolf." Jackal trots out the door, never once questioning whether or not Wren should be believed.

"Wren, you are in charge of the child and Lynx." Wolf crosses to the doorframe, pausing as he growls, "I have to admit that your story sounds plausible. Yet I know your reputation for being an impeccable liar. So, hear me, Wren, when I say that if I find out that you've lied to me about any of this, I will kill you myself. Very, very slowly."

"On your feet, Lynx," Wren commands, one hand pressed to his lips in a gesture of silence. "We will go to your tent and pick up any basic supplies you need. You are moving in with me, so I can keep an eye on you at all times." Wren winks once to assure the woman, pointing to the door. "Now move!" he barks harshly.

Lynx follows his orders, and as they pass the living room, Wren notices their fearless leader in the shadows, watching the scene for any signs of treachery. Breathing a sigh of relief, he keeps Lynx moving at a breakneck pace, hurrying away from the House of Piranhas as quickly as their feet can carry them.

"Wren," Lynx wheezes as they reach her tent. "Please tell me —"

"Shut up, woman!" Wren bellows, raising a hand as if he intends to strike her. Lynx recoils, cowering low with her hands over her head. Hauling her up roughly, he shoves her toward the tent's canvas folds. "Not out loud in the open like this," Wren mumbles under his breath. "Eyes and ears everywhere." He hopes his fragmented words are enough to explain their need for secrecy.

Lynx grows pale, her cheeks turning wan as she understands. "Later?" Her lip trembles as she eyes her son.

Wren nods once, understanding what she seeks. Tonight, he will find a way to explain his plan to her. One way or another, he will make sure Lynx and her son make it to safety. And the sooner it happens, the better.

CHAPTER 3

"For someone who's so hell-bent on training the new Cadogans until they are dead on their feet, you sure are easy on yourself," Siri snipes from her perch on a stony outcropping overhead. She's been sitting up there all day, hurling her taunting insults at me as I attempt to harness my abilities as a Gwen to see the future. So far, I've only managed to give myself a headache.

"This is different," I spit through my clenched teeth as sweat drips down into my eye. "Mental training is much harder than physical." With the sun beating down upon the blistering sand that's sifted into the Pith caverns, I feel like I'm roasting over an open flame. *My skin is starting to crackle and char, Siri. I need a break!*

"You *need* to learn to control your thoughts!" Siri barks back, all traces of humor fading from her demeanor. "Then you need to learn how to guard your mind. Right now, you're practically begging any mind-reading magician to walk right in and steal your thoughts out of your head. Or worse, a skilled mage could manipulate your mind into seeing things that aren't real. Do you want to spend your days chasing phantoms?" Siri stands up, pacing back and forth above me as she continues her rant. "What if you happened to be in the heat of battle when a real vision overtook you? Or what if someone deliberately planted a vision in your mind to lead you into a trap? What if they slipped into your thoughts and filled your mind with emptiness, blinding you to an attack? Do you think your enemies will fight fairly? Will they wait until it's convenient for you?"

"Of course not!" I bellow, my knees buckling and my pulse growing faint. "I know we've been lucky so far. But how do I force a vision?" I've been asking myself this all day long, and I'm still no closer to an answer than I was when I started. I snarl my fingers into my hair as a frustrated plea escapes my lips. "How do I control something this unreliable?"

"I've been asking the same question of Suryc about my Asíle abilities. So, if you've come up with an answer, I'd love to hear it," Cyrus mumbles as he staggers into view. His shirt is damp with sweat, and I see a bone-weary dullness in his glazed eyes. With the slightest breeze, I think Cyrus will topple into the sand and sleep for a week straight. Cyrus stares at me, and I practically feel his gaze raking over my skin. His mouth pinches together as if he's just bitten something sour, and he plops down beside my Ddraig, feet dangling off the outcropping.

My spine stiffens at his presence; the last thing I want is an audience for my repeated failures. I pick up a stone, planning to hurl it at Cyrus's leg. Instead, I feel it tumble through my fingers, and I wince as the sharp edges rake across my bare feet before it thuds back into the dirt. Staring down at my toes, I watch my blood well up from the scratches. The sight carries my mind deep into a vision, my body dropping backward to the ground.

Blood. Everywhere I look, I see it. Coating the floors, covering the walls, and staining my skin. I stagger, searching my body for signs of the injury. A hacking cough fills the air from beside me. Turning my head, I see Cyrus, his throat split open from ear to ear. His body still heaves, unaware that his soul is already claimed by Death. I can tell by the way his eyes have faded, their dilated pupils fixed on me, that he is gone.

A sob rips from my throat, and my heart shatters as I claw my way closer to his side. I hear my voice wailing, the depths of my grief making my words unintelligible.

Even though I continue to drag myself across the floor, my feet feel as though they are weighted by lead. Looking down, I see that there is a long, heavy chain securing me in place. Scanning the room, I search for signs of Wolf. Deep down, I know this must be his doing. "Where are you?" I whisper, struggling to keep my voice from cracking.

"I never understood how you could choose him." Wolf's voice is as cold as iron as he steps out of an alcove on the left side of the room. "In all the time we spent separated, I thought about you. I obsessed about you; I literally went mad over you. What were you doing? Were you alive? Had you finally come to your senses? Were you searching for me? I pined for you, Iris."

"I know," I wheeze, my stomach lurching as Cyrus's body heaves its last sigh. All sound in the room seems to pause, the absence of his breathing louder than any scream. A part of my heart turns cold. Looking down on my hands, I see my Dadeni lines flickering on my arms, their white purity tangled by small, coal-black etchings. Cyrus and I have bonded; we are coupled. I've just lost my mate. The words ring in my mind, emptiness roaring into the silence that follows the thought. My love, gone.

"Then, after everything went to hell, I find you in his arms," Wolf continues as though he has not noticed his brother's death, brandishing a long, spiked whip in my direction. He grips the leather so tightly his knuckles turn white. "I gave you everything you ever wanted, Iris. Didn't I?"

"It was never about you and me," I whisper, tears shivering down my cheeks. I cannot tear my eyes away from Cyrus's soulless body. The gash on his throat mocks me with its gruesome smile—"Just like the one you gave my father," it seems to say. "You know my decisions were about—"

"Those stupid Ddraigs!" Wolf interrupts with a snarl, his voice echoing off the walls like a howl. "Well, I've dealt with that problem too, haven't I?" Wolf flourishes the whip with an audible snap, his mouth curling into a smile. "You'll find that I am far better at keeping my word than you. I told you I would take out the Ddraigs. She put up a fight, Iris. You'd have been proud!"

My stomach falls as my last shreds of sanity begin to crumble. I feel my mind breaking a minute before he confirms my fear. "Siri's dead?" But I don't hear Cane's response. Instead, a dull roar engulfs my ears. Every sight before me becomes coated with a thin film of translucent blood, and a pressure builds so powerfully in my eyes that I fear they will pop out of their sockets. "No, NO! You rat bast—"

Then the voices begin. Siri's memories burst forth like an undammed spring. They fill me so quickly that I cannot follow any of them to fruition, passing through my mind at a breakneck pace. My emotions shift with each one: heartache, anger, fear, sorrow, ecstasy, grief, terror, panic. They pour from my heart, each passing second a different feeling. My mouth opens, but only a low moan escapes me.

The last thing I see is the darkness in my skull as my eyes roll back into my head. Then my mind is too far gone to register any shred of my former self. At least in this insanity, I can forget my many failures....

"Iris!" Cyrus's hand slaps me hard across the face. Sputtering, I snap out of the vision with a cry.

Wrapping my arms around his neck, I hold him fiercely close to me, reveling in the sound of his breath. In this moment, our confused relationship means little to me. The fact that he and Siri are alive is enough for me. *It wasn't real; he and Siri are still alive. I'm not going crazy.*

Cyrus's hands brush my back strongly as he rasps, "My gods, you had us terrified! You went all pale and started screaming—"

"And you vomited." *And wet yourself, I think,* Siri adds privately to avoid more embarrassment. Her silver eyes seem to glow above me, hovering like an angel of silver fire over my head. *I saw it all,* she whispers with a grim frown. *I'm sorry.*

Releasing my hold on Cyrus, I wipe my hands over my burning eyes, gasping for every strangled breath. Each part of my body feels raw, as though I've just been pulled out of a raging fire. "Are these truly glimpses of the only possible future, Siri?" I struggle to make my words understandable, my voice hoarse from my fear. My eyes keep fluttering between Cyrus's concern and Siri's shuttered expression. "Is there a way to change what I've seen?"

"I don't know," Siri answers, her voice unconvincing and flat. "A Gwen is a rarity among our Cadogans. I can recall only one mentioned in our histories. Her powers were never detailed clearly, but I do know her visions were never wrong. Still, there are some Ddraigs in our ranks that are older than I am. I will see if they can recall anything I have forgotten." She hurries off to do as she wishes, never looking back at me. I suspect she knows more than she's shared, but I keep my mouth shut. I'm not yet prepared for any kind of bad news, my body still in shock from the intensity of this vision.

"Everything seemed so real," I mumble, wiping a clammy hand across Cyrus's throat, tracing the place where his blood had poured. "You...you died right beside me. And Siri—"

"She told me," Cyrus whispers as his hand runs across my sweat soaked hair. "When you started screaming, Siri used your connection to watch what you were seeing, and she told me everything. I'm so sorry, Iris. That must have been a terrible thing to endure."

"We've got to change it," I cry, resolve burrowing into my heart and quietening my fears. "I can't let her die." *Or you.* I catch myself before I speak the words aloud. Cyrus would mistake my meaning, and deep down, I'm not proud of myself. My reasons for keeping him close are selfish. I want an ally, someone who can be beside me when I need assistance. Not a romantic partner or a bonded mate—just a true friend I can count on to have my back in the war that is brewing.

"You were only worried about Siri?" Cyrus questions,

pressing the issue, seeking to hear that I value him. I gasp as his brows furrow, his eyes turning as black as onyx. A tiny smile creeps along his lips as he smirks, "Liar." Then he's back to normal, all signs of his Asíle abilities gone. The change happens so quickly I wonder if I am still hallucinating. *What did he see? I wonder* as a blush heats my cheeks. *What does he think he knows? This truth-reading ability of his unnerves me!*

Cyrus's demeanor relaxes, but I cannot shake the feeling that he's mistaken my worry for something deeper than it is.

"What triggered your vision, Iris?"

"I hardly want to talk about that now!" I wail, stopped from running away by his steely grip on my shoulder. *I need space. Freedom. The chance to process everything I've just witnessed. And I need to do this part alone.*

"I understand what you're saying better than you realize," Cyrus begins, his hold tightening when I attempt to jerk myself away. "But think about this: the best time for you to analyze what just happened is immediately after it's over. The events are fresh in your mind, making them easier to review. A little discomfort now could save you hours of work in the future. Think about it! How much better would it be if you could control these visions? If you can learn how to force yourself to see the future, then you can anticipate what needs to be done to alter it. You can change this fate, Iris."

My nose begins to bleed, the warmth of my blood oozing down over my lips, some of it slipping into my mouth. The metallic flavor makes my stomach heave. Every blink is a new lesson in pain too. My eyelids feel like sandpaper as they scratch over my pupils. Pinching the bridge of my nose, my voice comes out sounding whiny. "I...I saw blood right before it began. Blood on my feet. The vision began with blood too, so maybe the similar circumstances propelled me into the hallucination."

For a long while, Cyrus does not speak, his thoughts far away as he considers my insight. I stay beside him, gagging as the scents of my own filth slowly assault me. Embarrassment heats my cheeks at the thought of how helpless and vulnerable I must have looked. *I hate being weak, especially in front of him.*

"There's got to be more to it," Cyrus finally decides, turning a dubious expression on me once more. His eyes narrow as he watches me squirm under his gaze, and he growls, "What aren't you telling me?"

"What do you mean?" I turn my face up to the cavern's entrance, so I do not look down and draw attention to my soiled clothes. *I'm a mess. Gods, this is revolting!*

"Well, what you described is a self-fulfilling circumstance and completely out of your control. You can't anticipate how a vision is going to be triggered without knowing the future, right? And you won't know the future unless you use your Gwen abilities." Cyrus pauses as I try to wrap my brain around his explanation. "Your mind couldn't know you needed to see blood to trigger a vision unless you already knew the future. It's circular logic, don't you see?"

"It's a paradox," I agree, nodding my head as I untangle the web of emotions in my mind like a ball of yarn that's been used as a cat's plaything. "I can't know the future and be walking blindly into these visions at the same time. I get it."

"So, whatever triggered your powers had to have been more complex than just seeing blood." Cyrus nods. "Similar circumstances aren't enough, so what else could it be?" When I do not answer immediately, Cyrus stands and begins pacing back and forth in front of me. He prattles on under his breath, and I use his distraction to handle my appearance.

I stumble on my shaky feet when I stand, but Cyrus is too preoccupied by his thoughts to notice my movements. In the corner of the cave, a small pool bubbles up from a cold spring. My body quakes as I strip off my soiled clothes, slipping into the freezing waters as soon as I am naked. The water is arid, gliding across my skin in waves that feel more like foam than fluid. I let the roiling frigid waters rinse away my embarrassment. My tears slip down my face; I hide my exhaustion in the springs. The water takes my secrets, easing them out of my heart as if I were bearing my soul to a close confidant. I won't even consider rising from the springs until my body and heart are numb.

"I think your gift is tied to your emotions!" Cyrus cries out in excitement, searching the ground where I had been sitting. "Iris? Where'd you go?"

I consider not responding, but his idea intrigues me. "Take off your shirt and turn around," I demand, waving a hand to alert Cyrus to my place in the bath. "Just toss it over your head, and I'll come pick it up."

Cyrus gulps, eyes wide as he realizes I'm washing in the springs. He scrambles to follow my wishes, his fingers trembling as he tugs at the buttons holding his shirt closed. I should probably feel some deeper level of mortification at our situation, but I'm just too exhausted to care anymore. Cyrus tosses me his shirt as I requested, immediately turning away so I can move freely.

The fabric is mixed with wool, making it a little itchy as it rakes across my arms. Still warm from Cyrus's body, I shiver as my skin absorbs his heat. "Now, what do you mean about my emotions triggering the visions?" I mumble, trying not to appear as flustered as I feel. Something about wearing his clothes feels too intimate, like another line between us has blurred, and no matter what I do, I'll never be able to erase the damage I've done.

"I...." Cyrus stumbles on his words as he faces me. His eyes drift down my frame, studying my damp hair and the way his shirt clings to my skin. It's a struggle not to fidget under this scrutiny. Sensing my discomfort, Cyrus clenches his fists and clears his throat to speak once more. "What were you feeling when the vision overtook you?"

My thoughts drift back over the moments before I was swept into the nightmare. "I was feeling exhausted and nervous. I was worrying over you, specifically your presence here to watch my training. I was afraid I would make another foolish mistake, and you'd see it." My cheeks flush red, and I bite my tongue to keep myself from talking anymore. Feelings have never gotten me far in this world and admitting to any type of weakness only leaves me vulnerable. Even with Cyrus, I should be careful.

"And how did you feel in the vision?" Cyrus questions, no sign of judgement at my explanation. Not even any trace of hurt flickers in his expression when he hears me say I did not want him around during my training. Instead, he presses for more information with an almost clinical detachment. "Were your feelings the same or different from the beginning of the vision?"

Exhaustion, nervousness, worry, and fear. I tick of the emotions on one hand as I replay the vision. "They were the same," I exclaim, a question immediately popping up to my lips. "But...how does that help me, Cyrus? Am I supposed to force myself to feel something if I want to see a vision?"

"I...I don't know," Cyrus murmurs, rubbing his chin as he processes the information. "But at least it's a start."

His calmness annoys me, and I cannot stop myself from lashing out. "Really? Because all I hear is that we are going in circles. Even if our abilities are connected to our emotions, that still leaves us with no means of controlling what we see. If anything, we've just damned ourselves to never understanding our gifts." *Emotions are dangerous, prowling beasts that hide in the lairs of our hearts and attack at the worst possible moments. They are unstoppable, uncontrollable, and unyielding.*

Cyrus pauses, turning to face me, a flash of concern causing his mouth to turn into a deeper frown, "Look, I get that you're frustrated, but—"

"No more," I plea, my mind swimming with too many questions to process at this time. "I need to rest."

Cyrus grabs my hand, halting my progress toward the path that leads deeper into the caverns. "Iris, I really think we could figure this out tonight if you'll just stay—"

"Enough!" I snarl, ripping my arm away as my temper boils with my frustration. "After all the horrors I just had to witness, I'm done, Cyrus. I felt myself losing my mind because my Ddraig was dead. I watched you die right in front of me. Now, I need to sleep and try and forget how all that felt. Can you understand that?"

I shove past him, elbowing my way around his still frame. The wool in the shirt's fabric scratches my skin as I hurry away, reminding me that I'm not in my own clothes. *He was kind to me; he's always been protective and kind to me in his way. He doesn't deserve my impatience or my scorn.*

I almost make it out of his sight without speaking again, but that nagging sense of guilt stays my feet at the edge of the cavern, forcing my mouth to whisper, "Thanks for letting me use your shirt."

"I'm sorry," Cyrus replies, his arms crossing as he scuffs the ground with his boot. "I know I'm pressing you to stay and talk more than you want. I just...." His words trail off as he silently argues with himself over what to say. He shifts from one foot to the other, hesitating on the edge of sharing his thoughts with me and keeping me out of his confidence.

"Please, tell me," I sigh, walking back to stand beside him, stifling a yawn as the shock of my vision wears off, fatigue rapidly filling the void in my thoughts. *Whatever it is, just make it quick!* My burning eyelids scorch my pupils as I blink, and I struggle not to fall asleep while I wait for Cyrus to make up his mind about talking to me. In truth, I am curious as to what is on his mind. Ever since we returned from the House of Piranhas, he's treated me with cold hostility or guarded fear. In fact, the more I think about it, the more I realize that this is the most civil conversation we've had in a long time. So, my attempt to be gentle and kind as I approach him once more is completely genuine. "What are you trying to say, Cyrus?"

Cyrus controls his breathing, his hands growing still as he makes a decision. "I just...don't want to be alone." Raking a hand over the back of his neck, the words finally pour out of his mouth. "My brother broke something inside me, Iris. I wake up at night in terror, screaming as I dream of all the nightmarish things he did to me. My dreams have been bad enough that they cause me to sleepwalk. I've awakened at the mouth of the cave, calling for my brother, begging him to kill me. Sometimes I fear I'm crazy." Pulling one arm away from his body, I see a long, jagged cut running from wrist to elbow, neat stitches keeping it closed. "Last night, I woke up when I'd sliced my own arm open, my last words a shout of triumph, proclaiming that I would finally die and rid the world of my wickedness. I'm still not sure if that's truly what I want or something my brother managed to implant into my brain. Either way, I am afraid I'll kill myself if I'm left alone too long."

"But you don't feel like you want to die when you're awake, right?" All traces of sleep disappear from my mind when I hear Cyrus's fears.

Cyrus shakes his head, his arms wrapping around his body as though he's keeping out a chill. I can see his teeth chattering. "I only feel this way when I'm asleep. Some hallucinations are so strong they happen when I'm awake too, but I've been able to talk myself through those," Cyrus confesses, wringing his hands a little as he focuses his gaze on the ground.

"How come I'm just hearing about this now, Cyrus? Does Suryc know?" I demand, wondering how he's managed to stay alive this long on his own. *It's a miracle he's survived this long!*

In a much softer voice, Cyrus rasps, "I couldn't tell Suryc. I couldn't handle the hurt it would bring him. I'm only telling you now because I actually drew blood this last time." Cyrus shivers, his eyes growing wide as he recalls the details of his last nightmares. "I'm afraid I'm losing my mind, Iris. The darkness in me is growing stronger, and I fear I cannot trust myself, alert or asleep."

My heart feels as though I've weighed it down with heavy stones and tossed it into the river. "How long have you been dealing with this alone?" *I would have done something if I'd known,* I tell myself to assuage my guilt.

"It's been coming on since I was captive with Wolf. After

we returned to the Pith, I started sleepwalking. I'd go to Suryc for comfort, but he spends his nights with Siri." *And I can't bear the sight of our Ddraigs together while you and I remain apart.* He does not say it, but I recognize the wistful longing in the way he stares at me. "The self-harm is really what terrifies me."

"Who stitched your wound?" I inquire pity causing my heart to ache. *I understand what it feels like to wake up screaming, to search for comfort and find none. Talking to Cyrus is in many ways like conversing with a mirror.* I may not be prepared to love or couple myself to him, but I can relate to his circumstances.

"I did it myself. Hurt like hell, but I managed." Feverish terror gleams in Cyrus's wild eyes. "Please. Help me. I know it's a lot to ask. I mean, you've already saved me once. But—"

"Follow me." My voice sounds tiny as I give the order, and I struggle to hide the quiver in my limbs as I consider what I'm about to do. *I wonder if we'll be able to make this work or if we will end up killing each other.* If I was a betting woman, I'd wager that one of us will die before the week is out. "We'll go to wherever you've hidden your stuff first. Bring what you need for the night, and then I'll show you where I sleep. From now on, you will bed down there too. We can move the rest of it tomorrow."

Cyrus sighs, reaching over and bear hugging me before I can react. His sudden nearness overwhelms me, and I brace myself against his chest, trying to quell my first instinct to push him away. When my hands hit his bare skin, I feel even more awkward. "Thank you," Cyrus breathes into my hair, the strands near my ear standing on end. He cradles me a heartbeat longer than necessary before he finally releases his hold.

"Come on then," I growl when I'm free to move. A strange sensation prickles in my hands, and suddenly, the further I move from Cyrus, the colder my world becomes. Cyrus doesn't seem to notice, staying a few steps behind me like a watchful puppy. Yet I feel the shift, and it terrifies me. For better or worse, Cyrus is becoming a source of comfort, an emotional crutch that I just cannot allow myself to indulge.

My vision alone was proof of that—if I allow my heart to get too involved with him, if I allow the coupling that Siri says is inevitable, then surely, I am setting the stage for that vision to be fulfilled. And the thought of watching him and Siri die at the hands of Wolf brings bile to my throat.

However, I cannot deny Cyrus's pleas for help, especially when it was my orders that caused him to endure the nightmares he's faced. I cannot abandon him to the ghosts in his mind. I'd never forgive myself if I woke up one morning and found him dead by his own hand.

"I...I sleep here." Cyrus interrupts my brooding, pointing to a tiny crevice in the wall. "It's a tight squeeze to get inside, but I figured that would keep me safe." He slides a hand into the crack, pawing at the ground on the right side. Within a few seconds, his hand snakes out of the hole with a carefully tied shirt that's serving as a makeshift knapsack.

"You...you were already packed?" I exclaim, wondering if I've just been duped into some strange seduction plan he's concocted.

"I never unpacked my stuff," Cyrus mutters, unable to meet my eye. "I guess I haven't felt safe enough to call this home."

Instinctively I brush his arm, whispering, "I'm sorry, Cyrus." Heat erupts under my fingertips, searing my skin until I am sure my fingers are charred. When I move my hand away, I still feel the pressure of Cyrus's skin against mine like an after-image from looking up into the sun. "Let's just go," I hiss, falling back into brooding silence before I can do any more damage.

***

"What's your greatest fear, Helena?" Ithel wonders aloud as they take a break during their third day of training for another meager meal of stew and stale bread.

"Heights," Helena retorts sarcastically as she slumps into a chair beside the guard, wishing she could knock him to the floor for all the horrible things he's made her endure. Right now, her nerves still flutter from her last attempt to climb up the palace ramparts.

Ithel had been truly sadistic this time and forced her to wear a blindfold, leaving her completely dependent upon her sense of touch. "Remember, your Windwalker magic won't be able to save you in the tunnel. You fall there, and you will die," Ithel whispered into her ear just before he secured the blindfold over her eyes.

Helena's heartbeat hadn't slowed since not even when her feet finally hit the infirmary's stone patio once more. "I thought we were supposed to *run* the tunnel, Ithel. Why do you keep forcing me to climb up the palace walls? Shouldn't I be focusing on building up my leg muscles and my endurance?"

"Climbing does that," Ithel bites back, stirring his broth with a crooked spoon. "The fact that it works your arms too is an added bonus. Besides, you don't know what's actually in the tunnel, do you? Maybe you'll need upper body strength too." Ithel smirks when he notices Helena's pinched, sour expression and reiterates his first question. "Now, what is your greatest fear?"

"Do they have anything other than broth in the kitchens?" Helena whines, refusing to answer as she slurps loudly. "Meat? Cheese? Even a few onions or greens would help give it some flavor. Or maybe a piece of bread that doesn't make me fear breaking a tooth as I bite down."

"This broth provides your body with all it needs to function. And that bread may be tough, but it's filling," Ithel answers, pointing his spoon at her with a low growl in his throat. "And you're damn lucky you get it. Now, quit complaining and eat."

"What do you mean?" Helena wonders, mopping the remnants of her soup with the hardest crust of her bread to soften its texture. The formless, tasteless lump is gummy in her mouth. *Still, it's better than starving,* she reminds herself, forcing her body to swallow the sticky mass before it becomes too thick to move with her tongue.

"I mean, oh Entitled One, that the kitchens don't supply

any of this for you. I make your meals, so you'll get what I give you or nothing at all," Ithel grumbles, lowering his gaze to the table as he waits for her to respond. "You think I like spending my evenings skulking in the kitchen kneading dough and stirring a kettle while you dream of finer things in the infirmary beds?"

"I'm...I'm sorry," she chokes, wondering when Ithel finds the time to shop for supplies in the markets outside the palace walls. *I am a kept woman.* She silently berates herself, hating the idea of owing Ithel for this kindness. Helena has no doubt that Ithel provides this food out of his own pocket; Alaric may have great wealth at his disposal, but he'd never dip into his coffers to feed her. Guilt and embarrassment churn in Helena's stomach as she whispers, "I didn't know, and I did not mean to insult you. Thank you for feeding me, Ithel."

"Wouldn't do you any good to starve," he grunts in response, his cheeks turning pink at her gratitude. "We'll see if you still want to thank me after this afternoon. Now, I haven't forgotten that you neglected to answer my question twice, Helena. Tell me your greatest fears. Immediately."

"What have I to fear?" Helena exclaims bitterly, pointing to the scars on her wrists from the prison shackles. "I've been captured, whipped, and branded a traitor. I've lost everything and everyone that I have ever loved. I've spent my last years in the dark, dank cells of this horrible place. I've starved and longed for fresh air and sunlight. I've witnessed murder and grief and experienced every other foul human emotion we've got! What more can be taken from me, Ithel? What could I possibly have left to fear?"

Her guardian ceases his meal, his jaw clenching shut as he stares hard at her. "Everyone has something that terrorizes them, Helena. Maybe you know what haunts your footsteps. Maybe you are truly blessed to live in ignorance of what terrifies you. It doesn't matter really; I'll find out soon enough." His words chill her to the core as she wonders at his cryptic meaning. "Are you finished eating?" Ithel wipes his face, reaching across the table.

As she hands him the weathered ceramic bowl, a movement catches her eye from inside it. Long, black claws curl around the rim. An eye appears next, then a wicked set of elongated, grimy teeth. "What the hell is that?" she screams, tossing the bowl to the ground. It shatters, pieces of glass skewering the shrieking monster that writhes at her feet.

"Hello, betrayer," An eerily familiar voice whimpers from the wide-open mouth of the creature. Though it never articulates its tongue or lips, the words are clearly spoken in the king's singsong tone. "You are a lovely liar, aren't you? Don't you think I know what you're hiding? Don't you think I've already seen what haunts your darkest dreams?" The monster cuts its dark eyes toward Helena when it hears her breathing hitch, its mouth finally closing into a cunning smile. It scuttles along the floor, creeping closer to Helena's side with long, grimy claws reaching for her pearly flesh.

"Ithel?" Helena whimpers, her head whipping to keep one eye on the creature while turning back to her guard. "I don't understand, Ithel! What is this?"

Yet Helena does not find Ithel standing beside her as anticipated. Instead, he lies on the stones at her feet, his body sliced to ribbons by the shards of her bowl. "Why do you hurt me, Helena? Why do you always hurt me?" His voice grows faint as she watches the light fade from his eyes, the piercing blue color leeching out of his irises with every rasping breath. "All I ever did...was love you. Was that so wrong?"

"No! Ithel!" Helena lurches toward his shattered body, her feet splashing in Ithel's still warm, sticky blood as it pools around her. Helena balks, jumping clear of the gore. And when she looks back down at her feet, both the monster and Ithel's body are gone.

"Remember what I told you about being drugged during our first training session?" The real Ithel asks as he edges closer to Helena's wide-eyed form, his mouth a grim line as he waits for her to comprehend his meaning.

"You rat bastard! What was in that soup?" Helena steps forward, only to hear the crunch of bones under her feet. Skulls, hips, legs, ribs, and all other bones from countless human bodies are now mortared into the floor. There's nowhere to step without landing on some poor soul's decaying body.

Helena shrieks, jumping up into the chair as she surveys the gaping maws and eyeless sockets of the skulls that seem to laugh at her from their cement beds. "Hello, traitor," they bellow and groan. "See what you've done? See how you've hurt us? How many must die before you see the real problem is yourself?"

Around the legs of the chair where Helena stands, a few grasping fingers, still connected by rotting ligaments and fetid tissues, clutch at the wood. These hands wrap around the rungs and feet of the chair, almost as if they are still alive, clinging to a raft to keep from drowning in the sea. Their haunting voices keen and wail as they reproach, "You did this to us, Helena! You betrayed us into the hands of our enemies! We are dead because of your selfishness!"

Then, these hands reveal their true purpose, slowly dragging the chair legs deeper down into the cement. Skulls light up with fire in their eyeless sockets, their mouths chattering with laughter as the monsters plunge Helena and her perch toward its mortar grave. "You will join us soon," their voices groan as their jaws creak and clack to form the words. "Your bones will lie among ours before the sun sets!"

"Ithel! Help me!" Helena wails, rocking back and forth on the chair as she searches for an escape.

"Helena! You've got to learn to focus!" Ithel's voice sounds like churning gravel, and when she looks at him, his eyes glow like burning coals. "Control it, Helena!"

She screams, jumping backward, only to wail when she demolishes another skull and hipbone under her heels. The sightless eye socket of the skull accuses her of the damage, its jaws clicking in disgust.

Ithel's hands grip her shoulders, his touch scorching her

exposed skin. She bellows and thrashes in his grasp, but the guard does not let her move. "Helena! Listen to me! You've got to calm down!"

"Please help me! It's all my fault!" She wails as the skull under her heel bites her foot. She feels blood pooling as she scuttles out of reach. "I'm so sorry, Ithel! Please, make it stop!"

"Slow your breathing rate," Ithel instructs, his tone gentle and soothing. It matters little; Helena screeches as his fingers elongate into tightly coiling snakes that wrap around her arms. Tighter and tighter, they bind, slithering closer to her neck with each passing second.

"Get them off! Get them off now!" Helena flails her arms in a feeble attempt to remove the hallucination. "Oh gods! Ithel! We've got to get out of here!"

Ithel's hand burns as it cracks across her cheek, but the pain manages to stifle her fears long enough to free her mind to listen. "Helena, focus on your breathing. There's going to be things around you that frighten you, but you've got to remember that they are not real. You've been drugged. Say that to yourself if it helps you calm down."

"I've been drugged," she repeats, shuddering as she takes a deep breath. Closing her eyes only brings a momentary comfort. Without Helena's sight to terrorize her, auditory hallucinations begin. A child's voice screams in terror while a deep man's voice whispers of his love and devotion. Both are far more devastating than anything she's endured so far, for deep down, Helena knows these voices are real memories bubbling up to the surface.

"Alaric may do something like this to you in the tunnel, Helena. You've got to be prepared. Keep your breathing in check. Stay calm and climb. Ignore the hallucinations and just keep your feet moving."

"I can't do this," she moans, her hands covering her ears as she attempts to block out the voices in her mind. "I can't see them again! I can't face the horrors that happened to them! I can't relive the moments when I watched them die!"

"You don't have a choice," Ithel replies grimly as he pushes her closer to the edge of the building. *If you could only see how much I hate this for you,* he sighs as he drags her flailing body to the edge of the patio. *I wish there was another way or something I could do to spare you this trial. I really do. I wish you knew I take no pleasure in what I've done to you; I hate myself for it. But this is the only way I can prepare you for what is coming....* As much as Ithel longs to tell her his true feelings, his voice is harsh as he pushes her over the edge and demands, "Catch yourself before you hit the ground, Helena, then climb back up to me!"

As Helena plummets toward the ground, the drug in her system wreaks havoc on her mind. "I am a vulture," she screeches, struggling against the wind as she attempts to hold her arms out at her sides as if to soar on the breeze and circle over the city. Despite her Windwalker abilities, she cannot control the gusting winds that whip around her helpless body. Not with the drugs in her system. "I cannot fly!" she cries, clenching her eyes tight as her stomach roils. The hallucination changes, twisting Helena into a small animal, scurrying to find shelter as a dark shadow looms overhead. "I will die! Ithel! Help me!" she bellows, her ears filling with an unseen beast's gravelly snarls. She imagines blood-stained teeth nipping at her legs as the monster slowly gains ground. Fire rips through her limbs as if long claws have sliced through sinew and muscle, cleaving joints and bones from their meaty flesh. A guttural howl bursts to life from her body as she falls, so lost in her mind's fears that she cannot see the ground hurtling closer and closer.

You fear the monster, you fear being prey; your only comfort is that you die this day, a grotesque image of Ithel sings as it floats beside her. His eyes are replaced by twin flames, and his mouth gapes wide. Where teeth still stand in those grey gums, they are cracked and bleeding. The monster's mouth closes to a grim smile, blood oozing down either side of its lips as it delights in her fear. *You are beyond worthless, Helena. You're good for nothing but the gravedigger's shovel. And even he won't have much use for you after you splatter yourself against the stones.*

"Not real, not real," she whimpers against the monstrous sight, scratching her hands until they bleed, focusing on the pain to regain some control over her mind and abilities. "I can't stop, Ithel!"

Then you will join me in death, the voice of the man she'd lived with in Cassè shivers up her spine. *And I will torment you for all the hell you put me through.* She sees the faint outline of the man, his eyes shrouded in darkness, and a too wide smile ripping through his ethereal face.

"No! No, please!" Helena fights, fixing her eyes on the stones that are far too close for comfort. Small changes in coloration, glittering veins of quartz and gold are now easy to distinguish. The murmuring cries of horrified observers rise up to meet her as she continues to drop. Feebly her hands shiver as she coaxes her abilities through the fog of hallucination and despair. Yet despite her greatest efforts, nothing slows her fall.

Ithel listens to every painful moment, praying Helena can get control over herself. He'd already made precautions, placing several healer slaves at the base of the palace to attend her if she failed. Yet that safety net doesn't do anything to ease his conscience. *This is an all-time low even for you,* Ithel chastises himself as he waits for the inevitable moment when Helena reaches the bottom. "There was no other way to prepare her," he reminds himself in a broken whisper. *But that doesn't make it right. I just pushed a drugged woman off the roof! What kind of monster does that make me?*

"She spoke of them," Ithel repeats the word as his mind replays Helena's last words. *The ones she left me for,* Ithel adds bitterly, the unhealed wounds in his heart breaking open once more. It was the first time he'd heard her mention the family she'd had in Cassè since she'd been freed from the prison. *The ones she loved more than she ever cared for me.*

A sour taste rises to Ithel's tongue as he recalls the early days of their relationship. He'd been the lead guard at the border station in the heart of the Devil's Spine when she'd joined his ranks. She'd marched into his office with her head held high and handed him the transfer orders. "Why come here? Thinking of making a name for yourself?" he sniped, surprised that someone of her background would take a job in a wild, rangy outpost at the border.

"I've come to see if the stories I've grown up hearing are true," Helena replied, her voice lacking all empathy and emotion. She'd been a colder, harsher woman in her younger years. "I want to see if the people in Cassè are really as barbaric as I've been led to believe."

"Dangerous choice," Ithel remarked with a smirk, secretly admiring her spirit. "Not many would willingly leave the comforts of the palace just to question their king's version of the truth."

"I'm not most people," Helena shot back, staring at Ithel in cool detachment. "I prefer to make my own choices."

"And what will you do with the information you discover out here?" Ithel couldn't help but wonder as she strode toward the door. "What will it solve?"

It was the only moment in Helena's introduction that her resolve faltered. In that single backward glance, she appeared completely vulnerable and lost. "I…I don't know what I'll do. I just have to see it for myself. I couldn't bear to sit through another meeting listening to the terrors of Cassè without actually experiencing it firsthand. Once I know the truth, I'll figure out the rest."

He'd let her leave the office and settle into the barracks, wordlessly adding her name to the guard's roster for the next evening. But he knew what she'd discover; he knew how bitter and disillusioned she'd become when she realized everything she'd been told was a lie. The people of Cassè were not monstrous at all. The life they led was just as refined and amicable as you could find in Déchets—and that was the real problem for their king. Alaric wasn't afraid of this neighboring land's barbaric ways; he was jealous that they were thriving without his leadership. He was afraid that Cassè was doing better than Déchets. It was pure greed that fueled the king's desperate feud with the people of Cassè, nothing more.

We might have changed the world together, Ithel recalls as a single tear slips down his cheek. *I would have followed you into Cassè. I would have helped you fight alongside them. I'd have given you anything you wanted if you'd only stayed true to me.* But Helena had strayed; she'd disappeared into Cassè without a trace once she'd learned the truth. *She found someone else over in that land; she loved another and had a family.* That realization is a rusty dagger slicing into Ithel's chest so that every next breath brings an excruciating ache in his heart.

Ithel lets his tears fall as he listens to Helena's terrorized sobs as she plummets to the ground. Then, silence. A blessed, terrifying silence. "Helena?" Ithel whispers the name, praying that her blood does not paint the stones below. Nothing. *If she'd gotten control, she would have answered. Even if it was just to call me atrocious names.*

"We're doing our best," one of the healer slaves shouts in response, his voice betraying the worry he feels for his patient. "But we may need more...." The healer's words die off as he gives his final breath.

Ithel races into the infirmary, shouting orders as he moves. "All available healers report to the ground floor. Priority patient in critical condition!" he demands, grateful to see a handful of healer slaves racing to the window, using their Windwalker magic to speed their arrival to their patient's side. *Hurry, hurry,* Ithel urges even as he follows them, lithe and graceful as he flies out the window and drifts down to the ground floor on the breeze.

It feels like an eternity before Ithel's heels strike the paving marble on the ground floor. He hears the soft wails of onlookers, frozen in place as the healers attempt to save Helena. Ithel's eyes land on a young girl, her mouth hanging open as tears pour down her face. "There was nothing we could do," the young girl's mother insists, racing over to cling to Ithel's arm. She desperately tries to pull her daughter's gaze away from the gory scene. "She was falling so fast; there was just no time to react," she adds as silent, grieving tears well in her eyes. "We tried to use our Windwalker abilities to slow her fall, but there wasn't enough time."

"It's not your fault," Ithel whispers hoarsely, wishing there was someone to blame besides himself. The little girl's haunted expression does not leave his mind's eye. *How many more will be traumatized this week? Because if Helena survives this, if she truly wishes to succeed in the tunnel, she'll have to endure this training. Again. And again, until she's mastered it.*

Ithel shakes off the woman's clinging grasp, forcing his feet to carry him closer to the scene. Voices hiss and murmur as waves of watchers part the way for Ithel to reach Helena's side. His stomach drops as his shoes slide on the stones, blood making them slippery. *Helena's blood. My gods, I've killed her!* Piles of sand form as the bodies of the dead healers disintegrate. More slaves take their place, pouring their life forces into her broken body. Helena's neck lies at a severe angle, her sightless eyes staring accusingly right at Ithel. Her legs are black and swollen from broken bones, and blood pools under her back.

Suddenly, she moans, and the sound is both soothing and excruciating to Ithel's ears. "She lives! But my gods, what kind of life will she have? The healers aren't miracle workers, you know? She'll wish she died, you mark my words!" someone shouts from the crowd of onlookers. Soon, Helena's screams are too gut-wrenching for them to witness, and they disperse from the scene.

"Ithel," Helena slurs as she calls his name, her shattered hand twitching as if she tries to raise it in his direction.

Ithel sinks to his knees beside her, pouring his own life force into her healing. *If I die, it is just. I caused this injury; I should be the one to sacrifice for it.* "I'm so sorry, Helena!" He chokes on the words, his fingers searching for a place he can touch her without causing more pain. His lips long to ask for forgiveness, but his tongue stays quiet. Such a kindness should not be offered to him. It would salve his conscience, but it would not stop her agony.

Ithel doesn't know how many healers perish in their efforts to save Helena's life. He passes his energy into her until he begins to sway. Despite his best efforts, his body refuses to give its last breath, self-preservation kicking in. Ithel drops to the stones beside Helena, noticing every detail in her broken face. His mind is so focused on her that Ithel neglects to hear the striking of fine leather boots on the stones by his back.

"So, you finally just killed her?" The king of Déchets sneers as he surveys the scene. "Can't say I blame you, but I never would have thought you'd have the balls to do it." Another healer races up to Helena's knee. "Oh, I see! An impulse reaction, and now you're filled with regret. My first assessment of you was correct, after all. Coward!" The king kicks Ithel hard, pounding his boots into Ithel's back as though he attempts to break his victim's spine. When that grows tiresome, Alaric saunters off, whistling merrily as he moves away from the grisly scene.

"Sir? What about yourself?" One of the healer slaves questions Ithel as she assesses his waning strength.

"Just take care of Helena. Keep her alive, whatever the cost," Ithel mumbles, his fingers curling into Helena's hair before he blacks out.

CHAPTER 4

Wren barely makes it inside his tent before Lynx springs into action behind him, pressing a serrated blade to his throat. "The only thing that's keeping you alive right now is the fact that my child is here," Lynx growls as she scans the tent for any weapon Wren might use against her. "Why did you sell me out as a spy? I was only following—"

Wren hisses sharply over her words, motioning to the billowing tent flaps. Anyone could be outside listening to their confrontation. Wren's overly paranoid nature swings into full effect determined that no one else would slip through his defenses and thwart his plans again. "Come with me."

"Why?" Lynx resists, tilting her head to check on her son, who lies peacefully sleeping in a basket by her feet. That distraction is all it takes for Wren to pounce, slamming his head back into Lynx's mask. While she recovers from the attack, Wren carefully slides out of her grasp. Before she has the chance to retaliate, Wren lifts his hands in defeat.

"I don't want to fight," he whispers as he slowly backs out of his tent into the cool night air. "Leave the child. No one will bother him. Follow me, and I'll tell you everything." Quickly scanning the grounds to be certain that no one else moves at this late hour, Wren sprints for the huge field that stands open and empty in his path. Just beyond it lies the ocean, whose unending waves drone on in a constant, monotonous roar that will drown out all sounds of their conversation. Noise cover and a clear line of sight — the two things that will ensure that the mistakes that put Lynx in peril are not recommitted tonight. Wren doesn't turn to see if Lynx obeyed his wishes. Every second his back is exposed is another opportunity to become Death's friend. He doesn't breathe easy until his feet muddle wet sand and the ocean's song is a relentless melody in his ears.

Keeping his back to the ocean, Wren halts suddenly in place while Lynx rushes up behind him. She barely manages to stop before running him through with her blade. Both of them breathing hard, they gulp a few breaths before Lynx shouts, "I want answers, Wren! Why did you name me a traitor? Why say you are trying to help me and then sell me out to Wolf?"

"It was the only way to keep myself safe." Wren winces as he says the words, hating the veracity in them.

"You mean you'd sell out a mother and newborn just to stay alive?" Lynx raises her blade once more, her mouth drawing back in a sneer.

"My safety is the only thing that's protecting you and your son, so don't get all high and mighty on me," Wren snaps, slapping the tip of her blade away from his chest. "I put the focus on you, but I'm going to be the one taking the big risks." *Playing both sides never ends well,* Wren reminds himself with a frustrated sigh. *How did I get mixed up in all this?* The image of that sleeping boy appears like a ghost in the mist. *You could not bear to see him harmed. That's why you'll take these reckless chances.*

The memory of the tiny Ddraigs sidling up to him when Suryc carried him to the hatching den flares up in Wren's memory too. Suryc had cornered Wren about his loyalties then, hoping he'd choose the side of the Ddraigs, preying on his emotions by showing him the helpless young. *That Ddraig just wants to protect his own, much like I seek to keep Lynx's child from harm.* Wren drops his head, wishing he could detach himself from the crazy ideas already taking shape in his mind.

He must have grumbled audibly as he recalls the black

Ddraig's plea for aid, and Lynx eyes him suspiciously, asking, "What's wrong?"

"I think I just decided to join the fight," Wren admits, cursing himself for getting too involved, even though a small part of his heart feels relieved to finally have a cause that matters this much to him. "And it appears that I'm going to be the proverbial wolf in sheep's clothing." *But it's nothing new to me, is it?* Wren declares, silently offering up a prayer that he'll find a way to survive this mess.

Lynx's mouth falls open as she finally comprehends Wren's plan. "You're saying that while Wolf watches me, waiting to see if I sell him out—"

"He'll hopefully miss the fact that I'm the real threat," Wren finishes, a thankful sigh of relief escaping his lips when Lynx's knife falls in the dirt. "I'll make him grow to depend upon me, to trust my judgment even more than he values the rest of his pack. I'll use Fox's leaving to my benefit, letting Wolf believe he's the betrayer, selling out Wolf's secrets to Iris and the Ddraigs. Whatever it takes to keep suspicion off me, I'll do it." Wren scans the field, his keen eyes watching for any signs of movement that might point to someone spying on them.

"Why?" Lynx demands, absently clutching her stomach as if the gesture could protect her son.

"Loyalty to my old house, my own damned love of intrigue, or downright insanity, I don't know. There are a thousand different answers to that question," Wren explains, his mouth hardening into a slim, straight line across his face as he prepares to explain his plan to Lynx. "If we're going to survive this, you're going to have to trust me completely. There may be times when I have to say and do things that hurt you. If Wolf tells me to beat you, I won't bat an eye as I do it."

"I can endure anything you put me through," Lynx whispers, her gaze on her shoes. "I've already been through worse, believe me. Just keep my son alive and safe."

Wren nods as if her demand was already anticipated. Then, with carefully practiced motions, Wren strikes out hard and jabs a fist into Lynx's jaw. She lands on the ground at the impact of the jarring blow, and already a bruise blooms to life under the edge of her mask. "That's to give us a story should any guards see us return to the campsite." He slips an extra shirt from the deep pockets of his coat, wadding it into a ball as he steps toward the fallen woman. "Carry this as if it is your son. If anyone asks, I'll tell them I caught you trying to escape my tent." In a softer voice, Wren murmurs, "I'm sorry it's come to this. Every time I end up hurting you, please remember that it's just a part I'm playing to keep us alive."

"Fair enough." Lynx hesitates to receive the outstretched bundle, rubbing her jaw as she exclaims, "But just how do you intend on becoming Wolf's right-hand man? He's not easily fooled."

"Neither am I," Wren adds with a mirthless laugh, hoisting Lynx off the ground carefully. "However, tonight, we were nearly caught because there's a bigger threat in our midst. But I think I know who it is, and I've already got a plan to get rid of him. I'm going to drive some doubt into Wolf's mind."

"Just like that?" Lynx scoffs, dusting off the coating of wet sand that covers her pants with grit. "You really think it will be that easy?"

"A few well cast shadows are all it takes to seed mistrust. The rest will happen naturally, especially since Wolf's already feeling betrayed and vulnerable. It won't take much for his mind to assume there might be more traitors in the camp. I just have to make sure his thoughts lead him toward Jackal and away from myself," Wren exclaims as he hands Lynx the shirt bundle that will pass for a newborn. "Trust me. If there's any one thing I'm good at, it's this kind of game. Wolf will never know what hit him."

"You better be right," Lynx acquiesces, still unconvinced as they turn and hurry back to camp. "We're depending upon you now."

***

"This is where you sleep?" Cyrus wonders as he steps

into the grand chamber that leads to the Pith caverns. I nod, unable to speak as Cyrus stares at me expectantly. When no explanation comes, he adds. "I just figured you'd have picked someplace deeper in the heart of the caves. Somewhere that's easily defensible and holds less painful memories for you."

Scanning the room, I understand Cyrus's assessment of the place. After all, this is where Antero was burned alive, where I'd first discovered he was a traitor, and where Wolf had first been separated from my side. "Yes, there are strong memories here. It's true. Some are difficult to recall," I agree, surprising Cyrus when I add, "But there are precious ones too, Cyrus."

"Like what?" Cyrus wheezes, and judging by his tense expression, I suspect he's silently praying my answer has nothing to do with Wolf. Already feeling vulnerable and emotionally threadbare, listening to me praise anything about his monstrosity of a brother would probably send Cyrus into a nervous breakdown.

I offer him a wistful smile, recalling my first moments in the cavern mouth. "This is where I learned that Ddraigs exist. That knowledge completely rerouted my life. Now, this is the first place to defend against any invaders who might seek to steal into our lands. As long as I'm here, I can be certain the Ddraigs are safe. If danger comes, I can raise an alarm. I can fight to keep them safe."

"You're acting as a patrol," Cyrus surmises, feeling a little small as he mutters, "How did you not see me the night I almost killed myself in this cavern?" Cyrus points to the lip that hangs over the steepest portion of the cave's mouth. "That's where I nearly...." He gulps as the feelings from that night take hold.

"You almost—" I drop my head to my chest, my eyelids falling closed, a chill seeping into my bones. *How did I not recognize that he was this broken?* I accuse myself, wishing I'd been paying better attention. "I sometimes spend the night up on land too. Sometimes the thought of being underground—of being swallowed up by the land itself—it's too much for me. On those nights, I sleep under the stars." My lip quivers slightly as I admit, "If I had been here, if I had seen how badly you were hurting, I would have helped you or tried to stop you. I... Cyrus, you have to know I would never wish you this kind of pain."

Cyrus nods, turning his face up to the cave's mouth. The angle of the entrance is odd, cutting off most of the night sky view. Still, Cyrus sees a few rebellious stars winking at him in the distance. "Maybe this is a bad plan, Iris. To be this close to the exit may only plague my dreams with ideas of escape. And I...I don't want to hurt you any more than I want to kill myself."

I point to the wall farthest from the cavern entrance. "Sleep there. I'll bed down a few feet in front of you. That way, you'll have to pass me if you sleepwalk again. I'm not a heavy sleeper anymore, so if you move, I'll be sure to wake up."

Cyrus obeys my wishes without another word, dropping his holey bedroll and blanket next to the rocks. He has no other items of wealth or usefulness that I can see. While he clears some wayward stones from his path, I set about building a small fire that will provide some comfort to us both on this first night.

It is awkward as we both prepare for sleep, attempting to adjust to each other's needs for privacy and routine. By the time we've both managed to drop into our bedrolls, the air is thick with silence. For a few blinks of the eyes, we turn and stare at each other, too lost for words to speak. Then we shift away, pointing our backs at the flames as we wait for sleep to claim us.

I must have been exhausted from the trauma of my earlier Gwen vision. For all my boasting, I slept too soundly for my own good that night. I did not hear the scuffles of shoes or the metallic zing of a blade loosed from its scabbard. Nor was I aware of the fluttered disturbance in the air close to my body or the light, careful footfalls of someone approaching my side. I missed all of those warning signs, twisting onto my back to give Cyrus a better aim at my throat.

It is his voice that warns me of the impending strike, forcing my eyes to fly open. Immediately I meet Cyrus's furious, dead stare, murder playing out in his nightmare. "You stupid, lazy oaf! If torturing you wasn't this much fun, I'd have killed you weeks ago. Why, the first time I saw you enter my courtyard, I could have ruined you! The only thing that kept you alive was my feelings for Iris. I know she'll want to be the one who deals the killing blow!" Cyrus's body slurs the words as he sways, and his body refuses to coordinate his motions. The tone of his voice is altered, as though his body is imitating Cane as he reenacts the hateful memory.

When Cyrus speaks as himself, I can hear the strange, subtle differences in his voice. His fear raises his tone, and the cadence of his words grows erratic. Cyrus's body trembles from the strength of the terror he still endures. It's like watching a person possessed, two distinctly different personas being portrayed in the same form. Or a play where two characters are acted out by the same individual. The way Cyrus shifts into and out of Wolf's mannerisms is eerily accurate, and it raises the hair on my arms.

"Iris," Cyrus wavers, tears spewing down his face. "She wouldn't send me here to die! I know she hates me, but—"

"But nothing!" Cyrus sneers as he shifts into Wolf, and I know the words I'm hearing must be from one of the many times Wolf tortured him. "She loathes the very thought of you! The only reason she sent you here is to suffer! She'll come here and rejoice to find you broken and begging for death." Wolf cackles, pointing a finger at an unseen addition to the dream. "And I hope the death she brings you is slow, brother. Slow and excruciating."

"No!" Cyrus goes white, covering his head with his hands. "Iris? It can't be true!"

Cyrus's body goes completely still, his voice changing to a high falsetto. Something about the way he stands suggests a feminine nature. "Miss me, Wolf?" he mumbles, brushing a hand down his cheek as he simpers. "Ready to die, Cyrus?"

"No, please, no!" Cyrus wails as he scuttles away from me, cowering into a ball as he screams.

He thinks it's me, I realize, growing cold as I watch him thrash, his brow breaking out into a clammy sweat. *He sees me in his dream, siding with his brother. He actually thinks I want him dead!* Dimly I recall the stories of the Vibría monster Wolf bartered for from Déchets, the shapeshifter he used to wreak havoc in Cyrus's mind. Worse than any hallucination, the Vibría tortured Cyrus physically and mentally, using my face as its own.

Hearing these hateful words breaks my heart for Cyrus. While I'd heard about the terrors he'd faced, nothing could prepare me for how terrible it was in reality. Rising from my bedroll, I race over to Cyrus's curled up form, hoping I can find a way to bring him back to the present. "Cyrus! Wake up!" I cry, attempting to rip the sword out of his clenched fist. It's a wonder he hasn't run himself through with it. His fingers are like long ice crystals, so rigid I fear they will snap when I try to pry them open. "Give me the sword, Cyrus!" I beg, reaching up to touch his face. I keep my voice gentle, hoping I can calm him with my soothing words. "It's okay, Cyrus. I'm here. Please, let me—"

The feel of my fingers only agitates him more. "Get away! Get away!" he screams, his arms flying out in an effort to push his ghosts away. "You're not real! You can't be real!"

The sword bites deeply into my throat, my blood spraying into his face and eyes. The sudden onslaught of warmth seems to pull Cyrus out of his terrors. It takes him a minute to shake the dream out of his mind, but I see the look of horror as he recognizes what he's done. The sword clatters to the stones as I fall to my knees. "Suryc! Siri!" His voice crackles with the force of his cries. "I need you now!"

I try to speak, but only a gurgling sound churns from my gaping neck. My fingers slide on my blood as I attempt to hold the skin closed, but I know it is a useless gesture. Every second is a step closer to death. My spine gives way, and I slump to the side, rolling onto my back. Immediately I choke on the blood pooling in my mouth, racking coughs lifting my body with their force.

Cyrus slides down to the ground, hoisting my upper body up to rest on his chest. I do not choke, nor do I breathe more than the faintest rustle. "Iris! Use my strength! Heal yourself, now!" Cyrus begs, his fingers entwining with mine as he puts pressure on the wound. "My gods, what have I done?! Iris! Keep breathing!"

My limbs quake and grow colder with every heartbeat. Despite Cyrus's pleadings, I cannot feel the mental connection that would allow me to heal myself. And even if I could, I wouldn't use it for fear of killing him in the process. Already I have slipped too far into Death's grasp. My vision turns gray and dim, and I hear my body's wheezing gasps slowing down each passing second.

This is what Hawk must have felt, I realize, my past deeds playing through my mind like a highlight reel of all the good and bad I've done. I know that when I reach the end of them, I will be dead. *It is a helpless feeling to slowly strangle on your own blood. He begged for such a fate from me; it's only fitting that I die in the same manner. And Warbler. My gods, what she must have endured! This is nothing compared to her sorrows.*

Iris? What's wrong? Siri whispers through my thoughts, and I can tell she is running in the tunnels. *Suryc heard Cyrus's cry, and I can feel your agony. Talk to me!*

Creeper, my mind continues its litany of the damned, heedless of Siri's pleas. *I earned this death for everything I put him through. But I don't regret it. I see his miserable face every day, and I remember how it felt to watch him breathe his last, but I stand by my actions. He deserved exactly what he got. It was justice for all the things he stole from Warbler.*

Siri, I suddenly call out to my Ddraig as my vision turns black, *tell Cyrus I'm sorry I took so long to see that he was the better man. I blamed him for a great deal of things that were really beyond his control. Tell him I forgive him. Keep him safe. And tell him…that in the end…I….*

IRIS, Siri wails, and I faintly hear the thundering of her feet as she enters the cavern where I lay dying.

I'm sorry, my friend. You were the best thing that ever came into my life. A light appears in my vision, a glorious warm pinprick of whiteness that grows ever closer.

"Iris," Cyrus moans, wiping my face with his bloody hands. "Stay with me, Iris!"

But by now, the light is calling my name, and I'm too far gone to care for the problems of this world.

***

"I won't do it! I won't let another slave die so I can be healed," Helena rasps from the infirmary bed, her head jammed into a pillow as if she can somehow escape the clutches of the slave approaching her side. His face is a mask of resigned acceptance, completely devoid of any traces of sadness or fear. *He doesn't even try to fight it.* Helena shivers as the healer's hand reaches for her wrist.

"It's not your choice to make," Ithel barks from his vantage point beside her, motioning for the slave to proceed.

"How many have died already?" Helena presses, shrinking away from the healer's touch. "How many more—?"

"As many as it takes to get you ready for the tunnel! Or have you forgotten your impending trial?" Ithel snarls, hating himself for the way terror colors his words. The sight of Helena's broken body filled Ithel with so much guilt that he'd attempted to give his own life force to heal her. While she'd drained most of his strength, an inner barrier shielded him from giving too much. *Probably something the king did when he connected guardians to prisoners, to make sure we don't die until the day of his choosing.*

Helena says nothing as she watches the healer slave's eyes glaze. A tear slips down her face when his body drops to the ground, already dust by the time it strikes the stones. "I hate this, and I hate you for it, Ithel!" she screams, her anger turning to anguish as the broken bones in her leg reset into their natural positions.

"I know," Ithel mutters, berating himself even as he waves more healers to her bedside. But gods help him, Ithel still felt something for the woman. Even after everything she'd put him through all those years ago, he still loved her. "I'll take your loathing if it means you're still alive to give it." Ithel's own heart breaks a little more as he recognizes how pathetic and desperate he sounds.

"Get out of here!" Helena snarls, gritting her teeth as her finger bones snap. "Stay the hell away from me!"

"I truly wish I could." Ithel wheezes as he moves out of the infirmary, giving Helena some space to grieve for the fallen healers. Stepping out into the sunlight of the infirmary's patio brings a little comfort. In the corner of the tiny oasis drips a cascading birdbath, and the sound of the trickling waters offers some small measure of soothing relief to Ithel's raw nerves.

Helena's curses rattle through the air at intermittent intervals, often right about the time when Ithel feels like he's finally beginning to settle down. Her voice is enough to drive him mad, a welcome and loathed distraction, like a thorn that itches when it's embedded in the skin — oh how it aches when it is finally removed, but oh how glorious it is as it scratches from the inside out!

She can never know how deeply I still care for her. It is a fool's wish anyway, Ithel notes with bitterness as he considers their morbid future. *If she survives the tunnel, she'll be sent back into Cassé, and if she fails in the tunnel, we both die. Either way, I end up empty handed.*

"You need your strength too. Take mine, sir," a small healer slave coos as she approaches his knee. Her long, dark hair shadows her face, cascading down her thin frame. She peeks through the tresses enough that Ithel can see the beauty in her emerald eyes and the glory of youth still tinging her features with childlike innocence.

"How old are you?" Ithel shudders as her tiny, cold hands touch his.

"Eleven," the child whispers, her voice no more than a sigh. Her voice is soft and completely devoid of emotion as she inquires, "Do you wish to take my strength? Or shall I give it to the woman in there?"

"Things are very wrong here," Ithel murmurs to himself bitterly as he drops to his knees before the little girl, wrapping his hands gently around her wiry shoulders. "Listen to me carefully. I want you to go down to the kitchens and speak to the maids that make bread. Tell them you were sent to meet Mercuri. They will guide you to him. When you meet him, he will ask you who sent you, and you tell him 'Helena's guardian.' He will give you some food, and he will take you someplace safe."

"But I'm bound to the king. My life is forfeit to the ones who need it more than I do." Even as the child protests against Ithel's plan, the glimmer of a future dares to shine in her eyes.

"Is that what you want, to die before your life's even begun?" Ithel snaps, gripping the child's arms tight enough to leave bruises. When she cries out, he drops his hold and whispers, "I'm sorry, girl. What is your name?"

"Raissa, sir," she whimpers, rubbing her arms as she shivers.

"How did you end up a slave, Raissa?" Ithel questions, keeping his voice soft and his hands at his sides.

Raissa shifts back and forth on her feet as she tells her story. "My family owed money to the king, and I'm the only child in the family that doesn't have Windwalker abilities. They sent me here to pay off their debts." Her head droops as she adds, "My mother's last words to me before she sold me to the king were, 'Finally found some way for you to be useful.' My father said nothing at all—he'd barely spoken two words to me after I did not show signs of Windwalker magic. They knew that when they sold me, I'd become a slave and probably die to heal someone else. They didn't care."

Ithel's heart breaks for the child as her lower lip begins to wobble, and he pulls her up in his arms for a gentle, comforting hug. "I'm going to tell you a secret, Raissa. The spells that the king uses on his slaves are indeed very powerful, but less so on children. You are young yet; I suspect that you can resist its draw if you fight it. Mercuri has some friends that can help you. They will make sure you find your way to freedom," Ithel assures, setting Raissa back on the floor and turning her so that she's facing the door. "Go quickly, and speak to no one in the halls. Can you do that?"

"You're sure?" Raissa gives Ithel a long look before she relents, wrapping her tiny fingers around his. "Thank you, sir," she exclaims as she scampers off in search of a new, free life.

It hardly feels like a victory as Ithel reseats himself by the waterfall, praying Raissa finds her way to safety. *How many more children have been forced to give up their life energies as slaves? How many of them could have been spared if they'd known they could resist Alaric's spells? How many good lives have been lost simply because they have no Windwalker talents? How long will this madness be allowed to continue?* Ithel wipes his eyes as he weeps for the lost ones, silently adding his and Helena's names to the litany.

As the sun gasps its final day's breath, Ithel stomps into the infirmary. Helena sits up in her bed, her body covered in a patchwork of bruises at various stages of healing. Her eyes are full of fire and hatred as she watches her guardian approach. Yet before her mouth can open to scold him, Ithel bellows at her, his voice hoarse and full of pleading.

"Listen here, Helena! You're going to beat the tunnel. Do you hear me? You're going to succeed. And when you do, you're going to find a way to dismantle the king's reign." He crosses over close to her side, leaning over so their faces almost touch. "And I'm going to help you do it—whatever it takes, Helena. Promise me you'll bring Alaric's reign to an end."

Helena stares hard into Ithel's eyes, defiance warring with her fears as she spits back, "How can you be so sure?"

"You hate that the healer slaves die to save you, right?" Ithel questions, pointing to the pile of sand swirling around the bed. "You hate what the king did to the people in Cassé? Don't you want to see him suffer for it? Look me in the eyes and tell me you don't want him dead!"

"Of course, I do," Helena agrees with a grumble. "But I don't want anyone else to die for me either!"

"Let them do their jobs, Helena." Ithel raises his hands to stop Helena's protests as he shouts, "I hate it too! And if there was another way, don't you think I'd have found it by now? But crying over these losses solves nothing. We can grieve over them once the world is right again — once you've had the chance to change the way Cassé is run. For now, let every death that heals you make you angry."

"It already does that, Ithel! I just want to stop it!" Helena cries, throwing off her blanket as she stumbles to her feet.

Ithel's fingers grip like a vice around her shoulders. "Then use your fury to beat Alaric at his own sick and twisted game!"

Helena's face slowly releases its furious scowl, slowly turning to a cold, emotionless expression. Her breathing slows as Ithel's words take effect. *Challenge your rage; let it drive your success.* Only the fire in her eyes shows any sign of her true feelings. Her next words surprise Ithel, her voice as frozen as the winter's snow. "Drug me again, Ithel. I want to be ready for whatever the king throws at me. And when I win this challenge — when the time is right — I will find a way to kill Alaric."

CHAPTER 5

"You seem rather chipper this morning," Jackal winks as he smacks Wren's elbow with a knowing grin. "So, does that mean we should be expecting another bundle from Lynx in the coming months?" His bawdy laughter erupts at his own crude joke.

"Hardly," Wren snorts, covering his rage in carefully controlled expressions. He schools his mouth to return Jackal's smile and forces his tone to sound conspiratorial as he adds, "I took great care to make certain she'd not carry my child."

Jackal roars once more, cuffing Wren's shoulder. "That oughta show her who's boss!" He slaps another cut of roasted deer onto his plate before he saunters off to find his men. Turning back, Jackal gives Wren another long eye before he inquires, "You want to come join my crew around their fire this morning? They'd love to hear all the gory details of you punishing the spy."

The longing to beat the stupid grin off Jackal's face nearly overwhelms Wren's carefully maintained disguise. "You go ahead. I think I'll give a report to Wolf first." Wren moves toward the stairs, putting as much distance between himself and Jackal as possible.

"Oh, that's not the kind of story Wolf would enjoy." Jackal scoffs at the idea, waving Wren to move closer. "Wolf's only interested in that sort of thing when the discussion turns to his precious Ddraig sympathizer. Otherwise, his snarling frown makes the men so uncomfortable that they stop talking mid-story any time Wolf approaches."

Perfect. Wren genuinely feels a slow smile creep across his features. *I can use that little detail to drive a wedge between Wolf and his second in command.* He revels in the simplicity of his plot to remove Jackal from his position of power. *It's almost too easy.* Wren dismisses Jackal with a wave as he replies, "Just the same. I think I'll go talk to Wolf first."

Jackal shrugs and saunters out the door, whistling as he makes his way to his men's campsites.

Wren waits by the steps a few heartbeats before hurrying to the kitchen table instead of up to Wolf's room. He hopes that Wolf will find him here alone and ask him why he does not join the other soldiers. *A simple, innocent question — that's all it takes to begin the greatest deception of my days.*

Wren chews his venison quickly, the flavor untasted on his tongue as he remembers the events of the evening. After formulating a bare bones plan with Lynx, he spent the remainder of the night determining his next steps. Thousands of possibilities and problems raced through Wren's wide eyes. He played each scenario like a mental movie, pausing and repeating each event until every detail was perfected. It wasn't until the wee hours when the sun was whispering its first light into the world that Wren finally slept.

Despite being bone weary, Wren feels at ease with his lies. Getting Wolf to question Jackal's loyalty won't be as difficult as Lynx feared. Breeding that kind of mistrust is as simple as breathing for Wren. A shiver of excitement races down his spine, and the smile on his lips is entirely genuine. *The thrill of the hunt has begun.* While the quarry may not be animal, the chase is very similar. The moment when Jackal is removed from Wolf's side will be just as rewarding as a kill shot.

"What are you doing here?" Wolf barks as he slides into the kitchen with his unearthly grace. The purplish bruises of sleep deprivation discolor the skin under Wolf's eyes. Almost absentmindedly, his fingers linger at his temple, attempting to massage away a headache that never seems to leave.

Wren notes each signal to Wolf's distress, forcing his mouth to frown in concern. *Unrested people are the easiest to irritate. Their emotions are already raw; I can manipulate that.* "I simply wanted to report to you that the spy is safely ensconced in my tent. She had very little information to share with me." Wren chews his next bite slowly, adding, "Are you feeling okay?"

"No," Wolf snipes, slumping into a chair beside Wren. He opens his mouth as though he's preparing to share all of his burdens, then closes it just as quickly. After a moment's thought, Wolf mutters, "I'm still deciding what to do with the wretch, so you'll have to keep her nearby for a while longer."

Wren nods, seizing the opportunity to begin sowing seeds of distrust. "Well, I had an idea about the spy. Perhaps, after she breaks and tells me how she's been getting information to the Ddraigs, we could use her to our advantage. We could plant some bad information and send the spy running back to Iris. Draw her out of her hiding place and lure them all into a trap. Get them to come to us, but make sure we have the high ground. She'd never be suspecting such a plan, and your brother—"

"Is too stupid to ever think of it either," Wolf agrees with a wicked gleam in his eye as he stands and paces around the table. "I like it, Wren! Go explain it to Jackal—"

"I think it would be best if it comes from you," Wren whispers, pinching his hands under the table to keep his smile from showing. A happy expression would disrupt his forthcoming lie. "Every time I try to join Jackal and his men at their campfire, they either quit talking or leave. It's the strangest thing." *Wrinkle your brow, pinch your lips together just a little, blink once or twice, not too much.* Wren walks himself through the body language that will make his words seem plausible. *There's time enough to revel in your victory when it's complete.* "Jackal and his gang will be sitting around the fire, discussing something in hurried whispers, but the minute I appear, their conversation stops altogether. The subject changes, usually to something forced, superficial, and mundane. It's almost as if—" Wren stops intentionally, dropping his eyes to his plate. *The crumbs are there; now, Wolf just needs to take the bait.*

"You think they're planning something?" Wolf whispers, his eyebrows raised as he pauses midstride and turns on Wren. "Surely not! Jackal has been an ally ever since I removed Fox."

"Right," Wren shrugs, picking at the venison on his plate without eating any more. "I'm sure he's been an asset." *Not enough, not enough.* Wren's mind races for something else that might paint Jackal as a traitor. "And the fact that Jackal was the one who caught Lynx out in the forest is just a coincidence. I guess I'm just tired." Wren rubs his eyes for show, coughing to cover his sigh of relief. *All the mental planning done the night before the deception begins always pays off in the end.*

Wolf stares at him hard, watching for any signs of betrayal or manipulation as he mulls the implication. "You know, Jackal's men clam up around me too." He leans heavily against the counter, exclaiming, "I'd have said that kind of behavior was because you come from the House of Vultures if it wasn't happening to me too."

"I'm sure it's because you're the leader. They'd have no reason to want to overthrow your power. Jackal is not strong enough to take your place, and the men know that." Wren pauses, biting his tongue to keep from babbling. *Sometimes silence is more important than the words that you might say. Let the other person's mind work the poison into its system while your mouth stays shut.*

"Jackal is well liked among the men," Wolf agrees, stalking over to the window where the first tents are visible. "But Lynx is the spy. You said so yourself."

"She's the only spy I've found, it's true," Wren agrees, cutting into his last venison strip to give his hands something to do.

"Of course, there could be others," Wolf admits, shuffling

on his feet in agitation. "That's only smart planning in case one spy is caught. Another takes his or her place unnoticed."

"Iris is a cunning threat," Wren replies, the implication being that he believes Wolf's reasoning is well-founded.

"But if anyone in this company would have reason to be a spy, surely it would be you," Wolf accuses, cutting his eyes to focus on Wren once more. "After all, you have the most history with Iris and my brother."

"I'm the obvious choice," Wren hedges, forcing his mouth to keep chewing and not reveal how unnerved he truly feels by Wolf's accusations. *Patience,* he reminds himself, forcing his throat to swallow his meal. *You can talk your way around his fears.* "Suspicion of me is natural. Surely your enemy would send you a less conspicuous threat." Wren picks up his knife, inspecting the teeth of the blade. He imagines how terribly it would hurt to drag this blade across his skin, to feel those teeth biting deep into his flesh, grinding and chewing as they search for his bones. The hurt he fantasizes makes his broken words sound genuine as he laments, "Iris left me behind when she came to destroy our camp with her horrible Ddraigs, remember? She chose not to take me with her—clearly, that shows that she considers me to be an enemy. Just like you, I'm sorry to say." Wren chances a glance at Wolf, hoping to find him convinced.

"Or she left you here to be her eyes and ears in my camp," Wolf replies, crossing his arms in front of his chest as he thinks.

"She has reason to hate me," Wren murmurs, taking a deep breath and hoping his next story will be enough to throw suspicion away from himself. "I tricked Iris when we were still in the House of Vultures. I made her believe I was someone else she trusted, and she ended up taking a beating and spending some time in the traitor binds for all the things I learned from her. So, let's just say that I'm not entirely surprised she'd leave me behind."

"I see." Wolf stalks over to the table, dropping into a chair beside Wren. When he speaks again, Wren can barely contain his smile, for the question Wolf asks only proves that he's begun to trust Wren's story. "So, for the sake of arguing, let's just say Jackal is a spy. How am I supposed to catch him?"

Wren pauses, purposefully hesitating to answer Wolf's query. *Don't be too hasty — a good answer given too quickly will make this seem like manipulation. He's got to think my response is carefully thought out yet spontaneous to this moment.* "Well, you already know that he clams up when you or I get close. And if you asked him about it outright, you know he'd deny it." Wren holds his breath a moment, closing his eyes as if he's lost in thought. "What if you let me watch him a while, gathering evidence from a distance? It's what I used to do all the time, you know, and when I have something concrete, I'll bring it to you."

"Fair enough," Wolf agrees, slicing off a piece of meat from the communal plate on the table. "Then I'll decide what to do when we know for sure that Jackal's a problem." Cutting his eyes at Wren, Wolf adds, "And if I find you are lying about any of this, I will kill you myself."

"Good thing I'm telling the truth then," Wren sasses with a sardonic smile, clenching his hands under the table out of Wolf's view.

***

Everything is bright white and astringently clean. Compared to the world I'm stepping into, I feel extremely grungy like I could never take enough showers to fit into this pristine place. Whispered murmurs catch my attention, but their words slip away from me before I can comprehend what is being said. My eyes blink but do not adjust to the light surrounding me.

Yet, the pain is gone. The blessed relief of finally being free of all my physical aches and emotional sorrows has come. I feel a genuine smile drawing up the corners of my lips, the first I have felt since the day I learned to fly on Siri's back.

The memory of my Ddraig brings me a moment of nostalgia. *Will she come to this new land? Will she be able to find me here? A Ddraig's life is a long one. How long before I will see my*

Siri again?

Hard as I try, I cannot see anything clearly enough to move into this new reality. Turning my head from side to side, I scan the horizon, searching for the faces of the speakers I still hear close by me. In the process, I discover a looming darkness at my back, a shadowy hole that swirls and writhes on itself. I turn around to inspect this hole, a sense of foreboding gnawing at my stomach.

"I wouldn't do that if I was you, Little Bird," a painfully familiar voice beckons me. Whirling around, I discover my father's stormy gray eyes staring at me, a glorious smile lighting up his face.

"Father? It can't be!" I wail, rushing over to wrap my arms around the man's neck, his deep laugh rumbling through his chest, warming my heart. Then I feel stupid for my outburst, for I know that I have died in my world just like my father. Why shouldn't I expect to see him again in death? "I've missed you so!" I sob into his shoulder, uncaring that I cry like a babe.

"I know, child, and I have missed you greatly," my father replies, gently pushing me back to look at my face. "And I would love to hear all about how you gained these strange markings on your face and hands. Yet it must wait; there are much more important things to discuss."

"Why? It seems we have all the time we will ever need now," I surmise, glancing back at the dark hole behind me, feeling oddly calm at the realization that I have died.

"No, Little Bird, you must go back," my father laments, looking a little wistful and sad as he leads me closer to the darkness. "The people over in your lands will need your help to defeat the king of Cassé."

"But why? Why can't somebody else step up and lead?" Immediately Cyrus and Drake's faces come to my mind, and I explain, "There are other Ddraigs and Cadogans—"

"So, you have already found the fabled Ddraigs of the Pith lands." My father laughs, shaking his head as he ruffles my hair. "Little Bird, you have made me prouder than you could possibly know." Dropping his hand to my shoulder, my father sighs, patting my arm in reassurance as he continues. "I suspect you've also discovered that your mother still lives."

"Yes, and she has Windwalker magic," I recall, replaying the scenes of her escape shown to me by the wretched Carreglas, which the Ddraigs guard so meticulously and the Cassé king desires so zealously. It seems like another lifetime when I recall those first days with Siri in the Pith. "I inherited Mother's magic too."

"My darling, there is something you must know," my father mumbles, his eyes full of regret as he presses on with his news. "Windwalker magic is only passed down through bloodlines where both parents are gifted. Not every child inherits it, but both parents must have the ability to wield it just the same." My father's hand tenses on my shoulder as he waits for me to comprehend his words. When I don't, he gently continues. "And you already know I died the day of Cassè's windstorm attack. I perished because I do not have those abilities." After a few more moments of silence, he clearly states, "While I have loved you as my own, you are not my biological daughter, Little Bird."

It takes my heart a few beats to catch up to the agony ripping through my bones. Tears stream down my cheeks as I wail, "I...I didn't need to know that! It doesn't change anything—"

"You did need this information, child, because the rest of what I must say hinges on this truth," my *father* interjects, and while I am curious as to the meaning of his words, all I can do is wonder what I should call him now.

"Why? How could that possibly matter?" I cry, eyeing the dark hole that will lead me back into my own reality. As beautifully clean as this land seems to be, it holds just as much sorrow as my homeland.

"Your mother was a dear friend to me, but she was never my wife as you believed. Her beloved was a soldier in the king of Déchets' border guards. Though it killed her to do it, she left him behind when she crossed into Cassè, and she did so for you. She wanted you to grow up in our lands, to see what life was truly like on our side of the Devil's Spine."

"To what end?" I snap, bitterness rising like bile in my stomach. "Why would she want me to suffer as I have?"

"Everything went to hell after the windstorm, something your mother had no means of predicting. She wanted you to see the good in Cassè; she wanted to bring you to this very moment. When the wretched King Alaric gets greedy again, she hoped you'd be ready to stand against him." My *father* takes a deep breath, a sound I've already come to regret hearing because it means more troublesome news is coming. "Your mother never told me outright who she was, but I know she came from nobility in Déchets. You are a full-blooded, Windwalker magic-wielding member of Déchets noble class. Your word has weight in the king's court because of your mother's title. Alaric will stand against Cassè, but because you are a citizen of his country, he is law bound to protect you." Lowering his eyes, my *father* gives me a moment to digest this information before he speaks once more. "It puts you in a very precarious position, Little Bird, and for that, I am truly sorry. But you are a noble of Déchets, and you stand with the Ddraigs and people of Cassè. You have an opportunity to bridge the gap between our nations—or lead a coup to overthrow Alaric for good. That choice will be yours in the end."

What a glorious gift from my mother, I sarcastically retort in my mind, clenching my fists as I consider the unfairness of it all. "I never wanted any of this."

"But it's yours just the same," my *father* replies, his tone reminiscent of the one he'd use in my early years, full of patience and tenderness. Looking over my shoulder, my *father's* mouth turns to a deep-set frown as he urgently ushers me to the dark hole. "This gateway between the living and the dead is closing soon, and you must go back to your world. I'm sorry, Little Bird, for I do wish you could stay here with me. There's so much more I wish I could tell you, but—"

"Now is not the time," I deduce as a sharp pain twists in my gut. Deep red claws reach through the gateway in front of me, ripping through the air and ether as they search for my soul. A voice beckons me, whispering my name through the darkness. I turn my tear-soaked face toward the man I'd loved all my life, completely speechless as I reel under the weight of all his revelations. Then, saying nothing more, I allow myself to be plucked from the light by those vibrantly gleaming claws, the terrifying darkness of reality swallowing me whole.

***

"She's coming around." Drake's gruff voice bellows over me, worsening my throbbing headache. He slumps beside me, his elbows perched on his knees, hanging his head low as though completely exhausted.

"Iris!" Cyrus whimpers my name, and when I turn my head, I see that he's pinned to the ground by Suryc. The black Ddraig's eyes are fevered, his long claws carefully securing Cyrus, preventing him from escaping or self-harming. "Say something to me, Iris!" Cyrus demands, and I can hear his crazed, mindless hysteria in his frenzied tone.

"I'm here," I croak, my voice gruff and barely recognizable as my own. "Let him come here, Suryc."

"Are you sure that's wise?" Suryc questions, turning his skeptical golden eyes on me. "When we got in here, you were dying, and he was beating on your chest—"

"I was trying to keep her heart beating," Cyrus snarls, struggling under Suryc's unyielding claws. "I wasn't trying to hurt her. I would never—"

"But you did!" Siri roars, cutting off my view as she steps between us, her silver eyes swirling with tears as she leans down to me. Smoke swirls from her nostrils as she carefully sets her chin on my stomach. Even without purposefully putting pressure on me, Siri's head causes intense, agonizing pain in my chest. "I think a couple of ribs are broken," Siri diagnoses while I gasp and try not to scream. "Clearly, there's a limit to your skills."

"Is she still bleeding from her neck wound? No! So, don't gripe at me for leaving a broken rib or two," Drake snaps, cutting his eyes hatefully at Siri. "The life-threatening injuries were all I could handle right now. I need to rest before I try again."

"You healed me? How?" I rasp, surprised that Drake, of all people, would opt to save me. "Those red claws I saw in Death, was that Ekard?"

"Don't say we never did anything nice for you," Ekard grumbles, his deep voice resonating through my body. The vibration jars my broken ribs, and I bite my lip to keep from screaming. It takes me a few moments before I realize I've been using Ekard's scaly side as my pillow.

"Apparently, I inherited some healing abilities when I became a Cadogan," Drake mumbles, slumping over to sit beside me, leaning heavily on Ekard's back too. "I wasn't prepared for that gift to be so exhausting, though."

"Thank you," I mumble, desperately wishing I could ask Drake why he and Ekard would choose to help me. Ekard's dislike of me and his longing to lead the Ddraigs haven't been far from my thoughts. If anything, I'd have thought Ekard would opt to let me die, removing one more obstacle between himself and his goals.

"Well, I wouldn't let you die, Iris." Drake sighs exasperatedly, and I wonder if he somehow heard my thoughts. "Despite the feud our Ddraigs seem to have with one another, I do not wish you harm. And I told you I'd stand by you unless you made a move against me. As long as you do not purposefully pick a fight with me, you will have my allegiance."

"I'm glad we're still on good terms then," I retort, wishing I had the strength to laugh. "I really do appreciate your efforts, Drake."

"I know," Drake smirks, leaning his head back on Ekard's warm scales. "Now, if you'll excuse me, my Ddraig and I need some restorative sleep to make up for all this life-saving we're doing." His eyes droop closed, and he begins to snore almost immediately after he finishes his sarcastic speech.

Maybe I've misjudged them, I force myself to concede, hoping we really have reached a truce. "Suryc, where's Cyrus?" I call out, wondering why I no longer hear his desperate voice.

"I'm here," Cyrus whispers, looming up beside me, his face turned aside as though he waits for me to yell at him. "I'm so sorry, Iris." He speaks the words, but it's as if he is asleep.

"It's okay, Cyrus."

Cyrus turns to face me fully, his eyes completely black as he hollers, "No, it's not! I killed you, Iris. If it hadn't been for Drake and Ekard, you'd still be dead. Nothing about this situation is okay."

"Cyrus, I do not hold any ill will toward you," I reply, hoping I truly mean my words. With Cyrus's eyes as black as night, I know his Asíle abilities will see through any lies I tell. *I must pick my words very carefully and sort out my feelings later,* I surmise, the agony in my chest making it difficult to breathe. "You were dreaming when you attacked me, Cyrus. I understand that you did not intend to hurt me. That's all I was trying to say."

Cyrus stands completely still, his black eyes harshly observing every word as it spills forth from my mouth. He cocks his head to one side as he watches me, waiting for some sign that I am lying. Yet I must pass his test, for, after a few heartbeats, his eyes fade back to their normal hue, and he mumbles, "You should blame me. The heavens know I certainly do."

"How long have you been having nightmares?" Suryc thunders clearly displeased to only just be learning of his Cadogan's troubles. "Why did you not think to tell me? I could have shielded your mind while you slept or helped you block out the painful memories that are plaguing you."

"I don't want to forget," Cyrus confesses, closing his eyes and staring up into the cavern's ceiling. "Blocking the past won't help me get through it. I don't want to spend the rest of my days depending upon you to protect my mind, Suryc. I have to learn how to cope with it myself."

"But you don't have to do it alone!" Suryc snaps, his long, spiny tail flicking in annoyance as he stalks over to Cyrus's side.

"He wasn't alone," I intervene before the arguing can begin. "He had me, and now that you all know, he's got you too." Reaching up my hand, I feebly attempt to catch Cyrus's fingers, fatigue weighing down my limbs. Cyrus hesitates, flinching away from my touch, the fear of hurting me filling him with terror even as a hopeful fire kindles in his eyes. "We're going to get you through this," I declare, a cough building up in my throat. It feels like someone is grabbing my spine and shaking me brutally from the inside out when I finally let out the wheezing hack that rattles my chest.

"I...I don't think I can trust myself around you right now," Cyrus admits, backing away from my side. He skulks toward the opening that leads deep into the Pith caverns, Suryc right behind him, muttering under his smoky breath.

"I'm not sure if I'm relieved that you're okay or furious you kept all this from me," Siri announces, laying down a few paces away from me. I'm still leaning against Ekard, and as much as I'd like to get away from the red Ddraig, I do not think I could handle the pain of moving.

"Siri, I saw...." My words trail off as I wonder for the second time what I should call the man I've always known as my father. Rather than speak everything aloud and risk letting Drake and Ekard know my secrets, I replay the key moments of my conversation with my *father* in my mind.

"Nothing, it seems, has happened by chance," Siri decides, dropping her head down to touch the cavern floor as she processes all I have shown her. "Your mother put you in a difficult position, demanding that you betray your country before you even had a chance to decide what you wanted." Siri turns her silver eyes to inspect me closely as she adds, "At some point in time, you will have to meet with the king of Déchets. If he opts to obey the laws of his land, then you will live. But I've never known anyone from that land to be that honorable, so I wouldn't hold much hope."

"I don't care what happens to me," I vow, Windwalker magic stirring in my veins as my emotions swirl with my conviction. "I am a citizen of Déchets, but I do not belong there. Cassè has been my home, but I don't really fit here either. Wherever the Ddraigs are is the place where I truly belong, and I will live and die to protect it."

"Your mother would be proud," a foreign voice hisses through the darkness of the cavern, a pair of yellowish green eyes glowing to life in the darkest corner of the space. "Shall we put your convictions to the test?"

CHAPTER 6

"Not so hard!" Helena growls, shoving at the doctor's hands as he prods her ribs. "Look, I realize it's the night before the big test, but I've had enough healers, and I see no reason to bring in a doctor!"

"It's the standard procedure," Ithel explains once more, clenching his jaw to keep from lashing out at Helena's persistent objections. "Alaric wants—"

"I know, I know! You've told me a hundred times already," Helena snaps, rolling her eyes as she turns her head away from the doctor, unable to look at his familiar face. "The king wants a doctor to declare that I am medically cleared for this impossible task he's put before me. Never mind the fact that nobody has ever survived the cursed thing."

"Don't think about that," Ithel snipes, tossing a towel at my face.

But why did he have to send in Pryce? Helena laments, turning her eyes back to the aged physician sitting on a stool in front of her, calmly listening to her bickering. *His hair is whiter than it used to be, and the grooves in his forehead look a little more etched and defined, but other than that, the years have been good to you, old friend.* A lump swells in Helena's throat as she waits for Pryce to begin his examination.

"I'd recognize that voice anywhere." Pryce leans forward, his fingers roaming across Helena's face, mapping out her features for his blind eyes. "The king finally came to his senses then, Helena? Why have you waited so long to send for me?"

"Not exactly," Ithel interrupts, dropping a chair beside the bed, the metal legs clacking hard against the marble floor. "She's got to run the tunnel to earn her freedom, Pryce. You've just got to say she's fit enough for the job."

"Even though I'll probably die in the first two minutes of the trial," Helena snorts, bitter gorge rising in her throat when she forces herself to acknowledge the truth of her words.

"Still doubting your trainer, I see," Ithel muses from his perch, crossing his arms as he mutters, "I've prepared you for the run, Helena. If anyone stands a chance at surviving, it's you."

"And you are still faithful at her side, Ithel. Some things are as steady as the sunrise," Pryce muses as he projects small slivers of energy into Helena's hands and feet. After a few more pokes and prods, Pryce nods his head once and announces, "Everything appears fine to me. Your bruises will heal on their own, and they aren't too severe to cause you any discomfort. Ithel is taking it easy with you, it seems."

"Hardly," Helena bellows, her heart breaking as she watches Pryce's face light up with his knowing smile. It is the same smile she recalls shining on his face when he told her she was going to have a child all those years ago. He'd been so excited to share the news with her, so thrilled that the border guards' barracks would "soon hear the cry of a wee babe." *Look how good that turned out.* Helena crumples as she recalls this bittersweet memory, cursing Alaric once more for sending Pryce to her bedside today. No doubt the king purposely orchestrated this moment to rattle Helena's already shaky nerves.

"Yes, I'd say I've been making Helena's life comfortable and easy," Ithel jibes, the only sign of mischief in the glittering of his eyes.

Helena's colorful curses rattle the glass in the windows. Pryce totters off in a fit of laughter, his footing sure despite his blindness. *Thankfully, he had enough sense to refrain from asking about the child,* Helena thinks to herself, breathing a sigh of relief. *I don't think I'm ready to tell Ithel that part of my story just yet.*

The silence lengthens, growing awkward and stale as Helena and Ithel sit in the empty infirmary, waiting for the dawn. Uncomfortable in the emptiness, Ithel shifts in his chair, his cloak draping over his lap as he finds a comfortable position. "Lay back on that table and get some sleep, Helena. We rise before the sun."

"I need to say this," Helena responds, pushing herself to sit on the edge of the small frame of her bed so she can look at her guard while she speaks. "My leaving the border guards and hiding in Cassè was never about you." Helena clears her throat, struggling to keep her voice steady. "I wasn't trying to leave you—"

"Helena," Ithel growls, a hand covering his eyes. "Not now, please."

"I just could not stand it anymore. Alaric's corruption and the vileness of his court was more than I could bear. I came out to the border lands in search of truth." Helena's chin wobbles, her resolve weakening even as a cold, despising glare shines in Ithel's eyes. "And instead, I found you."

"So, I wasn't enough for you then?" Ithel snaps, gripping the arms of the chair to keep from lashing out at Helena. "That's what you're saying, isn't it? You found me, but I wasn't enough for you. You still had to run off into that land, into another man's arms."

"I had to see for myself what was in Cassè. The border stations still weren't close enough to fully understand the country over the Devil's Spine," Helena replies, rubbing her fingers together to comfort herself as she waits for Ithel to respond. "I just had to be sure that attacking the people in Cassè was right, Ithel. I had to know."

"Nearly ten years you were gone. You must have been very indecisive." Ithel leans closer, a fire building in his brilliant eyes. "Ten years of waiting, of not knowing what had happened to you. I spent every day searching for news about you, pestering the guards that crossed over into Cassè for information. Ten years of wondering if you had died, if you had suffered over in that foreign place while I was helplessly waiting for you to come back. Can you even imagine how terrifying it was? And then, to find you the day of the major attack, alive and well with a new man and a daughter, a traitor to your people."

"I never turned against you or Déchets! I just—" Helena swipes a hand down her cheek, a low groan wheezing from her chest as she struggles to hold herself together. "It was beautiful there, Ithel. Cassè reminded me so much of Déchets that sometimes I'd forget which side of the Devil's Spine I was on. Nothing Alaric claimed about that place was true, Ithel! Yet we were blindly attacking and killing them, all for the king's incessant greed. Surely you see that."

"For someone so concerned about the people, you did not fight for them very hard. I was there the day they caught you, remember? You surrendered and took the iron shackles willingly. You said not a word as we tore the land apart. You didn't even cry when your new man disintegrated right beside you." Ithel surges forward in his chair, his nose almost brushing Helena's as he presses, "Why did you leave your child behind, alone in a world that was falling apart? What were you hoping to accomplish?"

"What else was I going to do, Ithel?" Helena snarls, her fingers clenching into claws as if she is a cat preparing to scratch out the eyes of another predator. "Should I have brought my daughter with me to the prison cell? Would you have her rot in that wretched darkness, or worse still, be a pawn that Alaric used to control my every move?"

"You could have asked me! I would have kept your daughter safe!" Ithel drops back in his chair suddenly, desiring to be as far from Helena's side as possible, when he whispers, "Did you even once think of me?"

Unnerved by Ithel's sudden mood swing, Helena moves to the farthest corner of her makeshift bed, lying down and facing away from her guard. "I just wanted to apologize before tomorrow's trial, Ithel. You are a decent man, and you deserved much better than I could ever have given you."

"I loved you so," Ithel breathes so quietly that Helena almost misses the words. "You were my life."

To repeat the sentiments would only hurt him more. Yes, she had loved Ithel, but in the days he remembers so fondly, her affection was like that of a child loving a favorite doll—an easy, superficial devotion. Her life away from the palace had given her the perspective she'd longed for. Her days in his arms at the border station had been glorious yet still sheltered.

Her time in Cassè had been so much harder. Trials and struggles had made her strong. She'd come to look back and appreciate everything Ithel had given her, including the beautiful moonbeam-haired daughter he'd never gotten to see. How bitterly ironic it is to look back on those days now, knowing that while her love for the man she'd left behind was only growing stronger, his affection was turning sour and bitter in her absence.

I should tell him he's a father, Helena concedes, knowing the words will never be able to escape her lips. *Yet that knowledge would accomplish nothing. If we live through tomorrow, I will have plenty of time to tell him the truth. If we don't survive, it won't matter anyway.* "Sleep. We have lots to endure tomorrow," Helena finally answers a willpower as strong and unyielding as iron forming in her heart.

Yet no sleep finds Helena, nor does she seek its solace. Silently she watches the stars and moon dance through the sky. *Let the rest of the world slumber,* she thinks as she traces their patterns in the sky. *If this is my last night, it will be passed, savoring every moment of life.* She imagines her beautiful daughter as a grown woman, strong and capable of anything. She mourns the loss of the man she'd shared a home with in Cassé, wishing his life could have been spared. She watches Ithel pretend to sleep, mapping the lines on his weathered face, drinking in the sight of his shuttered eyes.

Helena greets the morning sunlight calmly, her thoughts far over the mountains. *Today I gain my freedom or – no!* She cannot allow herself to consider defeat. Instead, she vows, *I will survive the tunnel. I will return to Cassè and find our daughter. I will protect her at any cost.*

***

"Attack! Get into the skies!" I bellow down the cavern halls that lead deep into the Pith before the intruder has the chance to move closer to me. "Siri! Ekard! Both of you and Drake get everyone out of here," I command, reaching for my weapon as I prepare to fight off the enemy. Siri hesitates only long enough to cast one loving glance in my direction before she and the crimson Ddraig hasten off to do as I ask.

"Relax, child," the strange being mutters as it slinks closer, keeping to the shadows. Its strange eyes glitter yellow and lime green as it moves. The creature's elongated slit pupils expand to adjust to the darkness, giving the already unusual eyes a creepy, maniacal stare. "I'm not here to harm you," the distinctly female voice taunts, but I do not believe her words. Brilliant white teeth gleam suddenly as the intruder smiles, and my heart shudders in my chest at the sight.

"Then why do you hide in darkness?" I wonder, keeping my hand on the hilt of my serrated blade. "Unless your words are lies?"

"I've been waiting and watching for this moment for a long, long time. But I am not a liar," the woman's soft voice hisses as she slinks out of the shadows. Her skin is mostly scales, similar to those of a Ddraig. Iridescent green, black, and gold, she practically shimmers when she moves into the moonlight. Everything about her is ethereal. She watches me with a cold, calculating gaze, her lips pulled into a tight, hostile straight line. My hair raises on end as I watch her creep closer, my feet glued in place. It's like she has charmed me into submission, forcing me to stand still as she comes close, drawing power from my fear.

"Wh…what do you w…want with me?" I stutter through

the question, half afraid that her answer will be that she wants me to die by her hand right here and now.

"I want revenge," the lady whispers, the word reverberating through the cavern ominously. She stands in front of me now, the long, dark claw-like fingers on her left hand reaching up as if she plans to trace my jawline. "We have a mutual acquaintance, and more importantly, a common enemy," she explains, her talons hesitating as they hover over my eye. Her smile gleams with malice, and I wonder if it takes a great deal of restraint on her part to keep from digging my eye out of its socket. The thought nearly buckles my knees.

"I...I don't understand," I confess, hoping my words don't frustrate the intruder, causing her to attack. "Please, lady, explain what you mean."

"My name is Vatusia," she hisses, leaning close as she inspects the Dadeni lines that trace patterns on my face. "And I knew your mother."

Surely to the gods, my mother never befriended a monster like you, I think to myself, my face growing pale as the Lady Vatusia begins to laugh. *Can you hear my thoughts?*

"Of course I can, child. The people in Déchets have spent years perfecting our abilities to see into minds, while you Cassians have been scratching away at the dust, struggling to survive." Lady Vatusia ignores my sputtering outburst at her revelation, clearly not seeing me as any kind of threat to her safety. She sounds rather bored as she adds, "And you are right; I was never friends with your mother. She was weak, too full of pity and empathy to be useful to me." Lady Vatusia stalks around me, and I feel like a cow she's sizing up for the slaughterhouse. "But the real reason I am here is the enemy we share."

"The king of Déchets?" I ask, guardedly watching her reaction for any signs of deception. *She sounded so loyal to that other land just a few moments ago. Was she lying then, or is she lying now?*

"I am loyal to my country, not the king," Lady Vatusia

snarls, turning hostile. Yet, almost as swiftly as her fury awakens, it fades into nothing more than a tight smile and a frigid stare. "Alaric and his war mean nothing to me or my people."

"What do you know of the king and his plans?" I wonder, hoping I can glean some useful information from the lady before she attacks me. No matter how I imagine this interlude, it always ends in a fight. So if I can learn anything of significance before the battle begins, everything I endure at her hand will be worth it.

"I am one of his most trusted, child. Alaric values me above all others in his court. I'd be his queen if I could condescend to take such a despicable man to my bed." Her slender nose wrinkles while she speaks as if the idea of tying herself to the king of Déchets is as detestable as a garbage heap.

"Why do you hate him so?" I question, unsure whether or not I believe what she says. Yet I am careful to keep a tight rein on my tongue and my thoughts, hoping I do not give away my suspicions.

"Do you know what I am, child?" she murmurs, looming in front of me once more.

"She doesn't. But I do," Cyrus growls, appearing behind the Lady Vatusia with a wicked looking club in his hand. Before I have a chance to shout, before the lady even has the opportunity to turn and face her unseen threat, Cyrus swings the club at her head.

I watch in horror as he moves, completely frozen in place. Breath rushes from my lungs as I anticipate the moment when the club strikes her. I wait for the dull thud as it pounds into her skull, and I pray it causes an immediate death. I cringe and close my eyes, waiting for the inevitable moment of the lady's demise.

Yet the bat passes through her as easily as if she is made of air. "You think I'd be so foolish to come to you in person?" Lady Vatusia laughs, waving off Cyrus as though he is a nuisance pest buzzing around her face. "If you truly are that naïve, then you should surrender now. You will definitely lose any fight you attempt against Alaric without a high dose of cynicism, mistrust, cold-hearted cruelty, and paranoia."

"How are you here?" I wonder, flinching when the stranger's ethereal eyes focus on me once more. "How is any of this possible?"

"I am a powerful Vibría, child," she replies, offering me nothing else as if her words require no further explanation. I feel my face grow cold as the lady scoffs at Cyrus, recalling all the atrocities he endured at the hands of the Vibría. "So, you must be the one that battled with my kinsman." Lady Vatusia waves a dismissing hand at Cyrus, declaring, "You don't look like you could have put up much of a fight."

Cyrus raises his club, uncaring that it will not damage the Lady Vatusia. I think he fully intends to swat at her ghostly visage until his limbs grow too weary to lift the weapon. I step between him and the Vibría, lightly taking Cyrus's hand. "You came here because you say we have a common enemy, but you have not explained why you hate the king. Why should we believe you?"

"My kinsmen and I are Vibría abominations because of the king's nastiness and greed," Vatusia explains, all traces of humor and mischief fleeing from her expression. "We are not his allies, child; we are his captives." Lady Vatusia turns her scaly face up toward the cavern's opening, closing her eyes as though she is being warmed by the soft moonlight streaming in overhead. Her shoulders slump as she prepares to tell her story, and I cannot help but feel sorry for her. Everything about Lady Vatusia in this vulnerable pose attests to her helplessness and desperate circumstances.

"I...I am sorry," I lament, wishing I could offer her more than words in comfort. Cyrus begins to protest, but I quell his words by brushing my hand on his arm. *Look,* I plead, hoping my eyes can convey what my words do not. *See her as she really is, Cyrus. She's a victim too.*

"It is not you that I blame for my situation, child," Lady Vatusia replies, crossing her arms and digging her claws into her own skin. Whatever magic she's using to project her form before us must be showing us a current image of herself. Tiny trails of blood trickle down her arms. But she's too emotional to notice the damage she causes, already too full of pain to feel anything more as she tells her story. "The Vibría used to be skilled magicians and seers, possessing wonderful abilities. But we were still simply human, in service to Alaric's father. He was a fierce but fair-minded man. He treated us reasonably, and we counseled him well. It wasn't a happy situation, but it worked well enough for both sides. When Ddraigs were discovered in our land, it came as no surprise to anyone that most of them bonded with us. The king gave them over to our care, and we never forgot his unexpected generosity.

"Then the king died without warning, and Alaric assumed the throne. We suspected that our king was murdered, but Alaric would not hear our cries for an investigation. Rumors began to circulate that Alaric might have killed his own father to take control of Déchets. That was when Alaric stole our Ddraigs from us. He—he slaughtered them all." Lady Vatusia's voice fades to a soft, wheezing gasp as she speaks of the loss of her Ddraigs, a wound that is still fresh in her heart.

"That's not the story our Ddraigs told us," I interject, my mind alive with the ramifications of this new information should Lady Vatusia's tale be true. *If the Vibría despise the king of Déchets, will they truly stand with us when we fight? Their change of allegiance would come as a huge surprise to Alaric. It might just be enough to help us defeat him.*

"Your Ddraigs probably heard the lies circulated after Alaric destroyed our Ddraigs. That tyrant will not allow himself to be cast as the villain in the eyes of his people. He commanded that his guards and his court spread the story that we, the magicians, killed the Ddraigs ourselves in order to become immortal." Lady Vatusia snorts at the thought, pacing toward us and mumbling under her breath, "He doesn't realize that all the people see through the lies anyway. Most of the people fear him; those that don't are doe-eyed fools."

"So, if he killed all of your Ddraigs, how did you become Vibría?" Cyrus questions, skeptical of the woman's story. Every time she moves or steps closer to us, Cyrus's body tenses as though he's preparing for a fight.

"I'll explain it all, if you'll let me," Lady Vatusia snaps, baring her teeth at Cyrus. "During the days when Alaric took the throne, I was the leader of the magicians. He blamed me for our dissenting opinions about his father's death. So, Alaric tied me to a pillar in his throne room and forced me to watch as he slew each Ddraig. Can you imagine what it was like? I watched every one of my kinsmen's most beloved creatures die. Alaric saved mine for last; I still hear the sounds of his roaring, grieving all the senseless, meaningless destruction." Lady Vatusia's eyes flow with tears, her scaly hands trembling as she reaches up to wipe them away. "Alaric got so lost in the murder and macabre of it all that he left me unguarded. While Alaric killed the Ddraigs, I cast a spell to keep their hearts beating. I had hoped I would be able to find a way of rebirthing the Ddraigs through the combined magic of my people. At the time, I thought I was doing good, finding a way to salvage all that we had lost."

"But you said he turned you into Vibría. How?" Cyrus demands, and I grip his hand tightly, urging him to be quiet. "What, Iris? You're not buying this—"

"Let her tell her story," I hiss, ignoring Cyrus's reply as I turn back to Lady Vatusia, intent on hearing what she has to say before I make a judgment. Something about the rawness of her expression, the agonizingly painful details of the tale, makes me believe she is telling the truth.

"I took the Ddraig hearts back to my people. We spent the next weeks in mourning, weeping and broken, completely inconsolable. Of course, when Alaric discovered what I had done, he was furious. He originally intended to kill us all, but something stayed his hand. Instead, Alaric blackmailed my second in command, Xanti, threatening to torture me and the rest of the female magicians if Xanti didn't follow his instructions. Xanti cast a spell that tied our life spans to the beating hearts of the Ddraigs. I know he did it to spare me and the other women from a death sentence, but Xanti's actions damned us all." Lady Vatusia clenches her fists so tightly that I fear her claws will slice into her palms. Her eyes glitter with malice as she announces, "So, if you truly intend to take Alaric down, you will have the support of the Vibría ."

"You won't fight against us?" Cyrus questions while I try not to imagine how terrible it must have been to watch the Ddraigs die, completely helpless to save them.

"If Alaric demands that we attack you while we are in his presence, then I am sorry to say the Vibría will obey him without mercy," Lady Vatusia explains, her visage glimmering and fading at the edges. Whatever power she's using to appear before us must be draining away rapidly. I suspect she has only a few more moments before she disappears from view.

Cyrus doesn't seem to notice, renewing his outraged outbursts. "Why? Why would you openly support a man you privately despise?"

"I think I understand. The king still has possession of your Ddraigs' hearts, doesn't he?" I surmise, wringing my hands while I consider her predicament. "That's why you will obey him, right? He'll kill you if you don't comply."

"Yes and no, child," Lady Vatusia answers cryptically, her words growing more agitated and forceful as her visage flickers brighter and brighter. "Xanti might have been the one who tied us all to the Ddraigs, but it was Alaric's decision to turn us into the monsters we became. It took only a day before we noticed the changes in our skin. The scales of our Ddraigs began to glimmer on our own arms and legs, our nails turning as black as flint and just as hard. Next, it was our eyes. The first time I looked into a mirror after my eyes changed, I screamed loud enough that my neighbors came to see what was wrong. I thought I'd gone mad because I saw my Ddraig's eyes staring back at me in place of my own. My reflection is a constant reminder of the things I've lost. Then the shapeshifting abilities began. It might have been an amazing time in our lives if we hadn't been dealing with such terrible losses." Lady Vatusia shivers violently, and I cannot tell if it is because of the horrifying memories she's recalling or she's over-exerted her magic. Her mouth bleeds a little at the corners, but she carries on with her story. "After Xanti completed the spell and the damage was done, Alaric hid our Ddraig hearts somewhere in his palace that only he knows. It was a cruel move, effectively assuring that we cannot even kill ourselves if we tried. Until he deigns to return the hearts to us, we cannot die. But Alaric can make our lives a living hell if we do not follow him." Lady Vatusia winces, lowering her voice to a faint whisper. "He can make us beg for death a thousand times over when he throws a temper tantrum. You have no idea what that monster is capable of doing."

"Why didn't you fight back? Or refuse to follow his orders?" Cyrus wonders, giving voice to a question that I must confess I am longing to ask myself.

"We tried a few times to protest and rebel against him," Lady Vatusia whispers, clenching her fists at her sides. "The first time we refused to fight, he destroyed our homes. Then we 'lost track' of key information that would help Alaric discover the Ddraigs on your side of the mountain. So, Alaric chose random members of his court to publicly execute. At each execution, he proclaimed that the death he dealt to his court was directly tied to traitorous dealings with citizens of Cassè, all of which were facilitated by the Vibría. We watched innocent men and women die, and still, we fought against him." Lady Vatusia's hands begin to shake, her breathing growing shallow as she says, "Then we showed mercy to some prisoners from Cassè that he brought before us, and he murdered our children out of spite. I learned that day that there are far worse things than watching your Ddraig die right in front of your eyes. Can you imagine what it's like to watch your own children die? Can you comprehend how completely helpless and broken we were as we buried their tiny bodies, knowing we cannot join them in death until the king decides to dispose of us? The only way to prevent any more tragedy was to obey."

"That's horrible," I whimper, my body shivering from the depth of the sorrow I feel coursing through my blood. Cyrus leans closer, his arm wrapping tightly around my shoulders. When I try to move away from him, Cyrus only pulls me closer, forcing me to stand still. "What are you doing?" I hiss, struggling in his grasp.

"Keeping you from doing something stupid," Cyrus snaps, seemingly unfazed by the dagger-like stare I aim at him. "I know how your heart bleeds at sob stories like this one, but you don't seriously believe anything this monster says, right?"

"You think she's lying? Who would make up such horrifying details?" I reply, even as doubt splinters my certainty, poking holes into my opinion of the unusual lady.

"She's Vibría! You remember what one of her kind did to me, right? How could you think she would tell you the truth?" Cyrus growls, keeping one eye on Lady Vatusia as he argues with me.

"I have spoken nothing but truth to you. Why would I seek you out only to deceive you? Do not call me a liar again," Lady Vatusia warns, pointing her clawed hand at Cyrus. "You know nothing of suffering, child. But if you insult me again, I will make sure you taste despair before the next sunrise."

"What about him? Cyrus was tortured by one of your kind and managed to kill him. How is that possible if what you say is the truth?" I ask, turning a skeptical eye back on the unusual woman glimmering before me.

"His body disintegrated into a black puddle of ooze, yes?" Lady Vatusia nods dismissively, exclaiming, "You didn't kill *him*, just his body. He regenerated back in Déchets; he's probably swapping stories about all the horrible things he did while he was in your lands."

"Convenient," Cyrus sneers, his eyes turning black as his truth reading gift takes hold. "Yet I see nothing false about her statements," he begrudgingly adds, looking a little disappointed to find her telling the truth.

"So why did you come here? Why tell me your story at

all?" I wonder, shielding my eyes from the way Lady Vatusia's image flickers. A strange buzzing sound fills the air, raising the hair on the back of my neck.

A wicked smile lights up her face, and her eyes gleam like tiny golden suns as she watches Cyrus squirm under her inspection. "I came at a sort of crossroads in your future, child. I know you're preparing for war with Déchets. If you wait for Alaric to come across the Devil's Spine and attack you, I can assure you that you will fail." Lady Vatusia lifts her clawed hand toward my head, and immediately visions of the future she's described spring to life in my mind.

Gasping breath wheezes from my throat as I give voice to the images in my mind, relaying each one to Cyrus before he can attempt to attack Lady Vatusia again. "I see a battlefield painted in blood, Cadogans and Ddraigs alike. I see the king standing over my broken body, laughing maniacally as he swings his sword at my head. I see Suryc and Siri captured, weeping over us, Cyrus. The images keep changing, but each one ends the same." Tears flood down my face as I watch the litany of death and destruction, helpless against the inevitable fate we face. These images from the Lady Vatusia only confirm what I've foreseen in my own mind's wanderings. "I can't allow this to happen. There has to be another way."

"There is." Lady Vatusia smiles, and the sight of her gleaming white teeth brings me no comfort. It's like standing before a hungry viper that's just seen its next meal skitter across the land. "You must bring the fight to the king in our lands, child. That is the one thing he will not expect."

"No! No way will we venture into Déchets on the word of an abomination like you," Cyrus bellows, pushing me behind him as he faces off with Lady Vatusia. "We'd be spotted by the border guards and captured before we ever made it to the king. You're only trying to trick us!"

Lady Vatusia says nothing, her eyes still focused on me. A searing pain streaks through my mind like white-hot lightning. In my ears, I hear the creature's voice, and I know by

Cyrus's lack of response that the lady is only in my head. *I don't mean your whole group must come to fight the king. Only you, child. You asked me why I came here today — it was to offer you my help. You have a place in Déchets and a title to your name. You will be harder to kill if you are standing by the king's side, pretending to support his throne. When you see I am right, when you decide to follow my advice, I will be in the fortress to assist you. The only real question is this: How long before you recognize the truth of my words? How many will you allow to die before you step up and fight the battle yourself? You weren't born into this war, but you can be the one to end it.*

I offer her a shaky nod, too overwhelmed to speak. The very idea of waltzing into Déchets, pretending that my own allegiance has changed to support the king, is repulsive to me. I couldn't pass myself off as such a wicked, fickle traitor.

"My time with you has long passed. The spell holding my spirit here is fading." Lady Vatusia coughs, blood spewing from her mouth. The strange buzzing sound in the air grows so loud that I must cover my ears, my spine shivering involuntarily. The light surrounding Lady Vatusia brightens until I must shut my eyes against its blinding brilliance. A howling scream erupts from the center of the light as Lady Vatusia's ethereal body explodes and fizzles in the air. Only a streaky spot on the stones shows any sign of her presence as the light fades and the noise disappears.

My body sags until I fall to my knees, shock and relief at war in my veins. Cyrus falls right beside me, catching me before I tip over and fall on my face. I let him hold me close, whispering his words of comfort into my aching ears. I barely hear them. My mind is far away, lost in a hopeless future that sees me forging myself into a ruthless, brutal weapon and traveling alone to my enemy's lands to bring down a tyrant king.

"Iris? Are you listening?" Cyrus gently brushes my cheeks, turning my face toward his own. "Are you okay?"

"I'm tired," I confess, leaning heavily on his chest as I struggle to put weight on my wobbly legs. *My heart is burdened by the heavy weight of a purpose I never wanted. I just don't think I'm strong enough to endure much more.* While I whisper the words in my secret heart, I keep them from Cyrus, determined not to add to the troubles he already carries. Instead, I pull on Cyrus's arm, saying, "Let's go find Siri and Suryc. It's time they hear the truth about the Vibría, don't you think?"

CHAPTER 7

"Are you ready?" Ithel asks for the seventh or eighth time as the medics leave the infirmary after their final examination before the big event.

"Enough, Ithel. I'm as ready as I can be. It's hard to imagine it is already time," Helena barks as she lifts her head from her hands. Seven days of maniacal, ruthless training completed, it is now time to face the tunnel. "I spent years in that prison cell waiting to go mad, wishing I would just die and get it over with. And now I'm here, nearing the one day of which I never dared to dream." Helena rubs her hands through her hair, still reveling in its silky texture and clean scent. "Now that I'm so close to escaping those cells for good, I can admit how badly I want to be free. I can almost taste it, Ithel," Helena confesses, crossing her thin, toned arms as she asks the question she longs and dreads to utter aloud. "Do you really think I have any chance of surviving the tunnel?"

Ithel rises from his perch on the armchair by her bed, moving until he stands right in front of Helena. His fingers walk down her cheek as he watches the bobbing of her throat. Softly he recalls the way it felt to brush his lips across her forehead, the tip of her nose, the hollow at the base of her throat. He groans at the memories, wishing he could pull Helena close. His hands clench by his side as he imagines placing them on the small of her back, holding her tightly to himself. He'd never let her slip away again. *No,* Ithel scoffs as past mistakes taint his memories. *I cannot let her break my heart again.* He'd keep Helena like a cherished locket, close to his heart at all times, but always on a chain, easily removed from around his neck. His fingers tighten on her chin, keeping her locked in place as he whispers, "I can't really believe no one has survived the tunnel. It's possible that every one of the spies Alaric's used in the past went through this same trial. Our king is not creative enough to use more than one means of determining a prisoner's mettle. Only the strongest will make it. And in my opinion, if anyone has a chance, it's you, Helena. You have the drive and endurance to face what lies in the tunnel. I have no doubt you will succeed." Then, before allowing himself to act on his romantic fantasy, Ithel drifts away on the breeze, mumbling, "Get dressed. I'll return when you're ready."

Helena's hands are cold as she reaches for the lightweight pants and sleeveless shirt Ithel chose for her. Her fingers tremble as she reaches up to brush her cheek, tracing the places Ithel had touched. Shivering as her eyes drift close, she can still feel the kiss of the wind he'd created as he fled from her presence. "Oh, Ithel...." Her voice fades, racing on the breeze as if it could somehow catch her former lover and drag him back to her side. *I wish you knew everything in my heart.*

After about a half an hour, Helena stands before the mirror one final time. "You can make it through this," she tells her reflection, her jaw setting as a determined fire flickers to life. "You have to—this isn't just about survival." *This is about revenge, about making recompense for a litany of wrongs caused by Alaric, perpetrated by his soldiers, and silently condoned by all the citizens of Déchets who did not speak up when they should have done. This is about protecting my daughter and Ithel and the Ddraigs and keeping the Carreglas from Alaric's greedy clutches. This is about saving another nation from ruination, even if it means I must bring down my own.*

Ithel returns to the infirmary with the sunlight blazing through the open windows behind him. Gulping once, Ithel moves closer and wordlessly ties a blindfold around Helena's eyes. His fingers graze the back of her neck as he tightens the thick material into her snarled hair. Her shoulders tense and pull toward her ears. *Ithel is a distraction I do not need right now.* Ithel lightly grips her elbow, silently urging her to move forward. *Calm, quiet, patient.* Helena breathes the mantra over and over with every step, her lower jaw beginning to tremble. Yet despite her resolve, Helena hesitates at the doorway and pleads, "Don't come with me, Ithel."

"Helena —"

"Please," Helena pleads, her heart fluttering in her chest as she cries, "It has nothing to do with us. I just cannot face this knowing you are watching. I don't want you to watch me die."

"I do not have a choice, Helena!" Ithel rips the blindfold away to stare into Helena's eyes. Her furious, angry, defiant eyes, the very ones that still haunt his dreams. "I am just as much a slave as all the people who have given you their life's strength to heal you every day since we pulled you out of the prisons. Can you not see that?"

"What are you talking about?" Helena demands, shocked by his sudden revelation. "You are a slave?"

"I mean, if you get hurt in the tunnel, I have been spelled to force my energy into you for healing, even if it brings my own death." Ithel's voice shatters as he pulls her unyielding form closer, finding comfort in her proximity even as he grieves his own circumstances. "Every one of the 'guards' used in this trial is a slave, Helena, including me. I am supposed to keep you alive at all costs. Alaric told me you'd enjoy the irony of the situation; he said you'd really get a kick out of standing over my body as your energy drains mine dry."

"But why didn't you tell me sooner? And how did you end up enslaved in the first place? When I left, you were still in the border guards! What happened?" Helena cries even as she struggles against his closeness. The familiar scent of his skin is almost too much to bear.

"I defied the king," Ithel breathes into her hair as he

pushes her gently aside. "After you left me, I lost my mind. Neither the palace nor the border guard stations offered me peace and rest; everywhere I went, I saw you hiding in the shadows, haunting my mind with memories. So, I joined the patrols that ventured up high into the mountains to escape you. Terrible things happen in the Devil's Spine, Helena. People — both Windwalkers and Cassians — are abused there. It's nothing short of torture and mass killings. And I participated in it all, doing what I was told and feeling no remorse. I was angry at you, and I used my rage to fuel my hatred of anything and everything that landed in my path. I did unspeakable, horrible things, Helena, and I was proud of it all." Ithel steps out of Helena's reach, bracing his hands against a window frame, his shoulders sagging in defeat. "I felt nothing but hate during those days until they asked me to kill a child. A young, innocent girl." His body trembles as he relives the moment in his mind. "She was the daughter of some high-ranking man in Cassè. The border guards had caught her and decided to send her back as a message — a defiled, deceased warning to her family. It was to be carried out by my hand at the king's special request to prove my loyalty."

"What did you do?" Helena places her hand against his muscled shoulder, already knowing the answer. The young unnamed child had belonged to her neighbors; she'd returned safely to her home after a couple weeks, unwilling to speak about wherever she'd been. *How close had the patrols come to finding us?* Helena realizes, feeling justified for keeping her child indoors as much as possible in those days. *How easily it could have been my own daughter!*

"I let the girl escape into the woods, with a pack of food and water and a general direction to travel to find her way home. When word got out that she hadn't died by my hand, I was sent back to the palace in disgrace. I was immediately stripped of my rank; I became Alaric's first slave."

Helena's lungs burn in her chest long before she realizes she has stopped breathing. "I'm so sorry," she wheezes, wrapping her arms around Ithel in a tight embrace. "It was all my fault; I should never have left you behind. You have to know that I truly believed you would be safer in the guard. I didn't want you to be labelled a traitor…like me."

"I'd have followed you anywhere," Ithel whispers, leaning back to kiss her forehead softly before slipping the blindfold back in its place. "Now go beat this trial, so we can finally be free."

Inside, Helena's very soul feels like a caged animal paces through her blood as Ithel leads her to the trial's unknown location. Every heartbeat fuels her rage. She welcomes the darkness of the tunnel. Something primal and wicked is awake inside her now. Nothing will stand in her path.

Ithel carefully removes the blindfold. Helena's eyes easily adjust to the semi-darkness of the cave. Though she knows the four other challengers are nearby, she cannot focus on them. Off to the left, a seat has been carved into the stone of the cavern's walls. It is a crude throne, yet it serves its purpose well enough for Alaric. Helena's furious glare is only for the king. He meets her anger with a smirk and a nod, too sociopathic to care about all the hurt he has caused.

"You will each run the tunnel separately. The order has already been arranged," a guard announces from his place beside the king. Unsurprised, Helena shrugs when her name is called to compete last. No doubt to cause her the most terror, to watch helplessly as the others try and fail to beat an undefeatable test. "Your task is simple enough. Reach the other side, and you will go to Cassè to gain your freedom," the announcer explains with a bored voice as if it is a simple feat to accomplish.

"What is in the tunnel?" the other female prisoner asks with a shiver. Silence greets her query as a guard steals up beside her. A quick slap with his metal-coated fist is enough to stop any further questions from us all as blood oozes down her chin.

"Dai, you're up!" the announcer shouts. The skinny boy who'd shown his fear at the very beginning of our trial shuffles up to the front of the line. He glances at each one of his competitors, terror causing his eyes to well with tears.

"What now?" he trembles as he rasps, his voice more of a croak. The announcer points up into the ceiling. While most of the room's ceiling is low enough to touch, there is a dark expanse right over our heads. A single rope ladder sways eerily, and Helena swears she can hear laughter echoing through the darkness overhead.

"That's the tunnel?" the stocky male named Bryn shouts as his face pales. "I always thought of a tunnel as horizontal, not—"

A punch from a nearby guard silences his words. Immediately Helena finds Ithel's watchful eyes from among the other enslaved guards on the right side of the wall. *It can't be a coincidence. How did he know the tunnel would require a climb?* He'd made her practice vertical maneuvers all week long. Ithel's face is impassive as he stares straight ahead, unwilling or unable to meet her eye.

The boy, Dai, barely survives ten minutes in the tunnel. A loud, terrified shriek fills the air as his body tumbles toward the cavern floor. A dull thud sounds on his impact, a crackle of breaking bones, then a gurgling choke as blood fills his mouth. Dai's body is purple with bruises that had formed during his climb. Far too quickly to have been the result of the fall.

Helena cares not if it hurts her pride as she shields her eyes from watching the boy's landing. Turning her face to the line of enslaved guards, she, unfortunately, stands witness as Dai's guard falls to his knees. His eyes roll back into his head, his mouth hanging open in an unvoiced gasp. He convulses, the king's spell sucking every last breath from his lungs in an effort to save the child. Finally, the guard's body crumples to the ground, turning to dust as it hits the rocky floor.

I should have kissed Ithel and told him I loved him one last time, Helena laments, tears streaming down her face. *I should have told him about his daughter. I should have explained that I took her into those lands to teach her about Cassè, to train her to be a weapon we could use one day to bring down Alaric. Now I'll never get the chance.*

"Great gods of old, some kind of monster attacked that boy! Look at those deep gashes and burns!" Bryn mutters his eyes on the darkness above him. "What is up there that could cause such wounds?"

"You're about to find out," the announcer says as he pushes Bryn forward. Kicking and screaming, it takes four men to push the stocky prisoner up the tunnel's ladder.

"What is your name?" Helena whispers to the shivering waif beside her, using the chaos of Bryn's protests to steal a moment with the child. The girl's hair appears silver in the dim light, her blue eyes seeming to glow with their own defiant light. *You could almost pass for my child,* Helena shudders, grateful her daughter isn't in Déchets. No doubt if she had been, Alaric would have forced her to watch her mother's trial and subsequent demise.

"Evaine," the girl whimpers, sidling closer to Helena for comfort.

"And what great ill did you do to the king?" Helena wonders, wishing she could smuggle Evaine out of this place.

"I loved his son, Antero," Evaine whimpers as tears glisten down her cheeks. "But I am low born. I was the kitchen maid that used to take him a tray when he worked in his room. It was a very common thing, and somewhere along the way, we fell in love. When the king found out...." Her words die as she sobs and wipes blood from her chin.

"I can imagine. I am truly sorry." Helena answers by patting the girl's shoulder. *Guilty of love. How terrible to face this horror for such an innocent crime.* Dai, Bryn, Evaine—Helena will remember these names until her final days. She will chant them like an anthem to keep her going when she feels defeated. "Good luck, Evaine." *May the forgotten gods look upon you with favor.* It takes Helena a few moments to realize she's already counted the girl among the dead.

Bryn makes it thirty minutes in the tunnel, a staggering,

unexpected feat judging by the king's bewildered expression. *None of us are expected to survive this.* Helena shudders as the realization settles in her mind. *Was he even serious about using us as spies? Or has Alaric grown bored and needs a diversion from his one-sided battle with Cassè?* Either, she knew, was possible.

Suddenly a sharp crack of stone radiates above them, and the wailing of the falling man heralds his descent. Judging by the sound of the impact, Helena is certain his body has no bones left unbroken.

This time Helena covers her ears, turning her back as Bryn's bodyguard dies. *What a waste!* Helena wishes to scream at the king. *What nonsense that you would kill us all for sport!* Glancing at Alaric, she finds him staring straight at her, smiling widely as he enjoys the sight of her torment.

Evaine's fingers, as icy as if death had already claimed her soul, grip her wrist as a guard tries to pull her away. "Remember me, Helena! I beg you, do not forget this place! When you return, tear it apart in my honor!" She moves to stand in the only circle of light in the room, her hair catching its beams and gleaming gold. "Promise me, Helena! Destroy it in the name of the girl who died for love."

The shouts and prods of the guards force Evaine to move into position, but she makes no attempt to step onto the rope ladder. Her eyes stay fixed on Helena, waiting for a response. One guard pulls his sword, approaching her from behind with death in his eyes.

"Evaine! For the love of the gods, move!" Helena shouts, her hands gripping her chest, watching helplessly as the guard inches closer.

"I have no fear of death, Helena. My love already waits for me." She smiles wistfully as she repeats, "Promise me, Helena."

"Yes, now go!" Helena screams, clawing at her own hair as she watches the guard's sword raise.

Evaine nods in acceptance and turns to face her executioner. The blade falls, and her head rolls gracefully off her shoulders. Her guard-slave's body seizes, his death just as sudden as hers.

The king, however, yawns as he waves a hand. "On with it then, Helena."

"You are a monster," Helena cries, grief roaring to life in her, erupting from her chest in a low growl.

"That's the nicest thing you've said to me in a long time." Alaric simpers at her words as though Helena's just offered him a glorious compliment. "At long last, we might find some common ground, Helena. How nice it would be to be on friendly terms again!"

Helena's feet trudge through Evaine's blood, leaving crimson trails. Her mind is numb as she stares into the darkness. The ebony void above her seems to reach down with midnight fingers to tangle into her hair. *How much can I endure in that emptiness before I go mad?*

"Speak truth, Helena! Whatever you do, speak—" Ithel's voice stops abruptly with the sounds of a struggle.

Her ears dimly register the words Ithel shouts, but she hardly cares about their meaning. She deftly maneuvers the rope ladder, and all too soon, Helena feels the bolts that connect the rope ladder to the rock. Patting the hard surface, she finds crevices to catch and pull herself up; her feet are slick from the muck on the floors. Helena slips off her bloody shoes, the calluses on her feet offering slightly better traction. The rocks tear and bite into her skin, but the pain just sharpens her mind.

Nothing seems dangerous. It is just a rocky expanse as far as Helena's eyes can see. A dim light shines high in the space. The freedom that no one dares hope to find taunts the prisoners from this high peak. The walls shimmer gray and blood-red—a glittering metal of iron ore that burns Windwalker skin and a strange stone-like substance that Helena does not recognize. Her fingers ache to touch one at about eye level, its surface almost as wide as Helena's palm. *I'm convinced that if I were to press my hand into it, I would come out covered in sticky, hot blood.*

"Why have you come?" A voice drones above Helena,

bored and passive like this is all some farcical joke. A startled cry rings from Helena as she turns her head and meets the eyes of the speaker. The sudden image of the specter is almost enough to make her lose her grip on the stones. It is due only to strength that she does not go tumbling to the ground.

"Why have you come?" the creature repeats, its face elongating, its jaw becoming more defined until it is Ithel's visage.

Speak truth. Helena recalls Ithel's parting words before beginning this climb. *Makes more sense now,* she snorts, eyeing the visage floating beside her head curiously. "There are many reasons I am here," Helena answers, hedging her honesty in vagueness until she better understands what she's up against.

"Such as?" The milky white face blurs and sharpens in pulse-like bursts.

"I am forced to do this to get out of prison. Ithel's life is tied to mine, so I must continue if I am to keep him alive," Helena replies, shifting her weight on the rocks as she struggles to keep her grip. She reaches for a higher hand hold, hoping to move beyond the strange ghostly visage. Yet everywhere she touches, the rocks suddenly burn like molten lava, scalding her fingers until tiny blisters burst to life. She hisses, staring accusingly at the face that eerily shifts to resemble Alaric.

"You go no further until my questions are answered," the image explains, its voice lacking all emotion. "Now, why have you come?"

"I want to return to Cassè. I was happy there," Helena mumbles, gritting her teeth to keep her mind focused on anything other than the agonizing pain in her hands.

Seeming to be mollified by Helena's answer, the strange image nods once, lifting a feeble-looking hand and motioning her to move higher.

Helena tries not to moan as the rock rips into her blistered hands. Some of the injured skin breaks open and oozes, making each handhold slick. Helena struggles to move deeper into the tunnel, but in only a matter of moments, the specter's voice breaks the unnatural silence once more.

"What do you fear most?" the shape-changer asks, its mouth opening unnaturally wide as its eyes glow crimson.

Do not let your fear rule you. Helena coaches herself to steady her breathing. *Do not focus on its looks. Ithel prepared you for this too. Do not trust your eyes.* "Why should I answer your questions? You'll only use what I say against me." Helena stalls as she shifts her feet to a better position. Her left hand slips out of its handhold, and as much as Helena desperately longs to place it back into the crevice, she fears that doing so would only cause her more burn injuries.

When she makes no move to touch the rock, an inhuman, red-tinged hand reaches out from a crevice above Helena's head and catches hold of her arm. Every place its fingers land on her skin burns with the heat of a hundred suns. The skin of her wrist is raw and blistered, parts of it white and flaking, as though one touch would cause it to fritter away like ashes on the wind. The agony of it steals away her screams.

"Do not try to outwit me, child," the voice repeats with a laugh, as though it enjoys watching the suffering of its victims. "Tell me what you fear most."

"I fear loss. Losing everything and living a lie, and I hate being afraid." Helena chatters through her teeth as the shock of her wounds erodes away her strength. Ithel's energy tries to force its way into her veins, but she pushes it away. *Not yet,* she replies, hoping she can keep him from sharing too much of himself so soon. *I can bear this. Save your strength until I am desperate; I don't want to unwittingly kill you later, Ithel.*

"Some would call you wise for such fears. Others would say you are foolish, for those things are inevitable. People leave or die. Lies come as naturally as breathing for most of your kind too. You cannot manage to go through life always self-sufficient and honest. Fear is necessary too, even if it is unpleasant."

"Are you a philosopher? Is that the great terror of the tunnel then? Will you torture me by speaking truths that I would not care to hear?" My stomach roils with a wave of nausea. *Are you that stupid, Helena? To provoke this strange beast that has already ruined your arm?* she chides herself, staring deep into the tunnel that rises above her head, wondering how far she must go before she finds freedom.

"Is that what you seek from me, child? You desire to be fearful? Then I can comply." The voice turns soft as a willow leaf on her cheek as the eyes of the creature turn painfully familiar. Small frame, shock of white hair, wistful smile full of unspoken sadness and longing...the last image that Helena remembers of her daughter.

"How could you know such things?" Helena asks as the form turns eerily solid, as though she could reach out and actually run her hand through her daughter's hair. Every detail is there, right down to the small dark spot just outside of her left eye.

"I know all about you, Helena. I am in your head and heart," the creature whispers with a sad smile, its voice changing to sound soft and ethereal. "Why did you leave me, Mother? Didn't you love me enough?" The creature edges closer to the cliff, her toes hanging off the sides. "Why didn't you bring me with you? Don't you know how much I have suffered?" The visage of Helena's daughter wails, tumbling off the ledge, her long ivory hair like comet's trail behind her as she flies.

Helena clenches her eyes against the sight. *Not real, not real.*

"Are you certain?" her daughter's sweet voice answers, the wraith's shape sitting on the ledge once more. This time her body is broken and bleeding, as if she had truly fallen and cracked on the ground. A part of her skull shows along her right ear, and a bone is protruding from her left arm as she reaches out toward Helena.

"Please," Helena begs, another bout of sickness turning over her stomach. "Leave my daughter out of this!"

A giggle that sounds like metal screeching against metal grates in Helena's ears. Throughout it all, Helena still forces her feet to keep climbing, her legs to keep pushing, and her arms to keep reaching higher. The only way out of this demented hell is to reach that light in the ceiling.

The rocks around her flare with a crimson light that pulses almost like a heartbeat. "What do you want, Helena?" The very crevices between the stones seem to cry out this question in mockery.

"Freedom," Helena whispers, biting her own tongue against the scalding pain of the rocks against her skin. They are burning hot, almost as though they had just come out of a fire. "I want to see my daughter again," she growls through chattering teeth.

"Is that all?" The strange voice seems to grow harsh, and a silent reminder and warning not to lie burns through Helena. The words she's kept from speaking inch up her throat, almost as if they are living, breathing monsters writhing inside Helena's chest. She shudders, fearing that when she opens her mouth, they climb out of her heart, spewing hate-filled blood as she bares the truth to all who hear. "Say it," the image of Helena's daughter demands, her broken body skittering closer on the rocks, moving more like a lizard than a human. "Tell me what you really want!"

"I want to end the king's rule...and his life." Helena's thoughts replay all of the faces of the forgotten. The three other prisoners who did not survive this tunnel. Ithel and the other slaves who had no choice but to endure their trials unto death. *What is life without the right to live it your way?* Her child and the man from Cassè who had taken them in and given them a home. All the friends and loved ones that she had left behind after the fall. Every evil, every injustice had the king to blame.

In her rage, Helena climbs despite the scalding heat in the rocks, never once daring to look at her hands. Blisters pop and ooze, her finger joints scream against the hurt, pain signals plead for her brain just to let her body fall to the land and end the pain forever. But her blinding will and furious heart urge her onward. "I want the king to suffer! I want him to pay for all of the things he has done," Helena cries, ignoring the pain lancing into her shoulders.

The creature of the tunnel matches her progress, a small smile forming on its thin lips. It changes form once more, this time becoming a young boy that appears to be around the age of ten. His frame is wiry and small, and his skin looks tan from many days out in the sun. His blue eyes pierce Helena, stopping her from climbing higher in the tunnel. "Are you sure this is what you want?" the creature asks, his voice full of optimistic hope.

"I hate the king," Helena confesses, wondering who this new persona is supposed to be. *Did I know this boy? Is he a face I should recognize? Or am I seeing the real face of the monster who has been tormenting me?* The idea that her assailant is a child fills Helena's heart with pity. *What would cause a child so young to be so cruel and heartless?*

Helena's revelation of vengeance seems to please the boy. He plops down onto a ledge, his skinny legs swinging over the side. "Very well, Helena. I hope you manage to accomplish this goal."

"Really?" Helena stops herself from challenging the boy, wary of his sudden change in demeanor. "That's it?"

"Yes," the boy replies, humming softly to himself before adding, "I've been waiting for someone like you, someone with enough drive to push on despite the pain. Someone who was so focused on their desire to see the king die that they didn't care what happened to themselves. Someone who would do whatever it took, even if it meant dying, just to reach their goal."

"Why do you hate the king?"

The strange being does not answer Helena's question. It dissipates into a crimson cloud that gets absorbed by a pocket of glittering gems nestled in the wall. The glowing rocks suddenly fade, all the damaging heat in them disappearing like smoke on a breeze.

The exit of the tunnel blinds Helena with its sudden closeness. A sob of relief escapes her parched throat as she clambers through the hole into the brilliant light of day. Her body shivers with a cold sweat against the sun-warmed stones of the king's private courtyard. No one is ever allowed to enter this place without Alaric's special permission. Heady perfumed flowers sway in the gentle breeze, their sweet aromas so cloyingly strong that they turn Helena's stomach.

I don't want to look, Helena confesses, taking a few deep breaths before she inspects her injuries. Her wrists and elbows ache and pop, grumbling in protest as she lifts them off the ground. Most of the skin is charred and blackened, and somehow the sight of them causes the pain to intensify in Helena's mind. A low, agonizing moan escapes her as she lets her hands fall back to the ground, her breath coming in short, rapid gasps. "Ithel," she whispers the name repeatedly, unable to say anymore.

"Helena!" Ithel cries as he races toward Helena, but the sound of his desperate voice does not stop her body's convulsions. Immediately his soothing energy and healing explodes to life in her blood, siphoning away the hurt as he heals her damaged skin. Ithel sags on the stones beside her, dropping to his knees as his body grows weaker.

When her hands are clear of blisters and her feet no longer resembling chewed meat, Helena finds the clarity of mind to speak once more. "How did you know?" Helena rasps, her terror-soaked screams from the tunnel causing her to grow hoarse.

"I was there when the tunnel was created," Ithel whispers, his fingers stroking her sweat matted hair. "I told you that you'd make it, didn't I?"

"Why not tell me what you knew sooner?" *I wish I had the strength to smack him,* she thinks wearily.

"Your surprise at the tunnel's unusual placement had to be genuine, or else the king would have realized his error in letting me train you. You would have probably died outright." Ithel shudders, his fingers tensing and stilling on her chin. "As it is, Alaric must have forgotten about my involvement in the creation of the tunnel, and I wasn't about to remind him. It worked in your favor, wouldn't you say?"

"You almost got yourself killed anyway, shouting advice to me from the sideline. Didn't your demand that I 'be honest' give you away?" Helena snaps, wrapping her fingers around Ithel's wrist, marveling at their smooth, unblemished flesh.

"I paid my price," Ithel growls, holding his other horribly burned hand up for inspection. "There are iron fillings in the wound. Do not touch it, Helena."

"I am so sorry," Helena mumbles, unable to keep her fingers from reaching for his hand. Even without touching the metal, she can feel the thrum of its power, like the heat of a fire as you wave your hands over its flames. "What can we do?"

"I'll have to wash it out and pick at the fillings that are too deep. It may take a while," Ithel grumbles, shifting until he lay beside Helena's prone form, facing up into the sunlight and closing his eyes. "For now, let's just stay like this a while. It won't be long before Alaric comes to find you."

"But those fillings will keep burning you if you leave them inside," Helena protests, reaching up to brush Ithel's cheek, hoping to get his attention and remind him of the urgency of his situation. Iron had a strange way of reacting to Windwalker's skin. The elders claimed it was the magic in the Windwalker blood that couldn't abide the material. They believed it weighs down the body, rendering magic ineffective. "Go get that wound cleaned now."

Ithel shakes his head, a stubborn set to his jaw. "I'll deal with it myself once we are safely away from here. I do not trust Alaric's medics. Those loyal to him might do me harm just to try and win favor from their liege."

"Please, Ithel—"

"Well, well, it seems your love withstood your jaunt in that wretched land after all," the king sneers as he stalks up to Helena's side. Alaric paces over to Ithel, kicking his leg hard as he gripes, "Seven days with this bitch, and you didn't kill her. You even managed to keep each other alive throughout this test." Moving up to Ithel's head, Alaric raises his foot.

Positioning it over Ithel's nose, the king prepares to step down as he mumbles, "You are more worthless than I realized."

Helena forces her exhausted, screaming muscles to move, hauling herself up until she stands toe to toe with the king. "I have earned my freedom. And Ithel's."

"Hmm…so you got cozy with her, too? You told her about falling from my grace." Alaric saunters around Helena, sneering as though she is a piece of art from his collection that he suddenly finds to be in poor taste. "Well, I guess you will do, Helena. You will travel to Cassè, find the traitor, and bring him or her back to me alive."

"And if I should fail?" Helena wonders, knowing full well she would not return to this land with her daughter. "I may be gone for months, years even, searching out your precious traitor."

"I've given that some thought and I think I've come up with a rather marvelous solution," Alaric replies with a wicked smile, the sight of which sends dread and bile up into Helena's throat. "I've decided I will be keeping Ithel in this land as my personal *guest*. Six months should be plenty of time for you to root out the rogue Windwalker, don't you think?" Alaric asks, smirking and savoring Helena's outrage. A guard appears behind Ithel's head. He silently reaches for Ithel's limp arms, gripping smooth and damaged skin alike, and drags the injured man back toward the dungeons.

Helena lunges toward Alaric, fingers curled as if to claw his eyes out. "No! You promised—"

"Nothing more than I have already given. After all, Ithel was freed the moment you escaped the tunnel. The fact that he chose to run up here to you, freely giving you healing when he so desperately needs it himself, was poor judgment on his part. So, I will keep the former slave for insurance. Either you return with the traitor, or in six months, I kill your ex-lover. Am I understood?" Alaric questions, smugly satisfied by Helena's silence.

"Helena! Helena!" Ithel wails as they drag him back

down into the depths of hell. "Don't worry about me! Just get out of here! Please—" The doorway to the king's courtyard slams shut, cutting off Ithel's words.

That wound, the iron fillings—how long until he is rife with infection? Will it cause him to lose the arm? Helena trembles, biting her lip to keep from crying. "I hate you," she mumbles under her breath, scowling at the king.

"Did you understand my terms, Helena?" The small, frail hand clasps Helena's elbow, its razor-thin fingers jabbing into her skin just enough to cause pain but not enough to draw blood.

"Yes." The word grinds out of Helena's mouth, and she struggles to resist the urge to rip her arm out of the king's grasp.

"Say it nicely." The hand twists ever so slightly until Alaric's fingernails slice deep into her flesh, almost as if the king is trying to etch her bones with the terms of their agreement.

"Yes, Your Majesty," Helena spits as though she has been poisoned, defiantly glaring into the king's eyes.

"Say it, Helena. Or I will draw a knife and really give you a reason to be hateful," Alaric challenges, his voice deadly calm.

I know exactly what he wishes to hear. The idea of even breathing the words makes me want to vomit on his shoes. Helena raises her chin, keeping her mouth tightly closed.

"For the slave's sake then? I will make sure his wound is cared for." Alaric smiles when Helena's resolve wavers, pleased to have found a bargaining chip he can use to keep her in line. "Healing for the ex in exchange for one special word. All you have to do is say it."

For Ithel, Helena's heart begs, even as the thought of uttering what Alaric wishes to hear makes her wish she could drive a knife into her gut. *For the one man of integrity in this horrible place. For the lover, I'll have left behind twice. I can say the word if it protects him, can't I? To save Ithel's life the way he has done for me, surely I can demean myself just a little.* Helena sighs, closing her eyes as she whispers, "Yes...Father."

"Wonderful!" A cackle of glee erupts from the king as his icy lips brush Helena's cheek. Alaric pushes the hair back from Helena's ear, leaning close as he whispers, "Remember, you have six months to find the traitor, my daughter, or I will kill your precious Ithel myself."

CHAPTER 8

This pounding in my head will be the death of me, Wolf sighs, rubbing his temples as he sits in the only good chair on the porch of the House of Piranhas. The roar of the ocean tunes out the clattering swords as soldiers spar in the sand. He can't even hear Lynx's child whimpering in Wren's tent. Yet Wolf feels his jaw tighten as another wave of nausea overpowers his stomach. He swallows hard, fearing he will lose the contents of his stomach in front of his men. Such a weakness cannot be tolerated. *All because of that damned woman! Now I have to relieve the withdrawal symptoms from losing her. Why couldn't she just stay with me?*

"Sir? Everything all right?" Jackal questions, stepping up onto the whitewashed porch. "You look ill."

"If I wanted your opinion, I'd ask," Wolf snarls, the blinding sunlight forcing him to squint. It feels like thousands of razorblades slice into his eye, hammering into his orbital socket in a reckless, relentless march to shred the fibers of his brain. Turning his face away from Jackal, he wheezes, "What do you want?"

"I was told you had orders for me," Jackal replies, his brow furrowing in confusion. "There was a notice on the table in my tent saying I was to report to you as soon as I could. Did you not leave it for me?"

Wolf struggles to recall sending for Jackal. Searching his

memory, he draws a complete blank. Yet rather than admit his mistake, Wolf states, "I decided to send Wren on my errand instead. Leave me, Jackal."

Jackal rocks back on his heels, his face a mask of rage as he challenges, "Was it really wise to trust that outsider? And why did you feel like you had to when you have me and Coyote and Hyena? We've been on your side since the very beginning."

"You dare to question my decisions now?" Wolf raises his voice, clutching the arm of his chair to keep his anger in check. If he should try to stand or make any sudden movements, Wolf knows he will pass out from the pain in his head. "If I decide Wren is an ally, then I expect you to do so as well. Is that understood?"

***

"Fine," Jackal hisses, stomping off without another word to his leader. He marches over one of the nearby communal campfires, grumbling to himself as he pulls a pot of stew from the fire. Serving himself, he plops down into the sand and slurps at his meal greedily. Only when he lowers his bowl from his chin does he realize he's sitting across from his enemy. "So, I see you've managed to get in good with the big boss, hmm? What's your secret, Wren?"

Wren keeps his face stoic, a difficult task when a wide smile of delight threatens to spread across his features. "I have no idea what you are talking about, Jackal," he replies, feigning innocence.

"I just can't figure it. You show up here completely refusing to take on a new mask and join our House—a feat that should get you beaten and sent to live among the nameless unchosen—and yet Wolf decides not only to show you mercy but to trust you. What errand did he send you to do? Did you meet with his border guard ally, Matthais? Or is Wolf up to something else?" Jackal's bowl trembles in his left hand, his right one slinking toward the knife in his belt.

Wren forces his brow to furrow, blinking a few times

as if he's confused. "I'm sorry, Jackal. I don't understand what you are saying. I've been here all day, and I've had no special mission from Wolf." *Keep still, and look him in the eye*, Wren tells himself, counting slowly in his mind and matching his breaths to the rhythm in his head.

Jackal hesitates, his head turning slightly to the side as he considers Wren's words. "I had a message in my tent saying Wolf wanted to see me, but when I got there, Wolf said he'd sent you instead. You're telling me that Wolf is lying?"

"I don't think so; Wolf doesn't strike me as a good liar," Wren replies, trying not to scoff at his own words. *Control. It's all about self-control.* Wren drops his gaze down to his stew, forcing his mouth to stay silent for a few heartbeats to give the appearance of thought. Then he continues, "But now that you mention it, I do think something's up with him. Wolf's been having headaches—"

"I know about that. He's been having those ever since the Ddraig-loving bitch left him. Withdrawals or something like that. I didn't quite understand it, to be honest," Jackal interrupts, standing up and refilling his bowl.

"Headaches and forgetting things—that's not a good sign. Is it possible that these headaches are doing permanent damage to him somehow?" Wren asks the question outright, sowing the seeds of doubt in Jackal's head.

"What do you care? You've not even officially joined our house," Jackal scorns, pointing his finger at Wren's subtle mask.

"My loyalty is here." Wren evades the impending conflict, speaking truthfully as he sees Lynx and her child step out of his tent. *I am loyal to that woman and her child because I want to keep them safe,* Wolf confesses in his thoughts, letting the veracity of these words color his verbalized lies. "But I worked with the medic in the House of Vultures for a while. He told me about this withdrawal from a naming bond. Headaches, hallucinations, forgetfulness, loss of speech, and eventually complete loss of mind and motor function." Standing up, Wren walks over to the barrel full of soap water and drops his stew bowl into the foamy suds. "If I were you, Jackal, I'd be making plans just in case what we are seeing is Wolf's downfall. Because if it is, wouldn't you be the natural choice to replace him?"

Wren saunters away before Jackal can speak again, weaving his way through the tents until he stands in front of Lynx. "What are you doing out here, wench?" he demands, winking even as he raises a hand as if to backhand the woman.

"Please, I just need a moment in the sunlight," she begs, scanning the tents surrounding them for any signs of eavesdroppers. "I think we are safe," Lynx whispers, looking up at Wren with a small smile.

"What's Jackal doing now?" Wren questions, tilting his head slightly to the left to indicate in which direction Lynx should look.

"He's called Coyote and Hyena over to him; they are huddled up and whispering. What did you do?" Lynx wonders, shifting her sleeping child on her hip.

"It's amazing how much mistrust one false note can cause." Wren grins, quickly filling in the details for her and turning his gaze to the House of Piranhas. "Now, I need to speak to Wolf."

***

All of the Ddraigs stand in the deepest Pith cavern, the strongest ones at the mouth of the opening to protect the baby Ddraigs. Glancing off to my left, I know the Carreglas is close; I can feel its gentle thrum as if it is a part of my heartbeat. Siri and Suryc thunder up to me and Cyrus, carefully scanning over us for any signs of injury. Ekard and Drake aren't far behind, the crimson dragon's guttural voice demanding, "What happened up there?"

"There was an intruder—one of the Vibría," Cyrus announces, his voice wavering with the depths of his unspoken fears.

"She didn't attack us. I think she wanted to help," I mumble, turning aside from Cyrus's withering stare.

"More than likely, she came to see if she could sneak into

our lair without being noticed, gathering up any information she could before she was caught," Cyrus snipes cynically, his hands clenching and unclenching. The wild look I've come to associate with his nightmares crosses Cyrus's eyes. Though he stands before me, I fear he's lost in his thoughts, fighting the Vibría that tortured him at the House of Vultures.

"She told us a great deal about her people," I gently protest, reaching up to squeeze Cyrus's shoulder, hoping the well-meant gesture will calm his nerves. "She claimed that her people are victims of her king's greed and cruelty, not soulless killing monsters." Glancing at Siri, I open my mind to her, replaying our conversation with the Lady Vatusia, carefully omitting the part when she said I should come to Déchets alone to take down the king. "Did you know anything about this?" I question, watching Siri's eyes darken until they are almost pewter rather than the silver hue I've come to love so dearly.

"Of course not! I've never heard such a wild tale about our kinsman over the Devil's Spine. The better question is, should we believe it?" Siri shifts from one foot to another, lost in thought. Her tail flicks impatiently behind her as she broods. "Cyrus, you were there — did your Asíle abilities pick up any lie in her words?"

"No," Cyrus grumbles, clearly annoyed by the admission. "But that doesn't mean I think we should trust her. What if there are ways to deceive a truth reader that we don't know about? What did she come here for anyway? To spoon-feed us a sob story about how the king has mistreated her, just to gain some sympathy? Or perhaps to get us to lower our guard, making us an easier target?" Cyrus shakes his head, crossing his arms over his chest.

Taking a deep breath, I voice my opinion, knowing it will start an argument. "She gained nothing by coming here, and her story was too detailed, too heartbreakingly personal. You found no deception in her words. So, I think we should cautiously trust her."

"Seriously?" Cyrus barks, wiping his hands through

his hair as his eyes widen with incredulity. "They are liars and tricksters, Iris! And she said herself that if the king ordered the Vibría to attack, she'd happily kill us all to satisfy him. Does that really sound like someone you can trust?"

"That's not quite how she said it," I mumble, heat flushing my cheeks as my temper flares.

"It's close enough," Cyrus whispers, shaking his head at me. "The Vibría hold no loyalty with their king; they just want him dead. Can you really believe someone like that will suddenly be trustworthy?"

"Haven't you asked the same thing of me?" I accuse, turning on Cyrus as hateful words spew from my lips. "You treated me like dirt in the House of Vultures, remember? But now that we have Ddraigs, now that I've learned we are supposed to be a couple, I'm—"

"Don't," Cyrus challenges, his voice softening to a lethal rasp, a storm of fury brewing in his eyes. "Don't compare me with that monster."

I swallow the remaining accusations, regretting that I hadn't kept a better rein on my tongue. "That was unfair of me. I apologize," I mumble, dropping my gaze to my toes, my arms wrapping around my middle in an effort to comfort myself.

Cyrus, however, is unwilling to let my insult go without a fight. "I didn't torture you for pleasure like the Vibría did to me. I didn't strike you for sport. I didn't attempt to break your mind or shatter the depths of your soul. Did I? Can you stand there and say that anything I did in the House of Vultures was for any purpose other than protection?"

"No." I shiver as if the icy, frigid bite in Cyrus's words somehow chilled my blood. "Cyrus, I'm really sor—"

"A better question that I can't help but wonder about is this: why are you so quick to trust a complete stranger over me?" Cyrus's hands come up to grip my upper arms, holding me still so I cannot get away from his questions.

"I—" My mouth opens and shuts helplessly as I struggle for an answer. "I'm worried about the Cadogans' slow progress with their Ddraigs, and any extra aid — even from an unlikely ally like the Vibría — is welcome."

"That's a partial truth," Cyrus sighs, his eyes flickering black as his Asíle abilities read the veracity of my claims. My hands grow slick with nervous sweat under the scrutiny of his dark stare, and I wish I had some manner of shielding myself from him. "Your supposed worry over the Cadogans is where the lie lurks. Your real motives are selfish."

Shocked by his blunt accusation, I sputter, "What? No! Not at all —"

"Liar! I see the filth of your deception expelled in the very air you breathe," Cyrus snarls, his fingers tightening around my arms like a vice. "What aren't you telling me, Iris?"

Cyrus's breath comes in ragged hitches, almost like he's become a wild beast chasing after its prey. I cower in his presence, longing to hide behind my Ddraig. However, one look at Siri, and I see no sympathy in her expression. *She blames me too, siding with Cyrus in this argument,* I realize, hurt putting pressure on my chest as if I've been physically struck a blow. "Suryc, how do I get him to stop?" I question, turning a helpless, pleading gaze to the black Ddraig beside my Siri.

"You tell the truth," Suryc informs, his voice grim and his golden eyes full of sympathy. "It's the only thing that calms Cyrus down when his truth-reading side takes over. Every lie will agitate him more; every truth soothes and brings peace."

Cyrus growls, his eyes glittering like a starry expanse of the sky at midnight. "You're not afraid that the Ddraigs and Cadogans are unprotected, are you? I think you worry over Cane. Either you fear that he will hurt you, or you wish you had stayed with him. Tell me now, Iris, which is it?"

"Of course, I worry about your brother!" I snap, wishing I could crawl away and creep into a crevice in the stones. I hadn't realized how dependent on privacy and self-sufficiency I am until Cyrus showed he was able to strip me of those luxuries. Having him use his Asíle powers on me is worse than standing naked in front of the entire army we've created. The thought of giving voice to my thoughts, baring my soul to Cyrus, smothers me. The way he demands to know what I'm thinking infuriates me. And the combination of these contradicting emotions is lethal, choking me and filling my head with raging words, stifling my will to act and making my blood boil with unspent anger.

"Finish it, Iris. Why are you worrying over Cane?" Cyrus commands, his fingernails threatening to break skin with every silent second that passes.

"How can I not worry over Cane? If he finds me, he finds the Ddraigs. And if he has his way, all of us will be dead. Do you want to see that happen?" I grumble, wishing I could just rip my arms out of his grasp without feeling the pain such an action would cause. I nearly bite through my tongue in an effort to keep quiet, but the rest of the truth—the words I hate to even consider—finally escape my lips. "He's hunting me now, Cyrus. I'm worrying over him because...I'm afraid."

A breath escapes my lips as Cyrus nods once, seemingly mollified. "More," Cyrus utters, and I find I cannot deny him.

"I don't want to be the one that brings us down," I whisper, words pouring out of my mouth almost faster than I can think about them. "I never wanted to be a leader because I was afraid I couldn't do it. Now, here I am, trying to keep my own head afloat, and all I can do is worry that I'm going to be the reason the Carreglas is found. I'm going to fail, and the Ddraigs will be caught. I'm going to screw up, and Wolf will find me." Clenching my eyes shut, I swallow hard against the final truth I cannot keep from rising to my tongue. Silently, I wonder if Cyrus's Asíle abilities allow him to pry the truth out of an unwilling speaker's thoughts as I hear my voice say, "I keep turning to you, Cyrus, and that scares me. I'm afraid I'm growing dependent."

The air, so full of tension and hostility, grows stale around us. Feeling vulnerable, I turn my face away from Cyrus's scrutiny. After a time, Cyrus's breathing slows, and he returns to his normal self. Easing closer to me, his hands brush my shoulders gently as he whispers. "And your feelings toward my brother? Don't you harbor any love for him?"

I shake my head, too raw and emotionally spent to trust my voice. Traitor tears slip down my cheeks as I remember the coldness, the unbridled lunacy I saw in Cane's eyes at the House of Piranhas. *I never loved Cane*, I remind myself sadly, wondering not for the first time if I am capable of romantic love at all. *I never cared for him as strongly as he cared for me. But now I know Cane sold our people as slaves. How could Cyrus possibly think I still feel anything for a brute like that?*

Love makes a man do crazy things. Siri's voice slips into my mind, her tone full of wistful amusement. *The thought of you loving another man is filling Cyrus with so much jealousy, I fear he will lose himself to madness. I know you don't want to hear it now, but you and he must complete the coupling, Iris —*

I mentally shove Siri's presence out of my head as hard as I possibly can. Glancing over at my Ddraig, I see her exasperated expression, smoke roiling from her nostrils as she huffs and creeps over to the farthest corner of the cavern.

Cyrus slips his hands up to cup my face, his nose brushing mine as his voice hitches, his eyes soft and full of wistful sadness as he explains, "Dependence upon another person isn't wrong, but it doesn't necessarily mean you love that person either. You can depend upon someone you despise. I don't want us to be in a toxic relationship."

"Nor do I, Cyrus," I mutter, using his shock to extricate myself from his proximity just to get a breath of unshared air to steady my nerves. "I'm still not ready to discuss us in any kind of *relationship* at all."

Cyrus chuckles a bitter, frustrated sound. Turning my head, I see him observing my rigid, crossed arms, and when he speaks, his words give me gooseflesh. "I know the truths that you dare not whisper. I can see your true feelings. Fight it all you wish, Iris. Your actions will change nothing."

"I thought I was the one that could see the future," I quip, my shoulders taut with tension as Cyrus stalks close once more.

"But I know that you are meant for me," Cyrus's replies, stopping when his toes almost step on mine. He lifts one finger up to my face, tracing my jawline and smiling when I shiver. "You don't want to admit it—you don't even want to feel it, but you are softening toward me. And that gives me hope." Cyrus steps away from me then, sauntering a few paces toward his Ddraig, whistling as he leaves. "I can wait a little longer."

Itching to move, I jump from my perch in the cavern, trotting as far in the opposite direction of Cyrus as I can get. In the deepest corners of the cavern, Anemone sits with her tail curled under her chin, babysitting the young Ddraigs as they attempt to fly. She laughs good-naturedly as they flutter, sometimes rising and catching them before they land on their heads. Smoke billows from her nostrils in time with her chortles.

Enomena is close beside her Ddraig, waving to me as I stomp toward her. Catching my mood as I flop down onto an obliging flat stone, she inquires, "What's got you riled?"

"Cyrus." I spin my hand in the smoke that curls around me, watching its mesmerizing dance on the breeze. "It hardly matters."

"Of course, it does," Siri replies, shooing away the babies as she looms over my shoulder, unwilling to leave me in peace. "You're mad because he's right, but you haven't forgiven yourself for being tricked by his brother. You've got to move on, girl. Let go of the past, and make a new future."

"With Cyrus?" I snort, unwilling to acknowledge that the very thought sends my pulse racing with anticipation. *Could I so easily switch loyalties? Not even two months ago, I was preparing to join Cane as his second in command, and now I am considering his brother instead? What's wrong with me?* Forcing my mind to focus on the issues at hand, I declare, "None of that matters right now, Siri. We have two enemies joining forces, and I have no doubt that they are coming after us soon. Cane and the king of Déchets are strong forces independently; imagine how much more lethal they will be standing united. How are we going to fight against them?"

"Right now, you need to focus only on the new Cadogans. We'll make a plan once they are ready to fight. For now, we can spend our time in hiding—"

I do not hear the rest of her words. My mind blots out everything, a white screen robbing my normal sight, and a dull roar that reminds me of the constant whirring of the ocean fills my ears. It is suffocating in its intensity, burning my senses as I transition into the strange world of my visions. I can feel my hands clenching for anything I can cling to, desperately struggling and failing to stay alert in the present.

The room I enter in my vision is dark and stony. I see two people sitting on the rough-hewn floor, their faces out of view. One wears a gray hood, and the other has his or her back to me. To the left, I notice an ornate throne shaped to resemble a giant snake. The armrests are twin viper heads as well, and jewels inset at the eyes glitter as if they are truly alive. Long, slender fingers brush these metal snakes lovingly, and my eyes draw upward until I am face to face with the king of Déchets.

He is not what I had expected, I admit. The king is thin and muscled, as though he spends most of his time on a battlefield. There's a dark, dead expression in his eyes, and as he watches the couple before him, he smiles. It is the expression of a man who just discovered he's cheated death. The sight of his wicked grin is enough to send fear shooting through my nerves like lightning intent on frying my brain.

"No!" I shout, my hands reaching toward the familiar face on the right side of the dais. I realize that I had still been hoping Wolf could be convinced not to ally himself with Déchets. Now, I cannot help but wonder if we are clinging to a hopeless cause.

"They are yours to punish, as we agreed." The king of Déchets raises a weathered hand to Cane, deferring to his wishes.

"Many thanks, Your Highness." Cane bows before slinking over to the hooded form, triumph written on his face. He swaggers around the pair on the floor, showing off his maskless visage and clean-cut attire fresh from the Déchets' seamstresses.

It is unnerving to look upon Cane's wildly excited expression. *His face is too symmetrical; it's not the face I'm growing to love,* I exclaim with a shock. I find myself searching for Cyrus's scars or that slight upturn to one corner of his mouth that always gives him a sardonic smile. *Cyrus's flaws make him beautiful,* I declare, knowing I don't just mean his physical appearance. *I'll take a flawed, real man over the perfect disguise of a coward any day.*

"Don't you have anything to say?" Cane mocks, kicking the legs of one of the people on the floor. "Aren't you at least going to beg me to spare your pathetic life?"

The pair huddle close together, leaning heavily on each other for strength. "I am sorry that it came to this, love," the hooded one whispers, and my heart grows cold as I recognize this voice as my own.

"I'd rather die with you now than live a thousand lives alone. I'm only sorry we had so little time together," Cyrus replies wearily, pressing closer to kiss my cheek.

"Get away from her!" Cane screams, drawing a sword as he approaches us. Yet, in this moment, the impending threat does not give rise to terror in our hearts. We stare into each other's eyes, our faces mirrors of one another. Sad smiles, unshed tears, longing and unspoken love all play out on our expressions. Cyrus drops his chin until our foreheads touch, his beautiful, haunted eyes closing as he waits for his brother to take his vengeance. Cane wastes no time, his sword slicing deep into Cyrus's side.

"No! Cyrus!" I bellow, waving my real hands as though I can somehow change the vision playing out in my mind's eye. "Don't hurt him, Cane! Please!"

I am helpless against the vision, forced to watch it unfold. Cyrus wheezes and drops hard, his breath already unsteady. Blood pools at my feet, and I watch as the spectral me rips the hood off her head and presses the fabric hard into his gaping wound. *Use your strength to heal him!* I silently order, wishing I could turn away and not witness Cyrus's last moments. "I can't save you, Cyrus! Why can I not —?"

"This place repels such magic," Cane explains giddily, grabbing my arm as he rips me away from Cyrus's side. "Now, you will join me at your rightful place, and we will watch my brother die. Then you will bring the Carreglas over to this land as a gift to the king of Déchets. Nothing will stand against us now, Iris! I am the king of Cassè just as you foresaw, second only Alaric, the ruler of this land. You will be my consort, and my brother will cheat death no longer."

I drop to my knees when Cane passes his sword over Cyrus's neck. Blood spurts across my chest, quickly draining from his gurgling body. My mouth hangs open in a scream, my fingers inching for Cyrus's boot. Suddenly pulling an unseen knife hidden at Cyrus's ankle, I launch myself at Cane. His face turns white as I gut him before he can take another breath, slitting his chest from navel to throat. By the time he hits the ground, his eyes have faded to sightless gray.

"Oh, my love," I mumble, weeping over Cyrus as his gurgled breaths slow. "Do not leave me in this place! Please! I need you, Cyrus."

"Well, well. That boy you just murdered wasn't lying to me after all. He swore you would be useful to me, and here you've proved him to be right." Alaric smoothly glides down from his throne, his cold fingers gripping my chin tightly, craning my head until my defiant gaze meets his. "Hmm…too bad you have to die. I'd have loved to break you myself. But time is of the essence, and I cannot let someone as strong as you survive to challenge me again. What a pity," Alaric sighs, dropping his hold on me and sauntering back to his throne with a flourish of his hand. My body slumps as a rain of arrows spear my back. As I fall, I hear Alaric announcing, "Send the border guards through Cassé with a proclamation that their lands are now under my rule. Find the Carreglas and have it brought to me. Capture any Ddraig that you find and kill their warriors. I have big plans for them." Flicking his icy cold gaze at me one final time, his gleeful voice taunts me as my sight begins to fade, "And to think, you wasted all of your effort to save your country only to end up dead anyway. Funny how things turn out, isn't it?"

"Iris?" Siri's concerned voice rips me from the vision. When my eyes focus on her scaly form, I wrap my arms around her leg, assuring myself that she is not a figment of my imagination. Her warmth seeps into my bones, and a strangled cry erupts from my lips. I cling to my Ddraig like a child crying on her mother's shoulder after a painful fall. "Iris, what did you see?" Siri whispers patiently, her body shifting until she forms a protective circle around me.

"It was awful!" I bellow, my teeth chattering as the shock of the events finally loosens my tongue. "If that was the future that awaits us, Siri, I can't bear it."

Siri's eyes widen as she reads the vision through our shared memories. "Perhaps it is best that you continue to hold out against Cyrus's advances. As long as you two aren't a couple, we aren't creeping closer to this end."

"Cyrus!" I gasp, recalling how it felt to watch him die. "My gods, that was horrible. If watching me die at the hands of the Vibría caused him to suffer even a fraction of what I just endured, then I understand why he hates them." Dropping my hold on Siri's leg, I clamber over her tail, frantically searching the gathering crowd of Cadogans for Cyrus's familiar face.

"Iris? Hey, let me pass," Cyrus demands, shoving his way through the onlookers to get to my side. "What happened? Where is she?"

A relieved sob tears through my chest as I rush toward my infuriating, complex, flawed friend. I don't care that we'd been fighting only a few heartbeats ago or that I'd clearly refused and rejected his love. All I know is that in this moment, nothing will satisfy me but to hold him close, assuring myself that he's alive.

Cyrus does not hesitate to wrap his arms around me.

"What's wrong, Iris?" he whispers into my hair, laying a soft kiss on my brow as he rubs small circles on my back. "What did you see?" he wonders, silently comprehending that I must have had an upsetting vision.

"I watched you die," I whimper between sobs, wrapping my arms tight around his neck. "Cane slit your throat, and I couldn't save you."

"The fact that you'd even want to means all the world to me," Cyrus replies, his voice lifting with his smile.

"Oh, don't joke!" I snap, wiping my tears on his shirt.

"I wasn't," Cyrus rasps, and my heart breaks all over again.

Looking over Cyrus's shoulder, I scan the faces of many concerned Ddraigs and warriors alike. The words of Lady Vatusia echo in my thoughts, and I wonder how many of these people will die if we must fight against the forces from Déchets. Between the Windwalkers, the Vibría, and the king's trained army, we won't stand a chance. No amount of preparation by a ragtag leader with no military background could ever prevail against such odds.

But there is another way, a traitorous thought shivers through my mind. *Take the Lady Vatusia up on her offer; go to Déchets as a spy. Take down your enemy's organization from the inside out if possible.*

I cling a little tighter to Cyrus, wishing I never had to let go. It would be so much simpler if we could just live out the rest of our days in the Pith caverns, content with our Ddraigs and each other. Yet the faces of the nameless unchosen and the knowledge that my people are living as slaves in Déchets is enough to rip this dream to shreds long before I can make it a reality.

"Cyrus, there's something I didn't tell you," I whisper, knowing what I have to say will anger him once more. "And I think now's the time we have to consider it—it might be the only way to save everyone."

CHAPTER 9

"Just the man I wanted to see," Wren calls out as he trots up to Wolf's perch in the rocking chair on the porch. A wave of revulsion roils in his stomach. The scent of burning flesh still carries in the air, and the burning pyre still smolders. No matter how much time passes, Wren fears that the taint of unjustified death will forever stain this stretch of land. Speaking to the man who caused all that useless destruction is even harder to bear. *Lying to him, however, is a far more satisfying endeavor,* Wren reminds himself, swallowing his own emotions long enough to carry out his deception.

"This better be good," Wolf grumbles, leaning back against the rocking chair's headrest, carefully keeping the wooden form from moving even the slightest inch. "I've got a terrible headache, and I'm in no mood for petty grievances."

"I am sorry to hear that," Wren replies, struggling to keep his words from sounding sarcastic. "But I thought you'd want to know that I saw Jackal meeting with two of his cronies, and judging by the intensity of their conversation, I think they were plotting something."

That idea causes Wolf's eyes to open wide despite the splitting agony that splinters his skull as the sunlight fills his view. "You think they are planning a coup? You really believe they seek to overthrow my reign even before it's fully begun?"

"I do," Wren admits, hiding his smile behind his hand,

rubbing his face as if he's deep in thought. "But why take my word for it? Go and see for yourself. The three men were sitting by the campfires closest to Jackal's tent."

"I doubt they'd be so bold to plot a mutiny out in the open in a campsite not even fifty feet from me," Wolf exclaims, his eyes drifting closed even as his mind grows more alive and active with the idea of the possible threat. "Who was with Jackal in this supposed meeting?"

"Hyena, Coyote, maybe a few others, I don't know." Wren offers the names with as little emotion as possible. "But maybe I'm wrong. An open planning session in full view would be a pretty stupid way to start a revolt," Wren smirks, dropping to sit on the white-washed steps. "If I was involved in such a clandestine affair like that, I suspect they go into Jackal's tent for privacy. They'd be far away from prying eyes that way. Of course, if they did, you'd have the perfect opportunity to sneak up on them and eavesdrop through the canvas. But you'd have to move quickly; if they are smart, they won't meet for any length of time."

Wolf stands, gulping down air as he struggles to stay on his feet. Nausea overwhelms his stomach, and his teeth begin to chatter. "I...I don't think I can get there," Wolf declares, his knees growing weak. Another piercing throb in his head brings stars to his eyes.

"Take a deep breath," Wren suggests, pointing to a small knot in the porch railing. "Focus on this spot right here. Will the pain away from your mind's consciousness."

"Had a lot of experience with neglected naming bonds, have you?" Wolf snipes even as he follows Wren's advice.

"Nope, but I've endured a few beatings in my day," Wren whispers flatly, his eyes growing dark as the unwanted memories fill his mind's eye. "Breathing through the pain and displacing my focus always helped me persevere."

"Only for a short time, though," Wolf wheezes, squeezing the arms of the rocking chair until his fingers turn white. "The agony rears its ugly head no matter what I try. I've got to find a way to break the naming bonds as soon as possible." Despite Wolf's reluctance, the method works well enough that he can stand and walk down the steps without getting sick. A hard, unreadable expression passes over Wolf's features as he exclaims, "Now, if you are correct about Jackal, then he and the other traitors will die. But if I find you are mistaken or willfully trying to breed trouble, you, Lynx, and her baby will be the next ones on the burning pyre. So, are you absolutely certain that you want me to investigate Jackal?"

"I have nothing to hide," Wren lies expertly, silently calculating how quickly he could jump down the steps, find Lynx and her son, and disappear if his plan were to fail. "It's time to find out if your so called second in command can say the same."

***

"I don't need any more healers, and I don't need any more food! I just want to a little peace and quiet," Helena bellows while she agitatedly paces around the infirmary.

A sympathetic looking young woman shakes her head, a tremor in her voice as she protests, "But the king has ordered —"

"I don't care what Alaric said." Helena's voice drops to a low, dangerous growl. "I will see no one else this evening. Do you understand me?" She clenches her eyes shut, shying away from the memories haunting her mind. She cannot unsee Evaine's tearless eyes and serene expression right before the guard brutally decapitated her. Nor can she forget the enslaved guards who perished in the effort to save the other prisoners clawing through the tunnel. And the dull thuds of the prisoners' bodies slamming into the rock in freefall still ring in her ears. "Leave me," Helena begs, more to the memories than to the slave still standing in the infirmary.

"But —"

"I won't ask you again." Helena's voice grows deadly calm, her hands reaching for a tiny scalpel laying on a tray near the next sick bed. "I've witnessed a great many innocent deaths this day, but don't think for a second that I won't add your name to the funeral list. What's one more?"

The young woman gulps, backing away from Helena as if she was a wild beast with bared fangs and outstretched claws. Helena tosses the scalpel half-heartedly in her direction. It zips by the girl's cheek, skewering the wooden frame surrounding the door. With a squeak of fear and surprise, the girl races out of the room, finally giving Helena the silence for which she's been longing.

Helena paces over to the windowsill, staring out at the horizon. In the distance, she can see the faintest outline of the mountains. *Tomorrow I'll be traversing those peaks again,* Helena sighs, the thought of leaving this place naturally reminding her of Ithel's predicament. *He should be the guard going with me. I should have been able to protect him.* Soon the silence Helena so desperately desired grows unbearable. Opening the window, a soft breeze twirls wisps of her hair, begging her to dance and play in its wake. Allowing the wind to stir in her blood, she lets it carry her out into the sky, hovering over the palace. Were it not for Ithel's captivity, she would disappear on this breeze and leave Déchets forever. Yet to keep Ithel safe, she must play the part of Alaric's spy. *Unless I can free him now,* Helena realizes wickedly, drifting on the wind until she's in the king's private courtyard where Ithel was drug down into the prison cells.

A shiver ripples through Helena's elemental form, the rank odor of the prison wafting up to her on the breeze. *I have earned my freedom,* she reminds herself even as her body freezes, refusing to enter the prison. *I can go through this door and come back to see the sunlight. I am a prisoner no more.* Yet Helena can barely hover above the doorway without gagging. Human waste and the sour stench of terror permeate the place. The scent of moldy food and filthy straw fill her nose, choking her, reminding her of the horrible days when she feared she was losing her sanity there in the darkness. Breaths come in short, ragged hitches while Helena tries to cajole herself into entering the prison. *The guards who took Ithel into those cells probably didn't venture deep. No doubt, Alaric wants Ithel to suffer at the doorway, constantly in view of freedom without getting to fully taste it.*

Forcing herself to drift lower, Helena's feet strike the stone walkways lightly as she materializes out of the wind. A reckless plan overpowers reason in her mind. Not allowing herself to think further and back out of her plans, Helena steps forward and opens the heavy dungeon door. The rank air assaults her nose, and Helena drifts back up into the wind, watching for the perfect opportunity to slip inside unseen.

The prison guard sitting at the bottom of the stairs does not miss the sudden fresh breeze wafting into the first level of the dungeon. "Who's there?" he grumbles, trudging up the steps to secure the prison once more. "Hello?" he calls out, searching the grounds for any signs of life and movement.

Helena wastes no time, dancing on the breeze above the doorway, allowing it to pull her inside the prison. Once she finds herself behind the guard, she pushes all the air she can toward the guard. The sharp gust of wind causes him to stumble out of the prison. Immediately Helena slams the door. *I hope my abilities are strong enough to carry us both,* Helena worries as she skulks down the line of cells, searching for Ithel. "Where are you, Ithel?" she whispers under her breath in frustration as each passing cell is found empty.

"Helena?" Ithel questions from the last cell on the first level of the prison. "What are you doing here?"

Helena hurries over to his cell, and a strangling sob burns in her throat as she peers inside at her friend. Ithel's face is bruised on one side, and a cut mars one lip. His left arm is bandaged from wrist to elbow, the poorly applied white gauze already covered with layers of grit and sludge from the filthy prison walls. "Helena, go now while you still can." Ithel's words are slurred by pain and medication, his eyes fever bright. "Leave me."

"I wanted to be sure that the king had kept his word to care for you." Acknowledging that monster as her father still left a bitter taste in her mouth. "I'm supposed to leave in the morning with a new guard, Ithel."

"I know…I have a few friends in the guards, and they keep me informed. Your new guard, Andras, is a decent man. He is quiet, but he will protect you well. You could have had much worse." Ithel coughs, a guttural rasp already forming in his lungs.

"I'm not leaving here without you!" Helena hisses, cursing herself for not coming prepared with a key to unlock this door.

"I'll only slow you down," Ithel murmurs, pointing to his arm. "Some of the iron filings are still in this wound, Helena. Alaric's agreed to send a surgeon to get them out a week or so after you leave."

Shaking her head, Helena pleads, "Come with me anyway, Ithel."

"How? I can't use my magic, Helena. As long as the extra iron is in my arm, I am grounded. There's no way we can both get out of this prison without our Windwalker abilities, and you can't carry us both." Ithel whimpers, sharp pains lancing through his wound, almost as if the metal in his arm bites deeper through the flesh, gnawing toward his bones. "Please, Helena, just go."

"I—I'm so sorry, Ithel," Helena sobs, carefully reaching through the bars to touch Ithel's pallid cheek. "I should never have left you behind all those years ago. I should have begged you to come with me to Cassè. You should have been with me when our—"

"Hush," Ithel mutters, a sudden chill quaking through his limbs. "Now's not the time for regrets, love. Just go and be safe. Live well."

"I will come back here," Helena vows, her heart breaking as a racking cough causes Ithel to double over. He slumps down to sit on the disgusting straw, leaning his head back on the grimy stone wall. "I'll do whatever it takes to free you."

"Helena, you are not that stupid. Find a way to ditch Andras and never look back." Ithel lowers his head into his hands. "Get to Cassè and rebuild your life there. Forget about me."

"No. I cannot leave you stuck in this cell. I know too well how it feels to be caged." Helena's eyes cannot focus on anything but the bars. Tightness in her chest blooms at the memories, all the days she had spent lost to madness in these cells. "I will find a way to—"

The door above the stairs bangs open as a furious guard stumbles inside. His chest heaves with effort, his eyes gleaming with berserk madness. "You! Oh, how I hoped you would do something this foolish! That it would be on my watch so I could deal with you. So that I could finally make you suffer!"

"You fell for that open door trick, but I am the fool?" Helena spits on the shoes of the guard, sneering as she recognizes the man's face. While she never learned his name, she remembered him from her days in the cells. He'd never laid a hand on her, but there were worse punishments than a physical blow for a captive soul; this guard had taught her that lesson all too well. Hackles rising, Helena tenses her muscles, preparing for a fight as she declares, "I picked your watch because I knew you would fall for such an obvious trick. Isn't that why you are here, guarding the traitor's prison? Alaric can't trust you with an assignment that requires actual thought."

The guard smiles, either unaware of the fact that Helena has insulted him or too lost in his own lewd thoughts to care. "I dream of you, Helena, did you know? I dream that I did more than just piss in your cell when I had the chance. I still fantasize about watching your monthly sponge baths and touching you when you'd fall asleep too close to the bars."

Unwanted memories flash through Helena's thoughts. The way she'd turn her face to the wall to hide her shame while he leered at her during the baths. They were the one day a month she should have been able to feel clean, and he always stole that sensation from her. She always tried to sleep against the far wall, but depression sometimes forced her closer to the bars. A few inches closer to free, fresh air was worth the risk— until her skin was covered in purplish bruises and sore spots from the guards' unruly hands. And the smell of urine in her cell—gods, that was a scent she worried would never fully be removed from her body. It was etched into her skin cells, into her very pores, as if there was no soap that could ever scrub her clean again.

"You rat bastard," Helena hisses under her breath, shivering as she fights the urge to cower in the guard's presence.

"To me, you will always be the Princess Whore!" The guard skulks closer, sensing her defeat. "Now there's nothing stopping me from taking what I desire, is there?"

The threat in his words is enough to make her heartbeat stutter. She starts to curl into herself, her arms wrapping around her body as if she could shield herself from danger.

"No, Helena! Don't go down without a fight," Ithel urges, clawing his way closer to the cell bars without any regard to his own wellbeing. His skin sizzles in a few places where his fingers and wrists touch the metal, but he doesn't care. His concern lies only for the woman his heart still longs to love. "You can take him, Helena. Don't you dare quit before the battle's even begun!"

Helena's attention snaps to Ithel. Her resolve strengthens, and she nods once. Then, with a calm spirit and steady nerves, she stands and faces her attacker.

"Oh-ho! Going to make me work for it, are you?" The guard scoffs, stretching his arms exaggeratedly and cracking the joints in his neck. "I'm going to enjoy this—"

A low growl builds in Helena's throat, rising to a guttural roar. Helena's hands tremble, her Windwalker magic whistling through the cells like haunting ghosts moaning their grievances. The breeze she creates swiftly becomes a forceful straight-line wind, slamming hard into the guard. Sand flies through the air, each granule like a miniature projectile. The guard is helpless against the attack, his exposed skin soon covered in long, thin scrapes.

"So, you're stuck guarding this prison because you are lowborn and without Windwalker magic," Helena taunts as the guard blindly attempts to catch her by the hair. Because he keeps his eyes shut to shield them from debris in the air, his hands grasp at the emptiness, never finding their mark. Helena smirks, relishing the view as the guard stumbles around helplessly. "You know this prison is for the ones the king finds embarrassing. Is that why he put you here too? Do you shame your country in your service? Or just in your lack of magic?"

A nonverbal cry rages from the guard as he races toward Helena's dancing form. The sword at his side shifts out of its scabbard. Helena's steel, strong hands clutch its handle, aiming the point at the guard's throat. "Move, and you die," she whispers, smiling to herself as his throat bobs nervously, almost slicing itself open.

"Fiend! You hide behind magic, but I will be waiting for you. They will bring you back to these cells one day! And when you return, you will never leave this prison again!" the guard bellows, furious to find himself beaten.

"My friend is in this cell," Helena explains, leaning forward to whisper a warning in the guard's ear. "And I will come back for him. If I find out that you or any other guard has hurt him, I will make your deaths painfully slow." She lets the blade scrape lightly down his neck as it trails down toward more sensitive parts below his belly button. Her eyebrows raise coldly in challenge, enjoying the way the guard's face turns white as the winter moon. "Do you understand my meaning? Lay low one hair on his head, and I will make you all pay for it."

"You will —"

"I will what? Regret this? Die? Pay for the embarrassment you feel because you couldn't control a woman?" Helena mocks, smiling to herself even as her voice lowers to whisper a deadly promise. "Think twice before you threaten me further, or else I'll make good use of this sword. Your death would not cause me even a moment's grief."

The guard, to his credit, has the wherewithal to keep his mouth shut. His murderous glare is the only outward sign of his hostility.

"I will take this sword as a reminder of my plans," Helena announces, slipping behind the guard and backing toward the stairs. Looking over the man's shoulder, she focuses her attention on the bandaged hand she can still see pressing close to the cell bars. "I meant what I said, Ithel. I will come back to get you out of this place" Then, with a final howling breeze that gently caresses Ithel's cheek, Helena disappears from the prisons, letting the wind dry her tears as she floats back to the infirmary to await the arrival of her new guard.

***

"Why? Why on earth would you keep something like that from us, Iris?" Cyrus demands, slamming his hands into our makeshift table we created from a dry husk of bark from one of the few trees brave enough to try surviving in the Pith lands. The gesture only manages to crack the already fragile wood, scattering our poorly drawn maps and writing utensils on the cavern floor. "That Vibría monster tells you the best plan is to come into Déchets alone —"

"It wasn't just that! My so-called *father* made it clear to me in my death dream that I had some standing in Déchets' as well. Lady Vatusia only confirmed his words," I interject, hating the fact that I sound like I'm whining and making excuses. "This might be the best course of action, and it would be foolish not to consider it."

Cyrus stares at me as if I'm growing a third eye in the middle of my forehead. His voice is full of hostility, growing louder with each word until he's shouting. "And you don't see that there might be a trap in this? Are you really that blind?"

"This is why I didn't tell you," I snap, my hackles rising as my temper flares in response to his attitude. "You're so angry you aren't willing to listen to me, to even think —"

"What? That one of the monsters that tortured me might have had a change of heart and wants to help us?" Cyrus's hands shake at his sides, his breathing growing shallow as he exclaims, "You can't seriously be that naïve. You saw what they did to me."

"But you aren't seeing the visions I'm having," I cry, my voice growing shrill. "No matter what course of action we plan, nothing about our future has changed! In each vision, we are caught, our Ddraigs are dead, and you die right in front of me. Gods only know what happens to the rest of the Cadogans who follow us." Shivering against the fear in my heart rather than a chill, I whimper, "I'm willing to entertain any idea that might change our fate, Cyrus." My lip quivers as tears threaten to fall. "I don't want to see you get hurt."

Cyrus hesitates to speak, even to breathe. After a few moments, he blinks rapidly as though waking up from a dream. "You—you really mean that."

"Of course I do," I reply, slumping to sit on an obliging stone. The weight of arguing with Cyrus wears me out, pushing me to a point of emotional and mental exhaustion I can hardly bear. "Despite our past issues and all the heated words we've spat at each other over the years, I've never wanted you to die." *I'm not a monster,* I grumble to myself, a dull ache burning in my heart at the implication that I could be so cruel, so unfeeling as to want Cyrus's death.

Silence thickens the air around us until I fear it will stifle the breath right out of my lungs. Pressure builds in my ears until it is physically painful to remain in this void of noise any longer. A soft sigh of relief wheezes out of me when Cyrus finally speaks again.

"Tell me this." Cyrus creeps closer, dropping onto his knees before me so he can see my face clearly. "Were you planning to go to Déchets alone? Did you have any sort of plan in place?"

"I—I hadn't gotten that far," I admit, pulling my legs up onto the rock, shrinking into as tight a ball as I can, as if I can somehow hide myself from Cyrus's scrutiny. "I wasn't even sure if I'd go at all. I was waiting to see if a better idea came to us before I decided to go to the Vibría."

"Did any of your thoughts include me?" Cyrus plants

his hands on either side of the rock where I'm sitting, leaning close. "Did you ever once stop to think that I wouldn't let you go off alone into that dangerous land? Because I wouldn't allow it, Iris. Do you understand? If you even try to leave me behind, I will follow you to Déchets. There's nothing you can say or do to stop me," Cyrus interjects before I can protest, his eyes soft and full of sadness as he murmurs, "Did you ever even think about asking me outright to come with you?" Cyrus raises one hand to brush the hair away from my face, the touch surprisingly gentle despite the intensity of his expression. "You are an exasperating woman."

"I didn't want to put that burden on your shoulders," I admit, feeling small. "You're already dealing with so much, and I—"

"I would have said yes," Cyrus interrupts, his tone revealing his weary resignation. "I think I would follow you anywhere if you'd only ask."

"I can't keep living in limbo like this, wondering when the Windwalkers will come for us, anticipating Wolf's inevitable attack, and knowing that he will find us unprepared. I can't bear another vision where the ones I lo—" I stumble over the word, a powerful quiver rattling my body with such force that I cannot still the motion. *Was I really about to say that I love Cyrus?* I question myself, chewing on my lip while I hesitate, struggling to sort out the storm of emotions raging inside me. "I'd rather take the risk—"

"And I'd rather you let me perish than put yourself in danger going off alone on a half-planned whim," Cyrus interrupts, standing suddenly and pulling me up into a tight embrace. "But let's not fight about that now. It feels too damn good to hear you *almost* admit honestly that you care about me, and I don't want to ruin the moment."

His warmth seeps into my skin like a balm soothing my open wounds. The sensation quiets the voices of fear in my heart, and I feel my eyes drift closed. *This is perilous.* Allowing myself to get close to Cyrus is a mistake, I know. Yet his touch is the only thing that's managed to still the trembling in my bones. *Still, this growing affection only affirms that we are drawing nearer to the future I've seen in my visions.* And as much as I feel like I need him to hold me now, I should ensure he stays alive in the future by pushing him away. "Cyrus, we can't do this. The closer we get to each other, the more danger we—"

Cyrus stops my words with a kiss, his hands cupping my face, holding me in place until I stop trying to put distance between us. When he breaks away, his breath is ragged as he whispers, "I know you're afraid, Iris. Believe it or not, I am too. But we can't let our fears keep us from moving forward."

"Even if moving forward leads us to our inevitable death?" I murmur, my fingers toying with the ends of Cyrus's hair at the base of his neck.

Cyrus pauses, and for a moment, I suspect my words have finally talked some sense into him. Strangely, though, all I feel is melancholic regret, and I wish I could rewind time and just keep my mouth shut. Then, Cyrus tightens his hold on me, leaning his head down until our foreheads touch as he lovingly replies, "I'll face any future that comes, Iris. As long as you are by my side. As long as you are open and honest with me. You already hold my heart; you always have."

Speechless, I lean my head onto Cyrus's chest, letting the sound of his heartbeat soothe me. However, the longer I stay in his embrace, the more I know I cannot bear to let him die. *When did he become such a vital part of my life?* I wonder, reflecting back on all the troubles we've endured in the past. Somewhere along the way, affection snuck its way into my heart, stealing into my veins so subtly that I never noticed its presence. "I'll do whatever it takes to protect you," I whisper, wrapping my arms a little tighter around his middle.

So, a decision is made? A foreign voice slithers into my thoughts. *You will come to Déchets to spare this man and your Ddraigs?*

Vatusia? How long have you been in my head? I inquire, my blood chilling in my veins at the thought that she might have been a silent witness to all my decisions so far. Worse still, a sudden fear gnaws its way into my brain: does Lady Vatusia have any power to influence my decisions or visions? Has she been pulling the strings, controlling what I see, leading me to make this choice?

Is it my fault that you leave your mind open so anyone can walk in? Vatusia's strange hissing laughter buzzes in my ears. I notice she completely ignores answering my question as she presses, *Have you made a decision, child?*

Are you sure it's the only way? I stall, trying to make up my mind in a moment on a question that has kept me indecisive for days.

The only way? No, child. There are many ways this war could be fought. But is this the only way to ensure that your man and your Ddraigs survive? Perhaps. Lady Vatusia answers me cryptically, and my suspicions take deeper root in my heart.

"Iris? Are you okay?" Cyrus whispers, pulling away from me enough to look into my eyes.

"She's here," I rasp, my hands knotting my hair as if I could somehow claw her foreign presence out of my head. "I hear her voice in my head, asking me if I'm coming."

The vision of Alaric's throne room fills my sight. This time I stand on a blood-red carpet, pillars of polished marble holding the high ceilings over my head. Alaric sits on a raised platform, his throne made to resemble a viper's open maw. As I step out of the shadows, he smiles. Wolf stands on Alaric's left side, Lady Vatusia at the king's right hand. She watches me as though my approach bores her. Wolf, on the other hand, bounds down the steps and pulls me into his arms, burying his face in my neck. "I knew you'd come to your senses," he mumbles, kissing his way up my jawline.

"Did you bring what I asked?" Alaric demands, his voice tight with impatience.

"I did," I reply, my voice sounding strange to my ears. It resembles my pitch and timbre, but something's different. There's a soft rumble in my throat I've never heard before.

Hesitating, I look down at my hands. Where I should see white Dadeni lines crisscrossing my skin, I discover that I now have pearly, shimmering scales that adorn my arms like expensive white gloves. My fingers now bear sharp, black claws for nails.

"I'm Vibría ," I gasp, backing away from Cyrus as the vision fades. "She wants me to go to Déchets and become Vibría ."

I see that you are still not ready, Vatusia whispers in my thoughts, cutting off my ability to hear Cyrus's reaction to my outburst. Her tone is grim and full of sorrow. *Your time is drawing short, child. I see a sacrifice in your future; maybe then you will realize I am right.*

"Iris? What's happening now? Iris?" Cyrus's persistent voice hammers into my mind as Lady Vatusia severs her connection to me.

"She's gone for now," I shudder, wondering how long it will be before she speaks to me again. "But I think she gave me a warning. Trouble is coming, Cyrus. We need to get the Ddraigs and get out of the Pith. We have to face the threat head on, somewhere we choose."

"I'll get Enomena and Drake to round up everyone," Cyrus replies, all traces of tender emotion fleeing from his expression. Before me stands no longer a timid, unsure lover; now I see the battle-hardened survivor I've always known. "We'll get them ready tonight and fly in the morning."

"Where? Where do you think—?" My words die out as I recall the house of my childhood. Its rickety form sat on the edge of a forest a few miles from the Devil's Spine. "Home. We have to go back to my home before the windstorm all those years ago."

Cyrus pauses, considering my suggestion. "The open fields would be decent enough for a battle. And we'd be in a perfect position to see when Windwalkers or fighters from Déchets cross into our lands. We could hide in the forest or in the caves...." Cyrus falls silent as well, the memories of our childhood days so distant and ethereal that they hardly seem to be anything more than an elaborate dream. "Home," he whispers, and a single tear slips down his cheek. Clearing his throat in an effort to regain control of his feelings, Cyrus announces, "I'll show the place to Suryc through our mental link. He'll pass the directions on to the rest of the Ddraigs."

"Thank you." I choke on the words, barely noticing when Cyrus walks away from me.

Leaning heavily on the stone wall, I slide down its rough surface, uncaring if it tears my shirt or scratches my back. Curling into a ball, I wrap my arms around my knees as if this position can somehow keep me from falling apart. Leaning my head back against the stones, I let the tears building in my eyes fall freely, and I wonder if I'll ever see a day when I don't feel like the world is out to break me.

CHAPTER 10

I wish I'd told Lynx to run. I should have gotten her to the stables, hitched up a horse, and sent her and her son to the Pith. It all just happened so fast, and I didn't think. So careless! Wren curses himself as he sits on the porch, waiting for Wolf to return from his attempt to spy on Jackal in his tent. *Everything should work out fine, but I wish I'd taken the extra precaution just to be safe. If Wolf tries to attack that baby....* Wren shudders, struggling to still his nervously tapping feet.

Wolf stomps through the sand, tugging a long chain behind him. Jackal, Hyena, Coyote, and a few other faces Wren doesn't yet recognize are manacled together, each one shouting and pleading their innocence. "Be silent, traitors!" Wolf demands, snapping the end of the chain back like a whip, uncaring which of the prisoners he hits.

Wren breathes a sigh of relief, raising his chin a little higher to portray confidence. "I take it they were plotting after all?"

"It seems you were right," Wolf answers begrudgingly, wrapping the chain around the porch railing and locking it in place.

"It's him!" Jackal accuses, snarling and spitting at Wren's feet. "He's the traitor, Wolf! No doubt he's set us up!"

"Really?" Wren leans back on the porch steps, forcing himself to smile and laugh as though he's just heard a hilarious joke. "Why would I—?"

"Because you're still loyal to the House of Vultures! You're a spy for Condor and Mynah!" Jackal shouts, the others offering their words of agreement.

"Why? Because I still wear this old mask?" Wren scoffs, shrugging his shoulders to emphasize his indifference. "Would you rather I try on one of yours and wear it instead?"

The implied threat of killing one of the prisoners is enough to silence them all. Jackal throws murderous glances in Wren's direction, but no other accusations are made.

"Well, it seems I'm in a difficult position." Wolf slumps into his rocking chair once more. "But I made a deal with you, Wren. You've gained my trust, and I guess these men will be added fodder for my funeral pyre."

"You could do that," Wren agrees, smiling at the way each man's throat bobs, gulping down air as they face their death sentences. "Or, you could imprison them. Let me see if I can get any information about their plans and rout out any other traitors in our midst. Then, when your friend from Déchets returns, sell them off into slavery as you did with all the others."

"Developing a squeamish stomach?" Wolf wonders, turning a suspicious eye on Wren. "Or are you feeling guilty because they are innocent after all?"

"Neither," Wren lies, pretending to pick at his nails. "I just thought you could turn a profit by selling them. It seems wasteful to just kill them; you gain nothing in return."

"Fair enough," Wolf agrees, standing up from the rocking chair and trudging toward the door. "We'll follow your plan for now. See if they have anything useful to tell you, then lock them up in the barn. I'll send a message to Matthais that we have six more slaves for our Déchets' king."

***

"I don't know if I should be proud or furious," Siri grumbles as she plods up to my side. She stops right in front of me, lowering her head until her silvery eyes are on the same level as mine.

"Please don't lecture me," I whine, burying my tear-stained face in my hands. "I really can't handle it right now."

"Too bad," Siri huffs, smoke whirling around me until I fear I'll choke. "But I'll wait until we get into the sky." *The other Ddraigs don't need to hear us fighting.*

"The nomads are ready to fly," Drake interrupts, stalking up to my side with a tight smile. "They wait to move on your command." I can hear how much he hates admitting the role of leadership belongs to me.

"Enomena, you and Lerual fly at the front. Keep sharp eyes on the ground for any signs of trouble. Drake, you lead the nomads out next. Cyrus and I will move last." I lay out the plan, stroking Lerual's chartreuse scales, smiling to myself as a deep hum of approval rumbles through her throat.

"What about us? Can't we help you?" Goldeneye asks, Grouse nodding her head emphatically.

"I've been flying with Lerual since she has no Cadogan," Grouse explains, looking hopefully into Lerual's vibrant yellow eyes.

"If she doesn't mind, then I'm fine with you riding along with her," I concede, chuckling as Grouse squeals in delight and races to stand beside Lerual, jerking Goldeneye along behind her.

"I'll stay with Drake," Bittern offers, and I notice Nepsa leaning heavily against Ekard's crimson scales. "I think my Ddraig has taking a shine to that red one."

Oh no. I struggle to keep my face expressionless as I imagine Bittern's tantrum when the Ddraigs tell her about the coupling bonds. *She will take the news even worse than I did.*

She already is partial to Drake's company; I don't think it will be as bad as you think, Siri interjects, her eyes following Ekard. *At least the budding romance is distracting that red lizard long enough to keep him from challenging me. Be thankful; Nepsa's bought us some more time.*

After an hour, Cyrus and I are the only ones left in the

Pith's main cavern. "Ready to go?" Cyrus asks, holding out his hand to me.

"You and Suryc go ahead," Siri commands before I have a chance to speak. "Iris and I have some things to discuss. We'll catch up to you."

"Iris?" Cyrus hesitates, planting his feet as if he will not move until I respond.

"I'll be fine," I offer half-heartedly, wishing it was the truth. I can feel Siri's simmering anger as she stares daggers at me. "Go on ahead."

As soon as Cyrus and Suryc clear the mouth of the cavern, Siri bellows, "Lady Vatusia tries to lure you into her lands, and you don't think it's important enough to tell me? I mean, I get why you kept it from Cyrus, but why didn't you trust me?"

"We were already fighting about Cyrus and the coupling bond you're so desperate we complete. I didn't feel like sharing anything else that would cause a conflict," I grumble, feeling a shiver race through my spine. What startles me the most, however, is that I'm enticed by the idea of binding myself to Cyrus, not repulsed like I used to be. *He's winning me over*, I admit to myself, wondering how much time we have before the axe swings and the rest of my visions come to pass.

"Well, I don't like it," Siri exclaims, her pearly white tail flicking with her agitation. "The idea that Lady Vatusia's been listening to your thoughts and guiding your visions to fit her agenda worries me. We've been basing our choices on the things you've seen, unaware that they might not be truth."

"You think she's altered my visions somehow?" I whisper incredulously, a mixture of terror and hope flooding my senses. "Is that possible?"

"If she's powerful enough, and I suspect she is, Lady Vatusia could be able to see multiple futures that hinge upon the choices you make. She might be using this gift to lead you down the path she wants you to take. And you can rest assured, if that's the case, she's chosen the path that works in favor of her own best interests, Iris." Siri sighs, lowering her head down to the stone floor.

I crawl over to lean against her sturdy back, savoring the warmth of her scales as it seeps through to my skin. "Lady Vatusia said something about me leaving my mind open. Does that mean there are ways to protect myself from intruders like her?" Immediately the cloudy sky I sometimes see through my connection to Siri springs to mind. "You use skills like what she's describing, don't you? You hide your thoughts from me behind some kind of clouded screen."

"Yes, and it seems it's time for me to teach you that trick," Siri murmurs, a low, dull roar rumbling through her chest like a sigh. "Though I fear once you learn how to shield yourself, you will hide your thoughts from everyone, including me."

"I wish I could say you were wrong," I smirk, leaning my head back against Siri's side, closing my eyes and pushing hard against the emotions roiling in my heart.

"Iris, you have to learn to trust me," Siri scolds, smoke circling in the air. I imagine each tendril shifting into long fingers, grasping at my throat. Blinking the vision away, I shiver, feeling trapped and very paranoid.

"Trust does not come easy for me, Siri," I exclaim, hugging my knees tight to my chest. "I am trying, you know."

"I know," Siri sighs, and I can hear the twinge of hurt and heartache in her tone.

"I'm sorry," I whisper, genuinely wishing things like trust, friendship, and love were easier for me. *You don't live in our world without having to harden your heart against those soft feelings,* I tell myself, sorry to hear the truth in my words. "Siri, in the vision, I saw myself becoming Vibría. Is it possible — ?"

"The Vibría are an abomination," Siri answers severely, her words clipped and sharp.

"What I was wanting to know is whether or not the Ddraig involved in the ritual must die," I press, my questions so full in my head that I cannot keep them unvoiced. "Alaric killed the Ddraigs over in Déchets, but that sounded like it was more for punishment than anything else. The Ddraig hearts had to be spelled to keep beating, so the Vibría didn't die. So, is it possible for a Vibría to be formed without killing the Ddraig involved?"

Siri does not answer me for a long time. So long, in fact, that I begin to suspect she's fallen asleep. The minutes tick by, and I sit there in silence, ruminating on my questions, determined to reason through to find the answers. I'm so engrossed in my own thoughts that when Siri does speak, I startle at the sudden noise. "To become a Vibría involves blood magic. The blood of the Cadogan and the Ddraig must be united; neither has to die for the ritual to be completed. Killing the Ddraigs was a terrible, unnecessary tragedy."

"I pity the Vibría then," I reply, a chill settling on my skin despite Siri's warmth at my back. "Why are they considered abominations?"

"Hundreds of years ago, Ddraigs and Cadogans constantly willingly completed the rituals to become Vibría. Back then, it was as commonplace as the air we breathe. The warriors affected by the ritual became powerful, and with that power, greed and boredom grew. The Cadogans of old forgot their purpose. Rather than protecting the unchosen ones, the Ddraigs and Cadogans set up kingdoms. They expected the Ddraig-less people to treat them like royalty. That kind of desire for power poisons the heart, Iris. Wars and territorial disputes broke out. Eventually, the Vibría of old destroyed themselves in their fighting. After they all died out and the Ddraigs were hidden in the Pith, we all agreed never to turn our Cadogans into Vibría again." Siri's voice fades to a thin whisper as if the words she must speak are physically painful to utter. "If you become Vibría, you will never be accepted by the other Ddraigs or Cadogans again. You and I would be exiled; we'd lose our position as leaders. Think of what you'd be putting Cyrus through — he'd lose you forever. And I'd lose Suryc."

"If it was the only way if I asked it of you in the future, would you bind yourself to me and become Vibría?" I ask, my voice growing hoarse and full of emotion.

"It would break my heart," Siri whimpers, writhing as if the thought causes her physical pain. "But yes, I would do it if you asked me. I love you most of all, Iris."

"Let's catch up to the others." I change the subject, my mind still processing the new information I've learned. *I won't ask unless it is the absolute last option for us,* I vow, already afraid I'd have no other choice in the coming days. *Could I do it? Could I break her heart and my own, exiling us from all of the ones we care for? Could I live with becoming an abomination?* "If it's the only way to save Cyrus, Suryc, and the rest of the Ddraigs, could I afford not to do it?" I question, turning my eyes up to the sky that mocks me with its bright, beautiful light.

***

As the sun rises and peeks into the infirmary, Helena paces restlessly between the empty beds. She nibbles absent-mindedly on her thumbnail, a habit she's never been able to break since her childhood. The sound of Ithel's hacking coughs still haunts her ears. The sight of the shock, fever and chills racing through his body stole every moment of sleep from Helena's mind. No matter how many plans she created, analyzed, and ultimately discarded, she cannot determine a means of helping Ithel escape. "I have to play along with the king's orders," she whispers with a sigh, resigning herself to the truth that leaves a bitter taste on her tongue. "I'm so sorry I must leave you behind."

"And here I half expected to find you in a fighting mood," Alaric quips as he strides into the infirmary, humming an indistinguishable tune in his good humor. "I heard about your escapades yesterday. Tell me, how did you like our accommodations for your former flame?"

Rage burns like a wildfire in Helena's heart, but she keeps her mouth shut. *I will not rise to his taunts.* "When will I meet my new guard?"

"So anxious to leave my presence?" Alaric feigns sorrow, raising a hand to his heart as he sneers. "Or are you anxious to leave Ithel behind again? Did the sight of him bring back old feelings? Or are you just running from guilt and shame, Helena? This time, I wonder, will the separation be permanent?"

Helena stalks over to the window, clutching the sill to keep her shaking fingers from revealing the depths of her anxiety. *There's some truth in his mockery. After all, what choice do I have? If the rogue Windwalker in Cassé is my daughter, I cannot drag her into Alaric's clutches. But what will happen to Ithel if I don't return?* Torn by the heartbreaking decision that lies before her, Helena struggles to keep her tone from betraying her sorrow as she replies, "I simply want to get all this business completed. I earned my freedom in the tunnel, and yet I am not fully —"

"Trusted. I believe that's the word that best completes your sentence, daughter. You are not fully trusted," Alaric interrupts, slinking up behind Helena, leaning forward until his chin almost rests on her shoulder. "You didn't really think I'd let you go so easily, did you?"

Helena's spine stiffens, and she steps off to the side, easing out of Alaric's proximity. The vision of her father's hands wrapping around her throat, tightening their grip until her eyes fade to pale gray, brings a slight hitch in her breath. *He's more than capable,* she reminds herself, crossing her arms to offer some semblance of comfort, however slight it may be. "I took you at your word when you explained the rules for all the prisoners. Succeed, and you earn your freedom. I believe that's what you said. It was my mistake to believe you would honor them."

"Haven't I?" Alaric exclaims, covering his mouth in contrived surprise. "Dear me, I didn't realize you were still locked away in a prison where there was no hope of ever seeing the sun." Alaric offers a smug smile as his sarcastic point is driven home in Helena's mind.

You will never be free of him, Helena reminds herself, feeling defeated as the truth of her words weighs down her chest. Her shoulders droop, and her head falls until her forehead rests against the glass pane. *Turn it off, Helena,* she warns herself as a stray tear threatens to slip down her cheek. *Don't you let that bastard see you cry. If he sees a weakness, he will prey upon it until he destroys you. Don't you dare give him a foothold into your heart.* An icy stillness slowly steals through her veins, calming her roiling emotions. *Let yourself grow cold. Emotionless. Sink into this emptiness; let this void become your sanctuary and your prison. He cannot hurt you here.*

Helena takes a slow, filling breath, focusing her attention on a wind vane far off on one of the distant houses. She feels her body straighten, her shoulders pulled back to their normal posture, her eyes open wide without tears. "When will I meet my guard, Alaric?" She repeats her question, her voice calm and her tone confident. "The longer it takes for me to leave this place, the longer your rogue Windwalker is allowed to remain free and unpunished."

Alaric's face grows somber, his eyes clenching a little as he studies his daughter suspiciously. "Time in the dungeons has served you well, it seems, daughter. I think you've toughened up."

Helena bites her tongue until she tastes blood. She waits in silence, determined to gain a small victory in this battle of wills with her father. Clasping her hands behind her back, she refuses to move or speak until he answers her question.

Alaric huffs, his hands itching to slap that smug expression off Helena's face. "You will meet Andras in the morning. I expect you to be gone before the sun reaches its midday peak. If you are still here by nightfall, you will join Ithel in the prison cells. And if you are still in Déchets by the next sunrise, there will be a death order on your head. Do you understand?"

Helena nods once, asking, "If you put a death warrant out on me, then how do you expect me to come back with the rogue Windwalker?"

"In the border guards, there is a man named Mattias. When you find the Windwalker, bring him or her to Mattias. He and Andras will bring the prisoner to me, and you will have gained the freedom you so desperately seek." Alaric's toes strike the stone floor impatiently as if he's now the one anxious to begin a long journey.

"And what of Ithel? Will you keep him safe?" Helena wonders, raising her gaze until she meets her father's wicked sneer.

Her heart plummets down to her toes when Alaric chuckles under his breath and responds, "So, you do care for him then?" Alaric leans over a nearby infirmary bed, making a show of examining a row of instruments laid out on the bedside table. "If you fail to bring the Windwalker to justice in six months, Ithel will die. Once I receive word of the Windwalker's capture, I will release Ithel from his prison cell."

"You will have the medics clean out his wounds and keep him healthy," Helena clarifies, her words sounding less like a question and more like a demand.

Alaric picks through the tools, his voice deadly soft as he whispers, "Naturally."

"And you will ensure that he is released from the prison without being harmed," Helena adds, silently noting that Alaric's definition of a prison cell could be vague. If, for example, Alaric's interpretation of a "prison cell" is a body that houses a soul, then Alaric's promise of freedom from that cell could mean a death sentence. *I'd be a fool not to believe Alaric might try to trick me,* Helena reassures herself as she watches Alaric's expression. Judging by the fact that he looks like he's just taken a bite out of a rotten orange, Helena suspects her worries were justified.

"Very well. He will be released unharmed," Alaric concedes, his voice tight. "But if you fail to bring me the Windwalker within a year, Helena, I will kill him myself. Very, very slowly. Perhaps I'll even send pieces of him to you as motivation. A finger or toe every month, just to keep in touch —"

"That won't be necessary," Helena scoffs, struggling to keep herself calm and emotionless. *I can't let him see how he gets to me.* "But why make we wait until tomorrow to start my journey, Alaric?"

"A feast, dear girl! We aren't about to send you back to that retched land over the mountains without some food and entertainment!" Alaric announces, clapping his hands a couple times as he sighs and whispers conspiratorially, "It's not every day that your only daughter is released from prison, you know. The court will want to celebrate your return to good graces."

The prospects of sitting through a meal and whatever sordid entertainment Alaric could find almost makes Helena's stomach lurch. However, Helena knows better than to argue. Make a fuss, and Alaric would probably increase the length of the feast just to spite her.

"Very well," Helena replies, resigning herself to being the source of amusement for Alaric's wicked court. "I'm sure you have preparations for such a grand event, so I won't keep you any longer."

"Dismissing me from your presence already?" Alaric pretends to pout even as he moves toward the door. "Oh well, we will have all evening to catch up at dinner, I guess." Alaric drifts out of the doorway on the breeze, a gentle hum the only remnant of his presence.

"Glad you're happy," Helena mumbles under her breath as the tears she's been holding at bay finally well in her eyes. She leans heavily against the windowpane, longing to throw it open and fly away from this wretched place forever. *I'll see it burn,* she vows, wiping her hand across her cheek. *Alaric's precious kingdom will go down in flames before the year is done.*

***

Once night falls deeply enough that all the campfires have died, Wren stands at the entrance to his tent, casting a wary glance at Lynx's sleeping form. Her son stirs in her arms, his forehead wrinkling as if he's in the middle of a nightmare. *If everything goes according to plan tonight, I won't have to worry about your safety anymore,* Wren realizes, selfishly regretting that he may soon have to cope with their absences. *I've grown used to seeing you both every day, to having someone to talk to regularly.*

You've let me imagine what life might be like with a child of my own; I will miss you.

But this is the right thing to do, Wren declares as he slips out of his tent and winds his way to the barn. Even with only the light the moon and the twinkling stars, he manages to move without hesitating footfalls or excessive noise. At the rough-hewn fence, Wren slips through the heavy logs without touching them and opens the barn door just enough to keep its hinges from creaking.

Jackal and the rest of the captives are tied around the poles that anchor the hayloft in place. Most of them sleep, their heads drooping toward their stomachs, leaning heavily toward the ground. "That's going to be hell on their shoulders," Wren whispers as he sneaks up to Jackal's side.

"What are you doing here now?" Jackal hisses, lashing out at Wren with his feet.

"Wolf wants me to question you all tomorrow to find out your plans," Wren replies with a mischievous grin. "Of course, we both know there's nothing for me to find, so —"

"You came here to gloat?" Jackal grumbles, a weary, broken chuckle rattling through his chest. "I knew you were tricky, but I didn't expect you to be cruel. What else do you want? You've already won Wolf's loyalty."

"I came to offer you an alternative," Wren explains, slowly drawing a knife from his pocket. "Only one will get this opportunity; everyone else will die tonight."

"I'm listening," Jackal murmurs, casting a wary glance at his comrades. None of the others appear to be awake. Breathing a small sigh of relief, Jackal questions, "What are you offering, Wren?"

"Freedom." Wren dangles the possibility like a treat before a hungry dog. "I will let you go free. In return, I expect you to take Lynx and her child and run to the Pith lands. Find Mynah and the Ddraigs; carry a message to them for me. Tell them we are getting ready to move over the Devil's Spine. After Wolf finds the dead bodies in the morning, he will be frightened.

I'll persuade him that it's time to join the king and make plans for a joint attack."

"And what if I agree but don't follow through on my part of the deal?" Jackal sneers, carefully picking at the ropes around his wrists, searching for any means of escape.

"Then Lynx will kill you and carry the message herself. Besides, what other option do you think you'll have? After Wolf finds the dead in here and discovers you aren't among them, he will naturally assume you killed them all to keep them from sharing your assassination plans. He will never trust your word; most likely, he'll kill you on sight. At least with the Ddraigs, you have a chance," Wren explains, raising his blade to inspect its edge as he lets Jackal consider his words. "Now, are you going to take this opportunity? Or shall I slit your throat and offer it to the next man?"

Jackal sighs, shaking his head a little as he laments, "I don't really have a choice, do I? Just kill them quickly, Wren. Don't make them suffer." Jackal turns his gaze to the other five men tied to the poles, recognizing this is the final moment he will see them alive. "Believe it or not, they are decent men. In a different world, they would have been some of the best."

"You could say that of us all," Wren quips, stalking over to stand before Hyena. In one fluid motion, he slices deep into Hyena's neck, cleanly severing the arteries. In a matter of moments, Hyena's body falls limp.

Wren moves quickly around the room, almost as if he's taking part in a morbid dance. Slice the arteries, twirl away from the blood spatter, step to the next man. Slice, twirl, step. Slice, twirl, step. He moves with fluid grace until he stands before Jackal once more.

"I hate you," Jackal declares in a hoarse voice.

"I don't blame you," Wren replies, sounding fatigued as he slices through the ropes that bind Jackal to the pole.

The sudden loss of support from the ropes causes Jackal to stumble and fall onto the hay-covered ground. He kneels in the muck, feeling the warmth of fresh blood seeping into his pant legs. The cloying air suffocates him. Breath comes in quick, ragged hitches as the scent of death begins to permeate the barn. "I can't...breathe," Jackal cries, clawing at his mask. He rips the tanned hide off his face, pushing himself off the ground as he races toward the barn door.

Wren beats him to the opening, forcing Jackal to stand still. "You can't go out there until you've calmed down. Otherwise, you'll alert the whole camp."

"If I get their attention, then you'll go down for this!" Jackal announces, preparing to bellow for help.

Wren clamps a hand over his mouth, bracing himself for a fight. "I'll just say I heard movement in the barn and came to investigate." Jackal lashes out with his elbow, connecting hard against Wren's stomach. Yet even while winded, Wren has a plan. Doubling over, he uses the momentum of his motion to slam his head into the center of Jackal's back. He lands a kick into the back of Jackal's knees. Then, in one quick motion, Wren raises the knife and poises its tip against Jackal's neck. "I could kill you now and be hailed as the hero that took out the traitor. I could send Lynx off on her own and still get the message to Mynah. I could even blame her escape on my distraction from dealing with you. Letting you live is a mercy, but it is one that I don't have to give."

"No, please," Jackal begs, falling very still. "I'll do as you wish."

"Good answer," Wren whispers in Jackal's ear. "I'd rather Lynx and her son travel with a man that could protect them if it was necessary. Unlike me, however, Lynx won't offer second chances. You give her any reason to mistrust you, and you won't live to see the next sunrise." Wren lets the knife fall slowly. When Jackal doesn't put up any more of a fight, he carefully steps over to the barn door. "The door squeaks. Slip through the opening without widening it, and wait outside for me. Do not try a stunt like this again; I won't offer you a third chance."

This time, Jackal does as he is instructed. Once Wren

slips through the barn door, he wordlessly motions for Jackal to follow him to his tent. They pick their way through the campsite, but their travels are far from stealthy. Jackal lumbers through the sand, accidentally kicking a few cooking pots and stumbling once into a firebreak. *I was wise to keep only one alive,* Wren grimly admits, wishing there had been a way to spare them all. The blood staining his hands weighs heavy on his heart as he struggles to guide Jackal to a quieter path. *It's a wonder Jackal hasn't alerted the whole campsite to our plans. Trying to do move stealthily with six other people would have been impossible.*

After stepping into his tent, Wren immediately throws a hand over Lynx's mouth. The motion startles her awake, her eyes bugging out wide as she suppresses a strangled scream. Her son rouses as well, a tiny cry piercing the silence. "What are you doing?" Lynx hisses as she bounces her son in her arms, hoping to calm him down quickly.

"Gather only what you can stand to carry on a long walk," Wren whispers, holding his arms out to take the child. "The basic things you need for yourself and the child. And move with haste, Lynx. There is little time."

Lynx nods, immediately springing into action. Within minutes she readies her meager amount of food, clothes, a canteen, a baby's bottle, and a blanket with its ends tied together to be a child's sling. "What now?" she asks, making sure the lacings of her desperately worn shoes are tight enough.

"Now, come with me and don't make a fuss," Wren commands, flipping back the curtain of the tent. Jackal stands directly in front of the entrance, shifting from side to side anxiously as he keeps a lookout.

"What is he doing here?" Lynx challenges, her voice sharp.

So much for not making a fuss, Wren groans, pointing toward the ocean. "Shh! Get out by the waves, then we'll talk."

Wren still carries the child as he, Lynx, and Jackal hurry toward the water. He keeps his eyes shifting and searching for any signs of trouble. *The gods smile upon us,* Wren believes when his feet hit wet sand without anyone from the camp noticing their movements. Once they stand beside the roaring water, he catches Lynx up on his plan.

"You can't seriously expect me to travel with this monster!" Lynx shouts angrily, casting a loathing glance in Jackal's direction.

"It's for the best, Lynx. He'll protect you and your son in the journey," Wren persists, wishing he believed the words even as he says them.

"He's a traitor! He murdered good people in the House of Piranhas," Lynx argues, unrelenting in her fury. "How could you expect me to willingly leave with someone so horrible?"

"You do see that I'm standing here, right?" Jackal interjects, his tone mocking as he huffs indignantly. "I can hear every offensive thing you're saying."

"Shut up." Wren rolls his eyes, turning his attention back to Lynx. "You don't have to like him or trust him. You just need to keep him around until you get to the Ddraigs." Catching Jackal's smug smile, Wren adds, "Or you can kill him and chance the trip alone. Makes no difference to me. But if you choose to kill him, do it far away from here. I need Wolf to believe Jackal ran off because he was the betrayer." To prove the sincerity of his words, Wren hands Lynx his knife, blood from the other prisoners' murders still coating the blade.

"I...I need time to think about this." Lynx hesitates, pacing by the water's edge.

"You don't have time," Wren presses, following close behind her. "You need to leave now and put as much distance between us as you can before the sun rises. If Wolf sends me after you, I don't want to accidentally find you because you were too close. Get out of here now while you can, Lynx."

"But what about you, Wren? What if Wolf suspects—?"

"He won't. If you all are gone, Wolf won't have any reason to believe I'm involved." Wren tightens his hold on Lynx's child, whispering, "I'll do exactly what I said I would, Lynx. I'll play both sides, spy, run myself into ruin if need be, and I will keep you and your son safe. So please, go while the chance is before you. Leave now so Wolf can't try to use you against me later."

Lynx stares out over the dark ocean, mesmerized by its relentless violence. "I'll go," she replies, her voice emotionless as she holds her arms out to reclaim her child.

Wren struggles to let go of the boy. Dropping his head, Wren kisses the child's head lightly before passing him back to his mother. The sudden absence of weight in his arms leaves Wren feeling empty as if he's just given away a part of his heart. *For a short while, I glimpsed what life would have been like if I'd had a family. It's a memory I will treasure,* Wren longs to say, clearing his throat as if he could wipe the words out of his mind. "Take care of yourselves," he pleads hoarsely instead, lightly brushing Lynx's arm.

The sudden contact sends a shiver rattling through her bones, but she nods in agreement. Turning to face Jackal, she points in the general direction of the horizon, where the forests can be seen in the sunlight. "Stay in front of me where I can see you," Lynx commands, transferring her son into the sling so she can freely hold the knife in her hand. "Give me even the slightest reason not to trust you, and I'll gut you where you stand."

Jackal's smirk fades as he watches Lynx's eyes. Seeing no trace of humor or insincerity, his spine straightens as he gulps and nods in agreement. Then, without any further conversation or exchanged goodbyes, they disappear into the night.

Wren walks down into the water, letting the furious waves cleanse his body of the horrors this night has brought. The thought of returning to his empty tent twists painfully like a knife in his brain. *They are really gone,* he declares, feeling a little foolish for how deeply this truth burns in his chest. *They have left me behind.* Wren steps down further, not hesitating to keep moving until he can barely keep his head above the water. *Goodbye, Lynx. Be well.*

Water rushes over Wren's head. *At least it carries away*

the scent of death, Wren tells himself as his lungs begin to burn, the need for fresh breath growing rapidly more urgent. *It would be so easy to just end it all,* he imagines, forcing his feet to bury themselves a little deeper into the ocean floor. *To let this place be my eternity, to rest in this watery grave…who would care if I disappeared? Wolf would think I'm guilty, but so what? He'll probably be heading over to Déchets soon anyway, so my work is done. There is no one else in this place that needs me now.*

The memory of the black Ddraig suddenly springs to life in his mind. He'd carried Wren to the den where all the young Ddraigs that weren't able to fight were kept. *Suryc rebuffed me for my lack of loyalties. Yet I think he would be pleased to see me now. I've helped Lynx and her son. And yet,* Wren sighs, forcing his feet to lift out of the sandy muck and start paddling toward the shore. *Drifting off into the sea would still be self-serving, wouldn't it? There's still too much work to be done.*

Coughing bitterly once he floats to the surface, Wren gasps to breathe fresh air once more. He opens his eyes to the starry sky, enchanted by the billions of tiny fires flickering above him. *I guess I've found where my loyalties lie, after all,* Wren confesses, slogging through the wet sand on his way back to his campsite, the memory of Lynx and her son burning in his mind. *I need to make sure Wolf leaves Cassè. Then it will be up to Mynah to bring down the king.*

CHAPTER 11

The constant roar of the River Sangre buzzes off in the distance. Tomorrow we will cross near the minor markets on our journey back to my old house. I can see the faint whisper of bushes and trees on the horizon. My eyes strain as I stare at these shapes, longing to have the keen sight of my Ddraig just this once. We've spent so long in this world of rocks, sand, caverns, and burned brush that I've almost forgotten what our old home looks like.

Home, I sigh, wondering how I will react to see my old house once more. *Will I cry? Will I suddenly recall all these strange, important details about my family and feel the need to talk about them with everyone I see?* Yet even as I think these thoughts, I wonder if I should feel anything at all. The man I thought of as my father wasn't actually related to me. The mother I thought was dead is somewhere in Déchets, alive and well after abandoning me. *Lion,* I shudder as I remember his always smiling face, recalling the day I stood and listened to him die, burying my face in Wolf's chest to keep from seeing the gruesome details. *But he wasn't really my uncle, was he?*

Dark claws rip through my conflicted memories as Siri breaks down my feeble mental defenses. She's been unsuccessfully trying to teach me to guard my thoughts for the better part of an hour now. "Try it again, Mynah," Siri growls, her voice carrying in the open air of the rocky terrain.

"Shh!" I snap, holding my hand to my lips as if the gesture could somehow magnify the sound's importance. We've only flown a few hundred feet away from the rest of the Ddraigs. I really don't want them to know about my weakness. "The whole camp doesn't need to know what we're up to, Siri."

"Then get it right, so I don't have to shout," Siri bites back, baring her teeth at me in frustration. "Although, if you ever do manage to keep me out of your head, I may roar louder than the river just to celebrate the occasion."

"I'm doing the best I can!" I hiss, sitting on a rock with my legs crossed and my arms tight around my chest. "Why can't you just shield my thoughts, Siri?"

"I thought I was," Siri mutters under her breath, stomping through the rocks to work off a little of her tension. "But believe it or not, I'm not perfect. Lady Vatusia managed to get through my defenses to get to you. This particular Vibría is strong; you need to be able to shield yourself too. Maybe she won't succeed again if we both have mental defenses for her to break."

My face scrunches up as if I've just smelled a five-day-old dead fish left out on the river bank. "That's not the answer I was hoping for."

"You look like a petulant child having a tantrum because you didn't win a game," Siri smirks, smoke hissing from her nostrils.

"Give her a break," Cyrus chides, leaning his head back onto Suryc's black scales. They've been silent witnesses to this entire training session, so I suspect Cyrus's nerves are about as raw as mine. He speaks through gritted teeth as he faces Siri and confronts her. "You just started all this mental training today; you can't expect her to figure it out after one practice."

"This is a threat that has to be taken seriously, Cyrus!" Siri exclaims, but her words lose some of their biting ire. "If she doesn't learn to guard her thoughts from external influencers, then anyone with the Vibría 's talents and strength can affect her visions. They could — "

"I get it, Siri! I understand the danger we're in," I

whimper, struggling to hold back tears. "Just try it again!"

"Fine," Siri snorts, focusing her silvery eyes on me. I see no pity or empathy in her; instead, she looks coldly at me. Emotionless, as if I am her next meal. "Block me out of your thoughts," she commands, but staring at the massive predator in front of me, I can do nothing but quake in fear.

Feebly, I try to form the image of a cloudy sky in my mind's eye like she taught me. Imagining myself in the center of these puffy, grey clouds, I examine the scene carefully, searching for any holes or weak points where Siri's thoughts could infiltrate. To me, the sky looks flawless. It's like a stormy day in the spring, and it's so detailed that I can almost smell the fresh, clean scent of the coming rain.

However, as I watch the clouds floating on their lazy paths, I see Siri's silver eyes appear in the darkest shadows of the vapors. Her dark claws scratch and rip through the cottony forms, shredding through the shield until I see my Ddraig standing in the middle of a field of darkness. She opens her mouth and roars, white-hot fire bursting into the surrounding black void, ripping me out of my thoughts and back into the corporeal world.

"Not good enough!" Siri growls, pacing around the cavern in agitation. "What's it going to take to get you focused, Iris?"

"Yelling at her won't help, Siri, so hush," Cyrus challenges, rising from his seat beside Suryc and walking over to my side. Without a word, he drops to sit beside me on my rocky perch, close enough that our shoulders touch. It's like an unspoken gift, a gesture of support, and I feel myself lean heavily against his arm, soaking up his warmth as if it could somehow bring me success.

"Siri, come with me. Let's go hunt for a while. I think you need a snack," Suryc suggests, spreading his onyx wings and rising up into the fading light. Wordlessly Siri follows, slipping out of sight like a silent ghost.

"What's going on in your head, sweetheart?" Cyrus

whispers, his voice gentle and full of concern.

"When did you get so level headed?" I grumble, wringing my hands just to give them something to do. "It hasn't been that long ago since I feared you were going to kill yourself or go insane. Yet you haven't had trouble in ages. What's changed?"

"Suryc's been helping me with my nightmares. He's already taught me a lot of what you're learning now," Cyrus replies with a shrug, staring out at the sunset. The sun drifts low on the horizon, painting the sky with hues of marigold. "A golden sky," Cyrus muses, one corner of his mouth lifting in a crooked smile. "Old folklore would say that when the sun sets in gold, the next day will bring triumphs untold."

"Maybe I should just quit trying this stuff until tomorrow then," I mutter, silently hoping that old rhyme is correct.

Cyrus sighs, sensing that his attempt to bring me out of my brooding has not worked. "Being closer with you has helped me more than anything. I don't feel so alone anymore," Cyrus explains, his voice growing soft. "Suryc tried the same methods with me, but I couldn't make them work either. For weeks I struggled and failed to keep my nightmares caged in a cloudless sky. Eventually, I just started experimenting on my own. To shield my mind, I needed something stronger. Personal."

"Like what?"

"Well," Cyrus hesitates, eyeing my expression warily before explaining, "I asked myself, 'Why does Suryc want me to use a cloudy sky?' And the only answer I could come up with is that Suryc loves days like that. It must be one of his favorite things, to soar high and skim the clouds, to feel their dew on his wings. So naturally, that made me wonder about what I love that dearly. What do I cling to so strongly that the very image of it would be enough to block out every outside thing?"

"That makes a lot of sense," I reply, growing excited as hope bursts to life in my chest. "If I think of my most beloved, cherished things, then I might be able to block Siri out of my head. Maybe that old folklore is right; tomorrow will bring me triumph after all." My mind races as I try to discern what it is that I hold most dear. Falling silent, I worry my lip between my teeth. "I...I don't know what to use," I admit, defeat crashing down on me, quashing the tender hope that was only just kindled in my heart.

Cyrus sits beside me, saying nothing. He focuses intently on the sunset, deliberately keeping his gaze off me. I can practically feel him willing me not to ask the question waiting on my tongue. Even to my own ears, I know the words sound terribly nosy. It'll sound like I'm asking Cyrus to rip open his heart, to lay his mind bare before me just so I can scrutinize him. *But I have to know what works*, I rationalize, giving voice to the query. "Cyrus, you don't have to answer if you don't want to. But could you tell me what you think about when you build your mental defenses?"

Cyrus loses the breath I hadn't realized he was holding, his eyes drifting closed. "You sure you want me to answer that?" he replies, his voice deepening with the rawness of his emotion. "Because I'll tell you. But if I do, and you don't like what you hear, you don't have the right to get angry at me for speaking. So be very sure you really want to hear these words, Iris."

I swallow hard, shivering as I consider my response carefully. My heartbeat thunders in my ears as loud as a stampeding horse's hooves. The silence grows unbearable. I suspect I know what he's going to say, and I know I should stop him. Yet, the need to hear these forbidden words spoken aloud is a nagging whisper in the back of my mind that I find I can no longer ignore. "Tell me," I rasp, turning my face to the sunset, struggling to calm down before my heart gives out.

Yet Cyrus will not let me escape. Gently he cups my cheeks, turning my head until I am eye to eye with him. "I think of you, Iris. You are my shield. I knit together a blanket of memories in my mind, and it is so strong that nothing can break through it. When the faces that haunt me appear, I hide in the memory of your smile. I trace the form of your cheek, brush my fingers through your shock of white hair. I get lost in every detail of your stormy eyes. I hear your laughter brightening up the darkest corners of my thoughts, weaving mischievously through each moment. I taste your kiss. I allow myself to spin fantasies of what our life together might be like if you will just be brave. You are the thing most beloved and precious to my heart, Iris. You always have been. When I think of you, I am strong. When I focus on you, nothing can break me."

I swallow hard against the knot in my throat, focusing on Cyrus's scars just to keep my mind clear as I process his words. Even though I knew what he would say, I have no response. Not because I don't feel anything—quite the contrary. I just can't seem to find the words to say what's in my heart.

We've come a long way since the House of Vultures, I admit to myself, my hands longing to trace the lines of his features. *I hated you so much then. How strange, then, that I can hold you in my heart as dearly as I do now.* My head grows heavy, and I wish that I could comfortably lean against his shoulder. That we could just stay right here and watch the sunset together, content to be in each other's company forever, letting the rest of the world fight its own battles as we embrace our little corner of peaceful paradise.

Despite all the emotions welling up in my heart, my mouth stays tightly closed. *It's fear.* I chide myself for not acting on my feelings. *The only thing that's stopping you is fear.* My throat bobs nervously, my lip trembles as my emotions plague me, but not a word do I speak.

My silence is magnified by the intensity of Cyrus's confession. "Say something, Iris," he demands, his hands falling away from my face. When I don't, he hops down from the rock, walking briskly away from me. He makes it about ten steps away, then stops, keeping his back to me.

The absence of him suddenly stifles me, and I feel as if I've just plunged myself head first into the River Sangre. All of my unspoken words choke me. I see him standing so far away, and my limbs beg me to run to him. My heart burns in my chest, the pain so strong that I wonder if I'm having a heart attack. "Cyrus," I wheeze, my hands clenching so tightly to my legs that I can feel my nails biting into my thighs.

Cyrus turns, glancing back at me with a hard glint in his eyes. "What?"

"Come…here," I rasp, my breath hitching in bursts as I try to breathe. It's like my lungs have closed to protect me from drowning. I claw at my chest, but I cannot draw a fresh breath.

"Why?" Cyrus hesitates, keeping his feet rooted in place as he watches me. "I keep pouring my heart out to you, hoping things will change between us. But it always ends up one sided; I always end up playing the fool."

"Please," I whisper, shuddering as my lungs finally open, gasping for clean air as the panic in my mind slowly fades.

"I can't keep doing this, Iris. Give me a reason," Cyrus replies, turning his back to me once more as he watches the sunset. "Or tell me if you can't so I can leave."

"Suryc and Siri would not—"

"I'd leave Suryc behind then," Cyrus declares, his voice hard as he calls to me over his shoulder. "If he and Siri cannot be parted, then I'll walk away alone. Is that what you want?"

Dropping lightly down onto the grass, I stalk up behind Cyrus as quietly as I can, thinking of what I could possibly say that might soften his heart toward me just once more. With each footfall, I hear my voice whispering all the words I would use to describe Cyrus. *Strong, certain. Pure, perfect. Mine.*

The last word catches fire in my blood, burning away the fear that has been holding me back. *Cyrus is mine.* Despite— or maybe because of—everything that has passed between us, he has always been mine. All the words I've been longing to say flow easily from my mouth now as if whatever hindrances were keeping them dammed up inside me have finally been removed. I close the distance between us confidently now, wrapping my arms around Cyrus's waist.

"When I was little, I used to think of you as a forest sprite," I whisper as I settle against his back, sharing my memories with a soft voice. "I used to sit at my window waiting for you to appear. I made up fanciful stories about how you were born of the trees, and I would watch the forest, hoping to catch a glimpse of you in your tree form." My eyes cloud as the memories of those childhood days overtake me. "When you stopped coming to my window, I was devastated. I cried for days."

"I thought you would hate me with my scars." Cyrus whispers, his voice rough. I cannot tell whether or not my sudden boldness or the topic of my speech surprises him most.

Guiding him to raise his arm, I slide around until I can see his face once more. His arms settle around me naturally, their warmth like a blanket on a cold winter night. Now, I let my fingers trace the scar from his forehead to his neck, stopping only once over his wobbling lips. "How could I hate the boy that brought the world to my window? I thought...I thought you had stopped coming because you thought I was boring."

Cyrus raises one hand, grazing his calloused fingers along my jaw. "You have always been fascinating to me."

"And you have always been mine. My heart chose you long ago. I'm only sorry it's taken me so long to listen. Whatever the future holds for us, I know I cannot keep fighting against you. The thought of losing you only brings me more anxiety and trouble." My voice wavers as I whisper his name, my fingers pressing softly to his lips to silence him. "So, don't go, Cyrus. Because I love you."

Pain radiates through my arm, shock appearing in Cyrus's eyes as he startles away from my touch. The ivory, crisscrossing lines of my Dadeni bond with Siri come alive, glistening with a molten fire. The initial spark of the fire in my skin fades to a dull, slow burn. Fascinated, I watch as thin slivers of silver, scale-like markings bleed out of my fingers into the air. They shift and blend before my eyes like smoke. Beside me, Cyrus has a similar peculiarity, the only difference being the color of the smoky apparitions before him.

"What is this?" he wonders as the whiteness of my

Dadeni lines swirl with the darkness of his. Everything slows when they touch, and I feel a flare of pain as the dark smoke writhes onto my skin, twisting like gnarled branches, knotting itself into the remaining silver binds on my arms. On Cyrus, I see my silver threads like spider silk caught on the dark brambles of his remaining marks. The scar on his face glows with my silver fire, and I wonder if he shows somewhere on my face too. It is over in a moment, the pain like the shadowed pressure from a burning kiss.

"My heart chose you," I repeat the sentiment even as I hear Siri's heavy footfalls crashing up in the grass behind me. "I believe that was the coupling bond Siri's been hounding me about."

"And I can't believe I missed it!" Siri howls, silver sparks of fire erupting all around us in her excitement.

"Stop that, or you'll start a wildfire!" I admonish with a laugh, captivated by the way the fire glitters in Cyrus's eyes.

"I'm going to tell the others Ddraigs; we have much to celebrate tonight," Siri announces, practically trotting like a dog as she hurries off to complete her chore.

"What about you, love?" Cyrus asks with a crooked smile. "Off to celebrate or plan for tomorrow's troubles?"

"We still have a lot to do," I agree, trying not to laugh as Cyrus's face grows somber. "But I think the worries and burdens we carry can wait another night. What do you think?"

Cyrus's soft chuckle and answering kiss is all the reply I need.

***

Helena's eyes fly open with the rising sun, her heart pounding forcefully in her chest. The strength of the spasm is such that her lungs will not expand. She desperately claws at her throat, digging her fingernails into her skin as if she intends to burrow into her trachea and release the spent air poisoning her lungs. Burning, lancing pain erupts through her nerves, pulsing in time with her heartbeat. It's as though her body is being struck repeatedly by lightning, and each strike grows in intensity as breathless seconds pass.

Until, finally, her autonomic senses retake control. Helena gasps wildly as fresh air enters her throat, rolling off the infirmary bed onto her hands and knees. A single, terrified sob racks through her as she struggles to calm down. Seconds drag into agonizing, slow-passing minutes before Helena feels strong enough to move. She crawls her way back onto the infirmary bed, sitting upright on the edge of the mattress.

"I was dreaming," she realizes, turning her head to inspect the surrounding sick beds, searching for any signs of life in the room. Finding no one, Helena lays her head back on the pillow, wiping a hand across her cold, sweat covered brow.

It was so real, Helena whimpers as she recalls her dream, a shiver shuddering through her bones. *I was crouching on the floor between two nameless guards, kneeling before Alaric and a strange man I've never met. Ithel was across from me, a grim, hard look of determination on his face. He seemed to stare over my head as if he could not be bothered to notice me.*

Doors opened at the back of the room, and I watched in horror as my daughter was dragged before the king. She was beaten, and not just in a physical nature. While her face and arms were covered with purplish bruises, it was the empty look in her eyes that really pained me. It was like staring into the eyes of a long-dead ghost. I called out to her, but she did not react. She was so far lost in her grief and agony that I'm not entirely sure she could hear me.

She offered no resistance as the guards jostled her into a standing position. She spoke not a word as Alaric taunted and teased her, his words incomprehensible to my ears. But I clearly heard the scream burst from my throat the moment Alaric released Ithel, giving him one simple command. "Kill her," Alaric declared with an airy wave, turning his back on the scene as he marched back to his throne.

"She's your daughter!" I tried to shout before one of my guards clamped his meaty hand over my mouth. I bit into his thick fingers, but my teeth couldn't cut through the hardened callouses of the warrior's hands. No matter how hard I fought, I could not break free. I could do nothing but watch as Ithel unknowingly choked the life

out of his own daughter.

Helena whimpers, clenching her eyes tight against the memory. "It was just a dream," she repeats nervously, the words sounding hollow and flat to her ears.

With the sunlight bursting through the window and the memory of the nightmare still clinging to the surface of her mind, Helena knows she will sleep no more this morning. Sighing, Helena moves away from the bed, dragging a ragged looking chair over to the window, content to watch the world wake.

She sits so still and quiet, so lost in her fearful musings that she doesn't hear a servant girl bringing her a food tray. Helena fails to notice the kitchen maid until she is close enough to touch. The sudden proximity of another human being startles Helena out of her chair. She deftly twirls her fingers into a spiral, effectively creating a wind tunnel prison around the helpless servant. "Who sent you?" she snarls, preparing to attack.

"Please! I just brought breakfast. And I was told to stay and see if you needed anything for the king's party tonight," the pitiful child wails, covering her face with her hands. "This wind is cutting me! Please, make it stop!" Blood splatters on the floor under the servant's feet, the red stains offering proof of her claims.

Regretting her hyper vigilance, Helena ceases the windstorm almost as quickly as it sprang to life. "Apologies, child. I will not hurt you anymore. But I would not sneak up on me again."

The servant nods, staring at her toes. Small, stinging cuts crisscross the child's arms. Her chin puckers as her mouth pulls tight. She wrings her hands and pinches the skin between her fingers to keep from crying. "D...d...do you need anything?" she asks with a sniffle, her knees wobbling as though they can barely hold her weight.

"Come here and sit down," Helena declares softly, instantly morphing from fighter to mother at the sight of a terrified child. She holds out her hand to the servant, trying to force her face into a pleasant smile. "I truly am sorry that I've hurt you. Rest assured, it will not happen again. What is your name, child?"

"Amie," the servant whimpers, shying away from Helena's touch as she moves toward the offered chair.

Regrets burn deep in Helena's heart as she watches the child cringe away from her. "And have you eaten breakfast yet, Amie?" Helena asks gently, pulling the table and tray closer. "The kitchens always send up more than enough food, and I'd hate to see it all go to waste."

Amie's stomach growls heartily in response, but the child does not move to take a single pastry from the plate. Her face loses all expression, her voice no more than a whisper as she challenges, "What do you want in exchange for this kindness?"

Pity swells in Helena's heart at the wary look in the child's eyes. *This fear runs deeper than just me, I think. What horrors could a child so young have faced to make her so untrusting?* "I want nothing—"

"Everyone wants something," Amie interrupts, her legs bouncing nervously against the chair. Her stomach roars once more, the grip of the hunger pain so intense that Amie clutches at her midsection until it passes.

"Well, how about we make a trade? You eat your fill, and in return, you answer some questions about one of the guards," Helena offers, her heart breaking as she watches Amie stare at the pastries, instinctively licking her lips.

"Really? That's all you want?" Amie hesitates, her hand twitching at her side. She tightens her fingers into a fist to keep from snatching food off the plate before a bargain is finalized.

"Yes, Amie. All I want is a few answers. Now, please, eat whatever you like," Helena declares, smiling wide when Amie lunges for the pastries, taking one in each slender hand.

Silence punctuated by smacking lips and sighs of contentment stretch between Helena and Amie. Only when Amie stops reaching for food, her eyes growing a little glazed at the intensity of the sugar rushing through her veins, does Helena begin her interrogation. "There is a guard in the palace named Andras. Do you know of him?"

"I do," Amie replies, her eyelids beginning to droop. "What do you want to know about him?"

"He and I are getting ready to travel together, Amie. I need to know everything you can tell me about him. What's he like? What are his strengths? Any weaknesses? Has he done anything wrong? Anything you can tell me that might be useful," Helena presses, trying to lightly steer Amie's thoughts toward the negative things that might be used as blackmail later.

"Andras keeps to himself most of the time," Amie replies, rubbing her now slightly swollen belly while she thinks. "You know, this may be the first time I can say I am truly full since I got to the palace." The pitiful child stretches her arms wide, her chin falling toward her chest as sleep drags at her mind.

"Amie, focus!" Helena cries sharply, reaching for the exhausted girl's hand. "Come on!"

"Andras comes to the kitchen after every evening meal for a cup of coffee or an extra piece of pie. I think he's sweet on one of the dishwashing maids, but he'd never tell her. He seems very shy," Amie mumbles, her words beginning to slur.

"Has he ever been accused of doing anything wrong?" Helena presses, clenching her hands into fists and firmly placing them on her hips to keep from shaking the child.

"No, he's good—" Amie's head falls back against the chair, her soft snores pitifully finishing her sentence.

A half-hearted sigh of frustration sucks the air from Helena's lungs as she slumps over to sit on a nearby infirmary bed, contemplating whether or not she should wake Amie. *For surely, there has to be more to Andras than that*, Helena muses, the bitterness of her cynicism burning on her tongue. "If Andras is so good, why does he stay here? What keeps him loyal to the king?" she wonders, leaning her head back on a pillow as she gets lost in the tangle of her thoughts.

Helena turns her head, eyeing the tray of uneaten pastries as her stomach roars in protest at its empty state. "Maybe the kitchen maid Andras is sweet on will be more forthcoming with information," she decides, sitting up once more as she prepares to hunt down this supposed love interest.

The sudden realization that a figure leans on the doorpost, however, is enough to freeze Helena's feet to the floor. Helena doesn't recognize the man, shuffling through her memories for some signal as to his identity. He is tall, broad chested and stocky — the kind of man who's perfect for the front lines of war. His eyes are dark, full of the spark of intelligence. He stands unnaturally still, barely even appearing to be breathing. It's a trained skill, Helena knows, and immediately her heart sinks to her toes as she deduces the man's identity.

"So that's where the little kitchen scamp ran off too," Andras smirks, calmly assessing the scene before him. "Eating your food while you root around in her head for my secrets."

"Don't blame the girl," Helena pleads, angling to put herself between the guard and the peacefully sleeping Amie. "None of this was her fault—"

"I heard enough to know that's the truth," Andras interrupts, waving off Helena's further protests. "Relax; I'm not after the child. But if she doesn't get herself back down to help the cooks, she'll have much greater things than me to worry about. The head chef has a cruel habit of smacking around the staff that shirks their duties."

"I'll make sure the chef knows her absence is my fault," Helena vows, an indignant fire roaring to life in her belly at the thought of Amie being hurt.

"Better let me take care of it," Andras replies, stalking deeper into the room with predatory grace. "The chef's a pompous, patronizing piece of filth that despises women who challenge his authority. If you try and reason with him, you'll only end up making it worse for her."

His footfalls are completely silent, Helena notices as she analyzes Andra's movements, searching for the reason why she hadn't heard him approach. She tenses as he sidles up to Amie's side, her muscles tight with unspent energy, ready to fight or protect the child if need be.

Andras smiles knowingly as if he's just learned some valuable information about Helena. He picks up a piece of bacon from her tray of food. Yet all throughout his movements, Andras's eyes never leave Helena, carefully observing her just as critically as she watches him. He bites off a piece from the bacon strip, chewing thoughtfully as he waits for Helena to make the first move.

Quiet and shy, my ass. Helena shivers under his scrutiny, all too aware that Amie's assessment of the man couldn't be more wrong. *This man's clever, hiding his constant awareness and assessment of others under such a guise. He knows exactly what he's doing. Even now, he wants me to speak first just so he can have the upper hand.* Helena swallows hard, her confidence fleeing as she asks, "What makes you so sure you can get through to the chef? If he's as bad as you say —"

"Oh, trust me, he's far worse than I've said," Andras interjects, glancing down at Amie's sleeping form. His face betrays no emotion or empathy for the girl's predicament; if he feels anything at all, he hides it well. "But the chef is also a coward. He will not go against me." Something about the flat tone in Andras's voice and the flinty, hate-filled look in his eyes is enough to keep Helena from pressing him further on this subject.

"Why did you come?" Helena stumbles over the words, raising her chin a little higher in an effort to regain some of her confidence. The longer she finds herself on the defensive with Andras, the more she feels like shrinking into the wall and hiding until he disappears.

"For the same reasons you sat here bribing that child with sweets," Andras shrugs, tapping his fingers on the back of Amie's chair. "Information; I want to know who I'm traveling with and whether or not I can trust you to keep from being a problem."

"I feel certain that Amie told me nothing useful about you," Helena announces, confirming her ideas about the man when Andras offers her a predatory smile.

"She told you exactly what I would have expected her to say. I've worked hard to maintain that image of a shy, simple soldier," Andras murmurs, crossing his muscled arms in front of his chest. "But you'd be a fool to believe the words of an adolescent kitchen slave."

Despite the easy manner Andras intentionally portrays, Helena senses that he is still on alert, cautiously observing her behavior. Helena lets her hands fall open at her sides, forcing herself to stay perfectly still, schooling her face into a blank, neutral expression. "And why would you intentionally play a part to dupe your friends?" Helena asks innocently, feigning ignorance to the strategy at play while she considers her next move.

Andras chuckles, raising one eyebrow as he challenges, "Come now, Helena, we both already know that you are no fool. Why don't we drop the pretense? You know what they say about honesty being the best policy—"

"When you're the one holding the knife," Helena interrupts, finishing the old saying with her hands held wide to prove she is unarmed. "Seems I'm at a disadvantage, Andras."

Andras nods, resting his hand on the hilt of the sword at his waist. His mocking smile only deepens the wound to Helena's pride. "I can afford to be truthful with you, I realize that. But I'd rather hoped we could begin this journey on better terms." When Helena does not respond, Andras shakes his head, mumbling, "In answer to your other question, surely you must know the merits of listening in on the gossip from the gabby kitchen maids. Most of their half-whispered secrets are full of juicy tidbits just waiting to be exploited by a cunning mind. I find it's in my best interest to play the part of a quiet man who can't muster the courage to meet their gaze, so they will speak freely in front of me." Andras moves away from Amie's chair, slinking over to stand toe-to-toe with Helena.

"Aren't you curious what they had to say about you?"

I hadn't realized he was so tall, Helena muses, lifting her chin as she looks up toward Andras's expressionless face. *There's much more to Andras than the bulky, dumb oafs Alaric used to hire to guard his palace. Escaping his custody will be far more difficult than I'd originally planned.* "I've no doubt the outlandish stories the maids must have told about me are completely untrue. But thank you for explaining your methods so clearly," Helena quips, forcing her feet to stay rooted in place, unwilling to cower in Andras's presence no matter how intimidating he may be. *Intimidation seems to be his weapon of choice. At least for now. Who knows when he will switch to a new tactic?* Helena shivers as the small flickering flame of hope in her heart sputters and dies. *I can't let my guard down around Andras even for a second. Who knows if the man I see before me is real? Or is this another illusion, an image he's created to deceive me?*

"Oh, I don't know," Andras smirks as if he knows Helena's innermost questions and backs away from her to lean against the window frame. "The maids had a great deal to tell me about your relationship with a certain jailed slave. Are you sure you aren't interested?"

"Seeing as how I've was only freed from the prisons a week ago, are you sure the maids are the best sources of information about me? You'd get more accurate gossip from the guards," Helena snaps, her temper rising. She presses her fingernails into her palms, fearing they will break the skin with her efforts to maintain her resolve.

Andras's smile grows as he notices Helena's discomfort. Sensing Helena's weakness like a predator after its wounded prey, he presses, "Yes, that was quite a scandal too. The king's daughter in prison for treason. Abandoning the man she supposedly loved and betraying her father and her people, only to be captured and dragged back—"

"Enough," Helena growls, even though she recognizes what Andras is trying to do. *He's baiting me to test my limits, to discover just how much pressure it will take before I lash out at him.*

"That's all it takes to get under your skin? I'm disappointed," Andras exclaims sarcastically, crossing his arms as he pretends to pout. "From everything I heard about you, I was expecting someone tougher. It seems you don't live up to your reputation." Andras's dark eyes narrow, his head turning slightly as he assesses. "Unless you are purposefully trying to appear weak to get me to lower my guard."

"Let's talk about you for a moment, shall we?" Helena demands, speaking out before he gets the chance to respond. "All of the guards are required to take a shift in the prisons at least once a month. So how come I never remember seeing you there? What hell-hole did Alaric pull you out of? If I had to guess, I'd say you've angered the king somehow, and he's using this as a punishment. Because let's be honest, if I know my father as well as I think I do, he's hoping this is a suicide mission. Or at the very least, that I'll screw up and give him another opportunity to try and kill me."

"Maybe I'm an assassin he's sending along to kill you and the rogue Windwalker," Andras teases with a tight, forced smile. He stands very still, keeping his gaze trained on Helena, daring her to argue.

Yet everything about his demeanor alerts Helena that she's hit a nerve. His clenched jaw, his purposeful stare, and his tense posture all point to his deception. "Nice try, but I'm not buying," Helena replies, feeling a sense of relief at finally being in control of the conversation. "The coming days will be long and boring, Andras. I look forward to hearing how you've fallen on the wrong side of the king."

Andras opens his mouth to speak, only to close it immediately. Absentmindedly rubbing his chin, his brow furrows as he struggles to come up with a response. After a few heartbeats of silence, the guard's face softens to his neutral expression once more. Glancing down at Amie, he says, "I'll take her down to the kitchens and settle everything with the cook. No sense in spending all of today sparring words with you, Helena. We'll have plenty of time to get on each other's nerves tomorrow."

After a surprisingly gentle awakening, Andras and Amie leave Helena in the empty infirmary once more. With nothing else on which to focus her attention, Helena's thoughts plague her mind. Dreaded anticipation of tonight's feast and the horrors it will hold builds with every passing hour. She replays her conversations with Andras in her mind, poring over the guard's words and manners, searching for any more information that might give her an advantage. Wistful desire that Ithel was allowed to come with her to Cassè pierces her heart. "Andras is a wildcard, an unknown variable that I cannot predict or control. How do I protect our daughter from him?" Helena whispers, imagining Ithel standing beside her, his comforting presence soothing her raw nerves. "I don't know if I can do this, Ithel."

Hopeless, bitter tears drip down her cheeks when no answer comes.

CHAPTER 12

Wren awakens to the cacophony of clanging alarm bells and angry, cursing soldiers. He lays in his bed with his eyes closed tight, unwilling to let the sounds rouse him into movement. His head pounds excruciatingly, each sound from outside the tent piercing his temples like barbed spikes.

After saying his goodbyes to Lynx and her son last night, Wren had returned to his tent and set the scene for his alibi. He'd scattered his belongings haphazardly as if there'd been a fight. With his skinning knife, he'd cut a few gashes on his face and both sides of his hands. Punching the air in a fantastical fight, the blood splattered his belongings in believable patterns. Then he'd wrapped one end of a leather cord around the sturdy center pole of his tent. Oh, so carefully, he'd looped the other end around his neck and walked away from the pole. He choked himself hard enough to leave faint bruises; the headache had been an unwanted necessity to pull off the ruse. Finally, as the sun began to peek over the horizon, he collapsed on his bed, waiting for this moment.

Soon enough, they will notice my absence. Wren replays his plan while he waits, leaving no detail uninspected. The voices outside fade as the stragglers finally make their way to the grisly scene in the barn. *Only a few more minutes now.* Wren breathes deeply, turning onto his side, so he doesn't face the tent opening. He maintains his slow, full breaths, feigning sleep as he hears footsteps approaching.

"Wren! Wake up, you fool!" Wolf snarls as he barges into the tent. His eyes dart wildly around the tent, noting every bloodstain and haphazardly tossed belonging. "Wren?" Wolf races forward to check and see if the man is even breathing.

"Hmph," Wren groans, shielding his eyes against the bright light of day. *I almost did too good a job,* Wren thinks to himself as he struggles to speak clearly, his voice coming out rough and garbled on the first few attempts. "What happened?"

"I was going to ask you the same thing," Wolf explains as he raises Wren's eyelids to check for a concussion. Ignoring Wren's grumbling, he continues his examination, prodding the cuts on Wren's face. "Looks like you and Lynx had an epic fight."

"Oh." Wren sits up, a wave of nausea hitting him hard in the stomach. "I remember. I found her rummaging through my stuff." He puts his hands on his head to try and stop the spinning sensation. "She was muttering something about getting out of here. 'Running back to Mynah,' or something like that. I tried to stop her, and we had words. She fought back, then something got tangled around my neck. I must have blacked out."

Wolf leans his head down to observe the bruises on Wren's neck. "Looks like someone choked you. Probably Jackal. It seems he and Lynx have disappeared."

"Jackal? What do you mean? Was he working with her?" Wren feigns surprise, picking at the dried blood on his hands to give his eyes somewhere to focus.

"He...he must have been," Wolf declares, wiping his hand over his face. "I can't understand it, but Jackal's absence suggests that they helped each other escape."

"I thought he was tied up in the barn," Wren questions, rubbing his temples to shield his face. Cutting his eyes, Wren peeks to see if Wolf is buying into the lie.

Despite the early hour, Wolf's bloodshot eyes and pale, hollowed out cheeks make it seem like he hasn't slept for weeks. He shifts from side to side, clutching his middle as though it pains him. "The best I can tell, Lynx went into the barn and untied him. She or Jackal killed all of the other men tied up with him in the barn, probably to keep them from talking," Wolf mumbles under his breath, his brow clenching as he struggles to solve the mystery. "I thought he was loyal to me. Hell, I thought they all were. What a fool I have been, it seems."

All in all, Wolf looks deranged, Wren declares, satisfied that his work has been successful. "Show me what he's done, Wolf," Wren exclaims, putting on a show in dressing hastily and rushing to the barn to inspect the crime scene for clues.

In reality, Wren's feet feel like lead weights. Icy sweat breaks out on his clammy skin with each hurried step toward the barn. The prospect of seeing his own handiwork in daylight has his stomach churning. Bile and gorge rise in his throat in expectation of the sight that lies just behind the barn doors. Taking a few steadying breaths, he forces the doors open and steps inside.

It shouldn't surprise me, Wren reminds himself as he wanders through the lifeless bodies strewn on the moldy straw. *I did this; all this blood is on my hands. Now, I must face it without showing signs of guilt. Emotionless, expressionless, cold.* Wren takes a few steadying breaths, trying not to linger too long.

However, when Wren stops in front of Hyena's body, he is unable to look away from his sightless, graying eyes. *You did this,* Hyena's open mouth seems to scream. *You are a liar. Betrayer. Murderer.* The horrendous scent of offal and posthumously expelled body fluids assaults Wren's nose. Around Hyena's neck lies a deep crimson stain. It would almost resemble a choker necklace if it weren't for the gnats and flies. They gather and stalk up to the bloody gash in search of a comfortable place to burrow and lay eggs. Able to stand no more, Wren rushes out of the barn, coughing out his disgust into the grass.

"I think I'm just going to burn the whole thing down," Wolf announces, standing a few paces away from Wren. "But I just can't believe it, Wren. I trusted Jackal; I thought of him as my second in command. He knew everything about my plans, and never once did he give me any reason to doubt his loyalty."

It takes a great effort for Wren to stand up and keep his knees from giving way. He closes his eyes, thinking back to all the words he'd rehearsed for this moment. *This is why you over plan everything,* Wren reminds himself, letting his mouth follow the script in his head while he regains control over his emotions. "But you have evidence that Jackal was plotting against you, remember?" Wren lies smoothly, wiping his chin and striding away from the barn without looking back. "Maybe the others wouldn't go along with Jackal's plan, and that's why he slit their throats. Maybe he didn't want to run the risk that they would raise an alarm before he and Lynx could get away. Or maybe those poor devils had served their purpose, and Jackal was just cleaning up loose ends." Before Wolf can respond, Wren adds, "It really doesn't matter. The fact remains that he and Lynx are long gone by now."

"Another one running off to join her," Wolf spits, clenching his hands into fists. "Condor, Fox, and now Jackal. How many more will she take from me?" Wolf's eyes glaze as he relives Mynah's supposed betrayal; it eats away at his sanity. Words spill from his lips in garbled, paranoid ramblings. "No doubt Jackal and Lynx will share our location with the overgrown lizards. Fox has probably told her everything about the way I run my camps, so I can't hide behind my usual defenses. And *she* will mount an attack, so desperate is she to take away my throne before I'm even fully declared king."

"Then let's get away from here," Wren suggests innocently, relief flooding through his veins at how natural it had been to steer Wolf to this plan. *So easy,* Wren sighs, ignoring the angry protests of the spectral versions of Hyena and Coyote. The faces of the dead don't seem to disappear from Wren's mind; their voices whisper into his thoughts despite his efforts to quell them. "Wolf, let's just go —"

"Where? She and her monstrosities will find us wherever we run," Wolf snarls, unable to stomach the thought of turning coward and slinking off into the shadows to wait for his enemies to find him. "There was a time when I'd never have believed she would be my enemy. But now, there is nowhere to escape from her. She will scour the land in her search, Wren."

"That's true if we try and hide on this side of the mountains," Wren interrupts, watching Wolf's face for any signs of opposition. "We have allies in Déchets, right? Maybe it's time for us to visit them."

"She'd never look for us there," Wolf agrees, the bright light of the sun boring into his skull, apparently causing his head to pound. *It's the thought of her,* Wren knows, watching Wolf grit his teeth as another wave of nausea roils in his stomach. Wolf sways, knotting his hands in his hair as a soft groan burns in his throat.

"You are not well; if we do not figure out how to break this bond, it will kill you." Wren shows his concern, carefully hiding his ambivalence to Wolf's predicament. "Perhaps someone in Déchets will have the answers we need to spare you this agony."

"Tell the men to break camp," Wolf mumbles, almost biting through his lip as another wave of pain slams into him. "We leave for Déchets in two hours. Whatever isn't packed by then gets left behind."

"As you wish," Wren whispers with a slight bow, walking back to his tent. *So easy and yet, so costly,* Wren thinks, grimly stomping through the rows of white canvas, shouting Wolf's orders to the men. The stench of death still clings to Wren's skin. The memories of sightless eyes and wide, bloody smiles torment Wren's mind as the soldiers hurry through the camp to prepare for departure.

Wren pauses, standing completely still in the middle of the chaos. He closes his eyes, getting lost in the cacophony of whinnying horses, grumbling words, and stomping feet. In the midst of the noise, Wren holds his body still, forcing himself to remain calm.

The hours pass quickly, and a hand clutches Wren's shoulder. "Get moving," a gruff voice demands, but when

Wren's eyes open, he sees no one standing beside him. A lone tent flaps in the perpetual ocean wind. The rest of the men have already stowed their gear and begun marching the caravan away from the House of Piranhas. Those that aren't so fortunate to have a horse are running alongside, their steps as eerie as rolling thunder.

Alone again in a wasteland. How much longer can I bear it? Wren mumbles to himself, savoring the silence for a few heartbeats before turning away from his tent and hurrying after Wolf and his men.

***

Rosined bows slither across their instruments as the king's players perform their sultry, mysterious tunes. A single bright light shines in the empty space at the heart of the room. All the court tables line the walls like they are purposefully skulking in the shadows, hiding the debauchery of their guests in the thin veil of darkness.

A mixed blessing, Helena thinks to herself as she stalks toward Alaric's seat, grateful not to see the horde of people that are certain to be watching her entrance. *I don't have to witness the court's depravity, but I cannot see if any of them are preparing to attack me.* A well thrown dagger or a precisely shot arrow could easily kill her before Helena can react. And Helena has no doubt that a few of the court nobles must be itching to bring her down. *Is this purposeful, Alaric? Are you giving your men a fair chance to kill me?* Helena wonders as she carefully inspects the darkness, searching for any sign of metal glinting in the low light. *Or did you set up your feast like this just to make me feel fear?*

A few bawdy laughs and outraged cries break through the music. *There will be more than a few unlucky kitchen maids covered in purplish bruises by the end of the night.* Helena's face betrays none of her pity as she stands beside Alaric's seat, trying not to sigh at his late arrival to his own feast.

"The king sure likes to make an entrance, doesn't he?" Andras's rough, rumbling voice whispers in Helena's ear.

Startled, Helena struggles to maintain her composure,

her heartbeat thumping wildly like the hooves of stampeding horses. "H...He's always been like that," Helena stammers, some inner part of her core trembling so forcefully that her voice wavers.

"I've noticed," Andras mutters, the corner of his mouth crooking into a tiny smile, surprised to see Helena so easily flustered. "He's been late to every one of these parties when I've been invited. Then whatever musicians he's found for the night stop playing, and the king makes his grand entrance. Between you and me, I think he just likes the control."

"I think you're right," Helena agrees, shocked that she'd never seen the pattern. Over the years, Helena had grown up wondering why Alaric would choose such a unique way to make his entrance into a room. Where most of the leaders she'd read about in the histories had music or an announcement of their arrival, Alaric had chosen utter silence. He expected everyone to stand completely motionless and silent. Alaric was to be the only person moving or making any kind of noise. If anyone so much as sneezed, he or she would find themselves thrown into the viper pit before they could see the next sunrise. There were no exceptions to this rule; Alaric had even killed one of his own sons just for interrupting his grand entrance to a feast. The boy was only six years old.

Now, hearing Andras's assessment, Helena wonders why she'd missed it. Alaric's late arrival to the palace was packed with people to bend to his will. The way he'd drag his feet and extend the entrance for as long as possible. It wasn't a dramatic effect; Alaric was reveling in the control he had over his subjects. He thrived on watching them grow uncomfortable with their silence. He relished the way their eyes pleaded for him to speed up his movements, sneering at the court guests like they were caged animals in his personal menagerie.

"What's the entertainment this evening? Do you know?" Andras asks, breaking into Helena's revelation as he steps over to stand casually behind the chair at her right hand. "Probably something grotesque or terrifying. Your father isn't satisfied until his guests are traumatized."

"And here I thought you were devoutly faithful to the king. You better be careful; it sounds like you don't approve of Alaric's antics," Helena retorts, cutting her eyes to watch Andras's expression.

"I am loyal to myself. I tolerate your father," Alaric replies in a soft, fury filled whisper.

Helena smiles, sensing that she's regained some measure of control over the conversation. "And is it this dissenting attitude of yours that got you into trouble?"

Andras's jaw clenches, his fingers digging into the wooden back of the chair. "We only met this afternoon, Helena. Don't assume you know me."

"Nor do you know me," Helena quips, quietly watching Andras's silent battle against his own temper. *Interesting,* Helena declares, curious to know more about Andras's loyalties. *Maybe he's more of an ally than I first believed.* "You know, Andras, if—"

"Hush, the music's stopped," Andras interjects, standing proudly behind his chair as he waits for the king to appear.

A tense hush descends, and Helena grits her teeth to keep from shattering the quiet by screaming. Her eyes dart from left to right, scanning for any sign of Alaric's approach, longing desperately to move her head. As the minutes pass with no sign of Alaric, every ache in Helena's muscles magnifies, each one screaming at her, demanding to move. Nerves fire off at random places on her body, her skin itching so torturously she fears she'll be the one who ends up getting thrown into the viper pit tonight. *It would almost be worth it,* Helena thinks as her nose, left eyelid, and chin all beg for a relieving scratch.

Ten agonizingly painful minutes later, Helena catches her first glimpse of Alaric. *He's barely halfway through the room.* She suppresses a groan, willing the king to move faster. *I feel like a flea ridden dog,* Helena grumbles to herself, longing to move her aching feet or scratch her upper lip. Anything to bring some measure of comfort.

A soft whimper bursts through the silence as Alaric

continues his painstakingly slow pace. He pauses, turning his head to stare into the eyes of the young woman who made the sound. By Helena's estimation, she looks to be barely fifteen. Her wide eyes and slightly aghast expression make it clear that she had no intention of breaking the silence. Offering her an icy smile, the king nods his head once, then continues on his procession. Yet his seemingly gracious reaction sends a shiver down Helena's spine. *That little cry signed your death warrant,* Helena laments, wishing there was something she could do to protect the young woman.

Another twenty minutes later, and Helena finally wheezes a sigh of relief when Alaric announces, "Please be seated." She picks at her skin, chasing the travelling itch down her knees and ankles, up her wrists, forearms, and shoulders, and around her lips, nose, forehead, and mouth. By the time she's done, most of her skin is splotchy and covered in thin pink streaks from her fingernails. But at least it no longer feels like it's crawling.

"Really, Helena, you look like one of the alley rat guttersnipes in withdrawal," Alaric muses, glancing at Helena's now disheveled hair. "I thought you would present yourself better. Like it or not, you are my daughter, and I expect you to represent my name well. It reflects on me."

"Surely, the fact that you locked me away in the dungeons reflects on you too, Alaric. If I have bad manners, blame it on the habits I've learned from your guards," Helena snipes, glaring at Alaric as she challenges him.

"I've been merciful," Alaric laughs, waving his hand to alert the servers that the first course should be served. "You're alive and free. That's more than any other traitor to my kingdom can say."

Before Helena can respond, one of the servants places the first plate in front of her. It is small, holding a single clear orb. Inside the jelly-like substance is a lifeless baby viper. "You seriously expect us all to eat snake eggs, Alaric?" Helena exclaims, pushing the plate away from her as she struggles not to gag.

"The brood has too many already," the king replies, picking up his knife as he prepares to cut into the egg. "Besides, it is considered a delicacy, Helena. A treat for all my subjects, wouldn't you say?"

Who decides what foods are delicacies? Whoever picked out this gem should be hanged. Helena scoffs, fighting to control her breathing and staring over the table at the empty place on the floor. She tries to distract her mind from the sounds of strangled gasps and scraping utensils as the guests grapple with their first course. Closing her eyes, Helena lets her mind drift on the breeze, focusing on nothing more than her own gratitude that by tomorrow she'll be far away from this place.

Alaric's icy hand brushes her wrist, startling Helena back to reality. "My menu is not good enough for you, daughter?" He growls, staring at the uneaten viper egg on her plate.

"Does refusing to palate your meals earn me another prison sentence? If so, I'll find my way to the dungeon," Helena bites back, refusing to meet the king's eye.

"Weak stomach? I'm surprised to hear that. It seems the guards in my dungeons haven't been doing enough to toughen up my prisoners, hmm? I'll remedy that tomorrow," Alaric explains, patting her arm lightly. "I'm sure Ithel will be so thankful for the changes I'll be making."

Helena stifles a groan, turning her head as far to the side as she can, utterly disgusted by the king's cruelty. *I'm so sorry, Ithel,* she laments, wishing she could speak to the man face to face. *I'm not even there with you, and I'm still causing you trouble.*

"You okay?" Andras wonders, his face looking a little green as he notices Helena's distress. Helena nods, unable to speak out of fear she'll say something that will only bring her more trouble.

"Are you ready for our entertainment then, dear?" Alaric asks, smiling too widely for Helena's comfort. "I planned it all especially for you."

Of course, you did, you bastard. Helena bites her tongue,

turning back to face the king. "What did you do?" Helena whimpers, clenching her fists under the table. The sharp bite of her fingernails into her palms helps Helena keep her expression neutral. *Show signs of weakness, and Alaric will invent new ways to display his nastiness, just to wriggle deeper under my skin.*

"I've set up a competition of sorts," Alaric explains, standing up to get the attention of the entire room. "You know how much I adore a good fight. Bring up the first contestants," Alaric commands, pointing toward the door on the far-right side of the room.

The heavy doors swing open, and six of Alaric's heavily armed men march through. Helena watches them stomp through the room, nervously assessing their faces. Not finding Ithel among their ranks brings a small measure of comfort, yet Helena still feels anxiety clinging to her bones. *What has Alaric done?* she wonders, casting a wary glance at the king.

The six guards suddenly stop their entry, turning to face the crowds huddled around the tables. One of the men steps out of the ranks, working his way around the tables until he finds his prey. Yanking a young woman out of her seat, he drags her along behind him despite the protests of her friends and family. Whispered worries and angry, rioting shouts fill the air as the company makes their way to the empty space in the room. The guards form a circle boundary, pushing the frightened girl into its center.

"What is your name?" Alaric asks, offering the girl the same terrifying grin he had when she whimpered during his grand entrance.

"P...P...P...please, sire, I didn't mean to disrespect you," the girl whines, wringing her hands as she cries. Recognizing her anxious habit, she drops her hands to her sides, her fingers immediately curling into the soft green fabric of her skirt. "I've been sick, sire, and my throat was tickling. I had to cough; I couldn't help it. Please don't—"

"Your name," Alaric growls, motioning to the guards so they draw their swords.

"Remy," the girl whispers, sniffling and wiping her nose on her sleeve. Behind her, a man and woman stand in the aisle, clinging to each other as they grieve, already mourning the loss of their child.

Helena pinches the fleshy area between her thumb and first finger, digging her nails into her flesh to keep from crying. *My tears would do them no good*, she justifies, staring coldly at the young girl while she waits to hear what Alaric has in store for the poor wretch.

"And where is the challenger?" Alaric spreads his arms wide, pointing to the hidden door where the servants slip down to the kitchens. Four more guards appear, dragging a young maid through the doorway. Judging by her rumpled hair, tousled clothes, and hoarse screams, she's been putting up quite a fight. The guards unceremoniously toss the girl into the ring, jumping out of her way just in case she spins around to attack them.

"Amie," Helena whispers the servant girl's name, her hands beginning to shake as her fingernails draw blood.

"What's that, Helena?" Alaric whispers, fighting to hide his smile.

"Nothing," Helena snaps, staring straight ahead as her heart breaks for both girls.

"There are five rounds in all," Alaric explains to the crowd, rubbing his hands together as he lays out his plans. "The last four rounds will require the contestants to fight to decide who will live and who will die. However, for this first round, I wanted to do something special." Alaric turns, lowering his hands to point to Helena with a winning smile, and a wicked, traitorous fire in his eyes. "As you all know, I am celebrating the return of my wayward daughter. After a few years in the dungeons, she has seen the errors of her old life and regained my good graces. So, to honor her, I will offer her the choice."

Helena hesitates, staring at the young girls who cower in front of the crowds. "I don't understand, Your Highness." Helena works to keep from rolling her eyes as she uses the king's title to show respect. "What exactly is my choice here?"

"Which one will die, of course!" Alaric exclaims with a light, airy laugh, clapping his hands together a couple times. Then he leans down low, his voice falling to a ruthless, terrible whisper in her ear. "Doesn't it feel good to know you hold their lives in your hands? Doesn't it make you feel powerful, knowing you will decide their fates? We are gods among feeble ants, Helena. It's time you start living up to your legacy."

"I won't do this," Helena snaps, balling up her fists as she prepares to attack the king. She glances at the table, searching for the knife in her place setting. The dulled edge looks like it could barely break the skin of a tomato. Looking back at Alaric's smug face, Helena decries, "This is barbaric, Alaric. I won't sentence either of these girls to death."

"Then I'll bring Ithel out here, and you'll watch him die instead," Alaric shoots back, offering her a dangerous smile. "Will my brood of vipers be dining on one of these lovely ladies for their first course? Or should I send my guards —?"

"You are evil," Helena hisses, lurching away from Alaric's nearness.

"And you love too deeply," Alaric replies, leaning over to whisper in her ear. "Don't you see, Helena? You're in this mess because you care too much. I can control you, string you along like a puppet, and manipulate you all because of your feelings. If you really want to be free of me, then let me kill Ithel. Get rid of love, and you'll find true liberty. Otherwise, I'll always hold the winning hand."

Could I do it? Could I watch Ithel die after all he's done to help me? Helena asks herself even while she tries to find a way out of this mess that keeps everyone alive. "I will fight in Amie's place," Helena counters, whispering low so none but the king can hear her proposal.

"Tempting," Alaric muses, tapping his chin as he feigns to mull over her idea. "But no. I've already got my plans for you. Choose now, Helena. Or I'll send for Ithel."

"Damn you," Helena wheezes, quickly assessing each

girl in the ring to make her choice. *The girl from the crowd is soft,* Helena declares, staring at her fleshy, undefined shoulder muscles and dainty hands. *She's probably never had to do a hard day's work in her life. She'll never survive a fight, especially in such a flowing skirt. At least Amie is strong — all those days kneading bread, lifting heavy pans, and mixing large bowls of ingredients have toughened her. She stands the best chance.* "I'm sorry...," Helena begins, cutting off her apology when Alaric's icy hand grips her shoulder. "Amie will stay in the ring and fight." Helena's lip trembles, her back going rigid even as a shiver snakes up her spine. "I choose Remy to die."

"So be it," Alaric agrees, waving to the guards to pull Remy out of the ring. Her parents wail as they watch their daughter being led over to the side of the hall where the viper pit waits. Tears flow freely down Remy's face, her knees giving way as fear overpowers her senses. One of the guards picks up her limp form, carrying her to the edge of the pit.

"She paid you a kindness," the guard whispers, gently setting Remy on the floor. "You'd have died a far more painful death in the ring. The vipers will make quick work of it."

"Surely a real kindness would have been to speak out against this madness," Remy accuses, facing the guard in a last, rallying defiance. Leaning around the guard, Remy shouts through the hall accusingly. "Why did you rejoin your father, Helena? Why do you no longer stand against him? He's just a bully with a crown! When you defied him, you gave the rest of us hope. You stirred rebellion in our hearts, and now by returning to his side, you are condemning us all. You are a coward, Helena!" Before the guards quell her words, Remy faces the viper pit, exclaiming. "I will not be pushed into this death just to be silenced. I will not cower as I face my demise." Remy's mother wails, her hands reaching as she watches her daughter leap into the viper pit, spreading her arms wide as if she was freefalling into a river.

The snakes in the darkness hiss and slither as they coil around their prey. Within a few agonizing heartbeats, the sounds cease. Helena trembles, her face pale as she clings to the edge of the table to keep herself upright.

"You failed," Alaric coos, echoing the words already rumbling through Helena's heart. "You still chose your heart over your freedom. I still own you, my daughter. Not that I'm really complaining, but I do wonder if you'll ever learn." Waving his hand, Alaric sends for the next contestant who will fight against Amie.

He's a swarthy, rangy looking man, and judging by his filthy appearance, he's been locked away in Alaric's prisons for a long time. "Give her a weapon," Helena pleads with the king as the man advances on Amie with a wicked grin that exposes his rotting teeth.

"Now that wouldn't make it a fair fight," Alaric replies, clicking his tongue as if he were a teacher admonishing a wayward pupil. "If she wants to be the champion, she must earn it just like anyone else."

The grimy prisoner snaps Amie's neck within five minutes after he steps into the ring. *She never stood a chance either, did she?* Helena laments, biting hard into her lip to keep from wailing. Amie's body falls between two of the guards; without any spoken command, they pick her up and drag her over to the viper pit.

"A winner!" Alaric announces, heedless to the soft cries from the spectators surrounding their tables. "Tell us your name, champion."

"Thayer," the prisoner barks, his voice gruff from years of shouting in the dank cells of the dungeon.

"Enjoy a moment's rest, Thayer. Then we'll send in your next opponent," Alaric replies, waving his hands at the crowd, urging them to cheer.

Helena doesn't notice any of Alaric's antics; her eyes are transfixed on Amie's broken body. She gasps as she watches Amie disappear over the rim of the viper pit, joining Remy in her serpentine bed. *My fault,* she whimpers, wishing Amie was still alive to hear her apology. *I put you in danger just by being in proximity to you. I'm so sorry, Amie.*

Helena faces Andras, determined not to witness another moment of this disgusting display. Until Alaric's long fingers clutch her chin, straining her neck as he pulls her face back toward the ring. "You will want to see who is crowned the victor, Helena. You are the prize, after all," the king sneers, relishing the way Helena's skin grows cold and clammy under his touch. "Don't you want to see who wins an evening as your special guest?"

A new competitor appears, this one making Thayer look like a clean, prim member of Alaric's court. Nauseous waves roil through Helena's stomach as she watches the fight, unable to decide which of the horrible men she could possibly hope will win. In the end, the new competitor reigns supreme when he bites Thayer's neck, chewing through skin and sinew despite the blood spraying from the wound.

One *more, then the one that really matters.* Helena counts through the rounds as she tries not to vomit at the grisly scene. She covers her ears with her hands, hoping to drown out Thayer's gurgling whimpers as his breathing fades. Time slows, each second grueling and prolonged, as if Thayer has somehow bent the rules of the hours just to prolong his own life. The minutes feel like hours, and Helena twitches in her seat, longing to get away from the sight. The breeze stirs around her as if it can hear her desperate pleas.

I could do it, she decides, subtly twitching her fingers to strengthen the breeze. *I could drift out of this place and just disappear into the night. It would be so easy.* Helena eases back her chair, widening the gap between her body and the table just enough that she can stand comfortably. *When the next fight begins, I will escape,* she declares, checking the surroundings for any open door or window she could slip through on the wind. The doorway to the kitchens catches Helena's eye. A few of the maids have propped it open to peek through the cracks. *Perfect,* Helena nearly hollers out loud, silently urging the next fighter to provide a distraction for her plans.

Then a sharp, blinding pain erupts between her wrist bones. "Still trying to leave me, hmm?" Alaric mocks, crushing a tiny iron nail deeper into her arm. The tip of the nail pierces her flesh, the metal burning through her blood with a sickening sizzle. "I've only driven the nail a few millimeters into your arm, Helena. I realize that's enough to keep you in your place. But try anything else, and I'll nail you to the chair just because I can," Alaric warns, holding a large, heavy mallet close to Helena's arm.

Helena shudders but does not move, sobbing softly as she turns her attention back to the fighting ring. Thayer has already been removed from the scene. The prisoner who's just defeated Thayer waves, offering her an exaggerated kiss and a wicked smile. Helena's face grows cold, sweat beading on her forehead as her injured wrist begins to throb.

"I open the challenge to the guards in the ring. Surely one of you would risk the fight for a night with my daughter," Alaric announces, waiting to see if any of his men would dare to take on the goliath standing before them.

Thayer's blood still drips down the monster's chin. He paces around the ring like an animal in a cage, challenging each guard by his growls. The prisoner spits on some of the guards' shoes, offering them a bloody smile to try and rile their anger.

One of the guards takes up the challenge and steps out of the circle, ripping off his helmet to expose his bald head. He sneers in Helena's direction, wagging his eyebrows as he asks, "Remember me, darling?"

The guard who used to watch me bathe in my cell, Helena recalls, a soft whine escaping her tightly controlled mouth. Helena grips her chair's armrests, hissing as the tension aggravates the damage Alaric's already done to her wrist.

"Seems you left quite an impression on old Grimshaw," Alaric muses, grinning widely as he waves the guard forward. "Very well, Commander. Best of luck to you; I'm sure Helena will be rooting for you as well." Alaric grins as Grimshaw's bawdy laughter ricochets off the stone walls, growing louder and more maniacal with each echo.

"He can't win," Helena pleads to anyone who might be listening, not allowing her mind to wander down the dark possibilities of what would happen if she had to spend a night with this man.

Her stomach drops as the prisoner and Grimshaw face off against one another. Evenly matched in stature, the men in the circle slowly pace around each other, searching for any signs of weakness or vulnerability. The prisoner wipes Thayer's blood from his chin, flicking the dark, congealing stickiness at his opponent.

Some of the droplets splatter against Grimshaw's ratty uniform. The guard glances at the stains, unperturbed by the prisoner's efforts to intimidate. "All that blood will soon be replaced by your own, you dog," Grimshaw exclaims, lashing out with his fists aimed at the prisoner's chin.

The prisoner sidesteps the blow easily, skittering over to the opposite side of the ring. On and on, they dance around each other, twirling in their furious waltz for what feels like hours. Helena's mind wanders far from her body as she offers silent prayers to any of the forgotten deities she read about in her childhood studies. When the crowd's roaring grows louder, she returns her attention to the fight, only to discover that the men are still clawing away at each other in search of victory.

Andras taps her unhurt arm, whispering low in her ear, "It's almost over now. The prisoner's getting tired. He'll make a careless mistake, and Grimshaw will take him down."

"No, no, please no," Helena mumbles under her breath, turning her head just in time to see the prisoner's protective fist droop down from beside his chin. Grimshaw wastes no time, plowing his fist into the prisoner's face. Blood spews from the prisoner's mouth, his eyes rolling back in his head as he drops to the floor.

"One more, my lovely," Grimshaw taunts, making vulgar gestures at Helena as he dances triumphantly around the ring. "One more, and then you're mine!"

Helena's shoulders quake as if she's sitting outside wearing a thin dress in the dead of winter. She clenches her eyes tight, fighting in vain to keep her breathing steady. Her frayed nerves cause every noise to be magnified; even the slightest scratch of a fork on a plate sets her teeth on edge and causes her to flinch.

"Helena, you have one final chance," Alaric whispers in her ear, the warmth of his breath making Helena's skin crawl. "Ask me to send Ithel in the ring. Tell me you are willing to let him die, and I will ensure that Grimshaw doesn't get his reward."

Helena hesitates long enough to keep herself from screaming an agreement to the king's request. *Think,* she demands, keeping her eyes focused on the wood grain of the table. *There's got to be a way out of this.* She traces the patterns under her fingertips while she crafts her reply. *I can't put Ithel in the ring, not after everything he's done to help me. His training made me strong, though; I can take the risk myself.* "I fought once to win my freedom, and I'm willing to do it again," Helena declares, offering Alaric a forced smile. "Put me in the ring against Grimshaw."

"We've been over this, Helena. I will not allow you to fight. How could you expect me to risk losing my only daughter?" Alaric mocks, placing a hand over his heart as if her words pierced his chest like knives. "I couldn't bear to face such a future, my dear. Besides, you're the prize, remember? If you died in the fight, what would Grimshaw win?"

"Then let me fight for her," Andras pipes up, rising from his seat at the table. "I'll take my chances against the guard."

"You're already facing many months with Helena. Why would you strive to earn one night more with her?" Alaric wonders, tapping his chin as he immediately grows suspicious. "Unless you've already formed some romantic attachment to her? Oh, darling daughter, has your heart already turned to another one of my guards?"

"Hardly," Andras snorts, leaning his arms against the

back of his chair. "However, if I save your daughter from facing Grimshaw now, I'll have a bargaining chip I can use later on in our travels. Starting out ahead against such a formidable woman is surely a good idea, wouldn't you say?"

"Hmm, it remains to be seen," Alaric mumbles, not quite convinced. "Very well, Andras. You may fight in the final battle."

The guard dips his head in the king's direction, immediately striding down the platform toward the fighting circle. There is no announcement or splendor in this final battle. Alaric stays silent behind his throne, stoically watching the scene. The rest of the crowds hush their tense mumblings, all eyes turning to Andras in curious wonder.

All expression fades from his features as he moves, stalking toward his prey with predatory grace. He assesses Grimshaw coldly, his hands steady by his side.

"Make a move," Alaric whispers, his voice betraying no signs of fear or panic.

Grimshaw stands still, his face turning pale, all thoughts of the king's contest fleeting from his mind as he pleads, "I have no quarrel with you, Andras."

"Yet I have one with you, Grimshaw," Andras sneers, taking a step closer to his quarry.

Grimshaw holds his hands up, immediately taking a step back. "Hey, I didn't realize the bit — Uh, the lady — was yours."

"She's not," Andras responds, shifting his weight onto the balls of his feet as if he's expecting to run. "But I don't like men who torment women the way you do, Grimshaw. You give us all a bad name when you instill fear in their hearts. She was prepared to fight you herself. I don't know if she'd have won." Andras pauses, his voice dropping low in timbre as he growls, "But I know I will."

Grimshaw whines softly and retreats until his back makes contact with one of the guards surrounding the fighting ring. "Please, Andras. You have my word; I won't bother the lady again."

"I know. And you'll apologize to her right before I cut out your tongue," Andras explains, unsheathing a small blade from the sheath at his waist. "And as your mouth fills with blood and you writhe in pain, I think I'll drop you over into the viper pit while you're still able to experience their attack. I'm sure the snakes enjoy living prey."

Grimshaw grabs for one of the other guards' swords, determined to face Andras with a weapon of his own. He charges Andras, screaming and yowling like a wild beast as he strikes.

Andras keeps himself still until the last possible moment. Then, right before Grimshaw can plunge his blade into Andras's chest, he lunges out of reach. The forward momentum upsets Grimshaw's balance, sending him down onto the stone floor. At an unnaturally fast speed, Andras appears behind Grimshaw and grips his head by his hair. "Now then, I believe you owe Helena an apology."

Grimshaw sneers, defiance roaring to life in his blood as he faces down his own demise. "I'll never say I'm sorry to that bitch. I enjoyed every minute I had with her in those cells. So, you might as well drag that knife across my throat."

Andras smacks Grimshaw hard across his shoulder blades. The force of the strike is enough to leave Grimshaw gasping for breath. Andras lithely winds his way around in front of Grimshaw, immediately pinching the ailing man's tongue. "I'm sorry, Helena," Andras calls over his shoulder as Grimshaw struggles in vain to get away from his captor's grasp. "I'm afraid you'll never hear this man show any signs of remorse for the way he's treated you. Yet you can take comfort in the fact that you'll never hear anything at all from him again."

Guttural, desperate shrieks ricochet through the hall as Andras slices through Grimshaw's tongue. Blood splatters across the floor, and a dull thud radiates through the room as Andras drops the useless muscle onto the ground. Grimshaw falls to the floor, both hands hovering over his mouth as tears and gore stream down his face. Andras says nothing more as he grasps Grimshaw's leg and drags him over to the viper pit. No triumphant words, no explanations or signs of regret for his gruesome actions. Andras simply pulls Grimshaw over to the viper pit and kicks him over the edge.

For a brief moment, Grimshaw's terrified, unintelligible screams pierce the stunned silence of the crowd. Andras strides away from the pit's edge, moving as calmly as if he doesn't hear the sounds of Grimshaw's demise. He stalks back to the platform where Helena sits pinned in her chair, and by the time he reaches his seat, Grimshaw is dead. The air brims with raw emotion as the king's guests whisper in hushed, frightened tones.

"Well, it seems we have a winner," Alaric stammers, feebly attempting to turn the attention of the crowd back to himself. Clenching his jaw when no one celebrates the victory, the king barks orders to the guards. "Clean up this mess and send the guests home."

One of the men raises his hand, protesting, "But the feast has barely begun—"

Alaric lashes out at the man, kicking his legs out from under him. The poor guard sprawls across the stones under Alaric's feet as the king stands dangerously close to his fingers. His heel grinds into the stone as if he's imagining what it would feel like to crush the guard's fingers under his boot. "I don't care. I want this room cleared out right now. Is that a problem with you?"

Trembling, the poor man shakes his head, skittering away from the king. Alaric turns back to where Andras and Helena sit. The king's mouth tightens into a furious, straight line as he stares at his guard.

Seemingly unperturbed by the king's irritated expression, Andras turns to Helena and winks. "Don't look so worried, Helena," Andras whispers, turning away from Alaric completely, just to prove he's not afraid of the king.

"He's going to kill you," Helena hisses, watching Alaric's face redden at the outright insult from his guard.

"He won't; trust me," Andras whispers, leaning back to put his feet on the table. "Why don't you get over here and remove the spike from Helena's hand? There was no reason for that nonsense."

Helena gasps, eyes wide as she holds her breath and waits for Alaric's response.

"Remember who you're talking to, Andras," the king growls, his hands gripping the sword hilt at his waist.

"I could say the same thing to you, Alaric," Andras replies, putting his hands behind his head as he reclines. He looks like someone who's just eaten a huge meal and is settling down for a long, lazy nap. Not at all like a lowly guard who's just insulted his king.

"I'm glad to be getting rid of you for a while," Alaric grumbles, but to Helena's astonishment, he does not reprimand Andras further. Instead, he waves his hand, and the spike he'd driven into Helena's hand disappears. "It was an illusion, Helena. The spike was never actually in your skin." Without another word, the king stalks out of the room, slamming the door behind him.

Helena raises her hand, marveling at the sudden change. All the agony she'd been feeling disappears as she stares at her unblemished skin. "I...I don't understand," she admits, waiting impatiently for Andras to explain.

"An illusion is when the mind is tricked into—"

"No, smart ass," Helena interjects, struggling against the sudden urge to slap Andras in the back of the head. "I meant I don't understand how you're still alive. If anyone else had talked to Alaric the way you just did, they'd have found themselves in the viper pit before they could take another breath. So why didn't the king kill you?"

"Fear," Andras replies with a shrug, staring at the bloodstains on the stone floor.

"Alaric isn't afraid of anything. Believe me, I've been searching for a weakness I could exploit for years," Helena contradicts, trying to keep her eyes away from Grimshaw's bloody tongue that the guards neglected to clear off. The muscle occasionally twitches as it dies, giving Helena the eerie feeling that Grimshaw is still trying to speak. Still desperately screaming, begging someone to save him. Helena shivers, turning her attention to Andras once more as she waits for his reply.

"Alaric's big weakness is so obvious I'm surprised you never saw it. He's afraid of dying, Helena," Andras announces, his tone mimicking one of a teacher patronizingly explaining something easy to his pupil. "And since I am his most successful assassin, it gives me an edge, wouldn't you say?" Before Helena can respond, Andras continues. "Oh, don't get me wrong, Alaric punishes me frequently for my indecorous attitude. He sends me on long journeys away from Déchets as a way of 'cooling me off and making me grateful.' At least that's the way he sees it. So, any time I want to get away from the palace, I just flagrantly insult him. And he tolerates it because he knows that if I chose to use my skills on him, he'd be dead before sunrise."

"Then why don't you?" Helena demands, eagerly sketching out a half-baked plan. "You could slit his throat tonight, then travel with me before sunrise as planned. By the time Alaric is discovered, we'd be well away—"

"No. I've thought it over for years, believe me. But keeping Alaric alive is better than killing him and watching someone worse ascend to his throne. At least with this devil, we know what to expect." Alaric smirks, reaching for a half-filled wine glass still standing on the table. He downs it quickly and adds, "Besides all that, Alaric pays me well, and he's afraid of me. I've got a good thing going here; why would I give it up?"

"Ithel was so wrong about you," Helena wheezes, all the fight leaving her as quickly as it had been stirred. "He told me you were a quiet, decent man. But he was wrong; you are just as bad as Alaric."

"Hey, I do what I can to discreetly help the people," Andras replies, slamming the wine glass on the table with enough force that it cracks at the stem and shatters.

"The best way to help these people is to kill the king. Start a revolution. Do something to make them wake up and realize they are oppressed, stifled under the thumb of a wealthy bully. That would be far more useful than playing along with the king's plans."

"What do you know about it? You've been in prison for years. You've stood all high and mighty on your principles, happily locked away where you couldn't actually do anything useful for these people to whom you claim such loyalty. You've been languishing in a cell. I may have dirty hands, Helena, but at least I've been doing something," Andras growls, leaning against a chair as the alcohol begins to affect his balance. "Now go get some sleep. We've got a long journey ahead of us."

"Fine," Helena huffs, floating away on the breeze before she can do anything rash. Her hands itch to go back and slap the smile off Andras's face. However, provoking the assassin she'll be travelling with hardly seems like a wise decision. *And he did just save me from Grimshaw,* Helena remembers, sighing to herself as she drifts toward her room in the infirmary. "Why does everything have to be so complicated?" she cries, wishing she could curl up in Ithel's arms and forget the events of this night.

CHAPTER 13

"Come on, Iris! Join the party," Grouse hounds me, grabbing hold of my arm and endeavoring to lift me off the ground. "Cyrus and Goldeneye want to dance again. Let's go!"

"You go ahead," I reply, refusing to move an inch. "We've been partying for at least two hours. I need a break from all the noise."

Once word spread through the ranks that Cyrus and I were officially coupled, the spirit amongst the Cadogans and Ddraigs lifted. Then Drake pulled out a few nomadic flutes carved from thick tree branches. Within minutes, the entirety of our crew was laughing and dancing, twirling around the campfires without any signs of worries or fears.

But my heart is no longer invested in the party. After about an hour, a burden like a heavy stone resettled on my shoulders. Nothing I did could restore my lighthearted joy. All I can do is sense the impending doom on the horizon, and I know I must act to stop it at all costs.

Grouse pouts but says nothing more as she scurries back over to Goldeneye's side, tugging on his arm and begging him to dance once more. Cyrus catches my eye, and I wave at him enthusiastically, offering up my brightest smile as my heart skips a beat. *I really do love him.* I recognize the sentiment with a soft sigh, wishing the knowledge of my feelings changed everything as much as Siri believed it would. *And it is because I love him that I must do what I can to protect him.*

Sensing my distress, Siri stomps up to stand beside me. "What's going on now, Iris?"

"I have to save him, Siri. The coupling bond brings us one step closer to the fulfillment of my visions."

"Not this; not tonight," Siri begs, but I do not listen to her pleas.

"And I've realized that in every vision I've seen that included death, Cyrus and I were together." Holding my breath, I struggle to quell the scream I can feel rising up in my blood. My stomach burns and aches so powerfully that I double over, putting my hands on my clammy forehead. "I love him, Siri. And it's because I love him that I will do what it takes to spare him from death. Even if that means leaving him behind. "

"You've decided to become Vibría then?" Siri asks, her tortured tone unable to mask the depths of her despair. "You're asking me to give up Suryc too. To leave behind all of the Ddraigs, to give up my place as their leader, to watch you walk into that wretched land — a place where I cannot follow. Do you see how unfair this is?"

"I don't like it any better than you do. From what you've told me, I'll be an abomination in the eyes of the Ddraigs. Exiled, hated, probably hunted by them. But if I am successful in bringing down the king and protecting everyone I love, won't it be worth the pain?" I wonder, leaning against Siri's warm scales, dropping my forehead down to rest on her side.

"You understand that this is permanent, right? There is no changing your mind and undoing the Vibría ritual," Siri stalls, searching for any weakness in my resolve, any argument that might persuade me to change my mind and forsake this whole scheme.

"I will not stand by and watch Cyrus die, Siri. What if the situation was reversed? What if you were facing a future where Suryc dies, and I asked you to let it happen? Would you honor my wishes?" I mutter as I stare into the flames of the fire, entranced by their swirling, writhing forms.

"You are asking me to live without Suryc now, which is just as bad," Siri explains, bowing her head as she speaks.

"If he and Cyrus truly love us, this change won't really matter, will it?" I ask, hoping my words are true.

"You don't know how extensive the alterations will be, Iris. Your power will magnify beyond the levels of all other Cadogans. Not to mention the changes that will happen to your body. I'm not saying you will cease to be human, but you will be dramatically different." Siri pauses, her voice lowering as she whispers, "And I don't even want to think about what I will become."

Siri's halting explanations leave me with a sense of foreboding. *She doesn't want to describe any of it in detail. What will I become? A monster?* "Siri—"

"You're forgetting the most important thing, Iris," Siri interrupts, smoke swirling around us as she sighs. "Cyrus hates the Vibría for what was done to him, remember? And you are willingly going to become the very thing he despises and fears most of all. Do you really think his feelings for you will be strong enough to endure a betrayal this deep?"

"It's not a betrayal, Siri."

"Isn't it? You know how he feels. Cyrus doesn't want you to become one of the Vibría. He wants to face the future by your side, and you are preparing to abandon him. He has made his wishes very clear, and it does not seem to matter to you." Siri claws at the dirt, raising her head to stare out over the tall grass.

"He will be angry, but Cyrus will—"

"He is haunted, Iris. He hides it well, and he has improved, but the horrors he has faced are still present in his mind. If you become Vibría, Cyrus will look at you and see a reminder of the monster that hurt him." Siri shakes her head, glancing up at the stars as she whispers, "If you do this, I fear you will lose him."

"And if I don't do this, he will die, Siri. So what choice do I really have?" I lament, my voice wavering as my body begins to shake. "Either way, our relationship is over before it's really begun. At least this way, I know he will be alive. He'll have a chance of finding happiness."

"He's happy now, but that doesn't seem to matter to you," Siri bites back, and I flinch at the sharpness of her tone. We sit in silence for a long while before Siri finally replies, "Let me go tell Suryc."

"No," I stop her, tears pouring down my cheeks. "If you tell him, Suryc will try to stop us. Or he'll tell Cyrus, and that will be even worse." My voice breaks as I choke on the sorrow in my soul. I know what I feel is a pittance to the sense of betrayal and hurt Cyrus will endure when he learns of what I've done. "Let's just do this and slip away in the night. Let the rest of them enjoy their party; they'll figure it all out soon enough."

Siri whimpers, dropping down until her chin rests on the ground. "I love you, Iris." Her soft, broken confession shatters my heart. "It's ironic, isn't it, that you who I love most will be the one to break my heart?"

"I love you too," I cry, wrapping my arms around her as best I can. "This isn't the end, Siri. We'll always have each other."

Siri lifts her neck, exposing the scales over her heart. Using her claws, she splits one scale, golden, ethereal blood oozing down her claws. "Hold out your hand, Iris," she commands, her expression grim. She presses her claw into my palm, piercing through my rough calluses with ease. Her blood mingles with mine, and immediately it feels as if my body is on fire. "Don't scream," Siri demands, carefully placing her claws around me like a protective cage.

I writhe in agony as my body burns. Time ceases to exist in my mind. Every second is a thousand years, with no end to my pain in sight. My thoughts shatter as my blood boils, and I convulse on the ground under Siri's claws.

In the shadows, I see a gleaming smile as Ekard approaches us. *So, you've become the abomination, hmm? I wondered how long it would take.* The crimson dragon slithers through the tall grass, his deep rumbling laugh causing the ground to shake. "I wasn't sure how much longer we could continue feeding you these false visions. It's been quite a drain on our powers."

"False visions?" Siri wheels to face Ekard, baring her teeth in a rage, "So you're to blame for all of this?"

"Healing powers," I question feebly, recalling the day when Ekard and Drake saved my life.

"Drake's gift, not mine. I'm the one who can toy with your visions. Didn't you know that the strongest Ddraigs can have special abilities too? Oh, I guess you wouldn't know that, would you—Siri doesn't have one," Ekard taunts, cackling in triumph. "But no matter. Once the rest of the Ddraigs find out that you are Vibría, they will disown you. I'll challenge Suryc, but with his beloved exiled, he won't be much of a fight. Then I will finally take control of the Ddraigs."

"All for power," I whimper through my clenched jaw, grinding my teeth so hard I worry that they will break.

"I have the nomads on my side. We have the numbers to fight. There's no reason we can't attack the border patrol station right now, but you've been too afraid to fight. You don't have the skills to win this war; I do. It's for the best interest of the Ddraigs that you just disappear," Ekard explains, looking smug as he towers over Siri.

"Don't hurt Suryc," Siri pleads, flexing her long claws as if she's fighting the urge to split open Ekard's neck. "He'll give up his right to rule as soon as he discovers—" Siri's voice fades in and out as her body begins to shift. Light appears overhead, flickering in time with her heartbeat. My body trembles, suddenly feeling as light as a leaf fluttering down to the earth on a gentle wind.

"The transformation is almost done," Ekard announces gleefully, slipping back into the shadows, calling over his shoulder. "I'll just go and inform Cyrus of your decision to become Vibría. It will give you both some time to adjust to your new forms."

All for nothing, I cry as my mind grows heavy and my

consciousness fades. *I became Vibría on the basis of a lie, betraying everyone I've loved in the process. It is cruel; I'm sorry, Siri,* I mumble, unable to keep myself awake.

A deafening roar bursts through the silence, overwhelming my senses until I curl up in a ball on the ground and cower. The light flashes so brightly that I must clench my eyes tight. "I love you, Iris," Siri cries as the light begins to fade.

"Siri!? Where are you?" I cry, temporarily blinded by the bright light.

"Oh, Iris." I hear Cyrus's broken voice somewhere in the dark expanse on my left side. "What have you done?"

End of Book 3

Don't miss Book 4, The Nameless, coming soon!

Maggie Claire is the author of House of Vultures, Pack of Wolves, and Attila the Hummer. When she is not writing, she is working in children's ministry or spoiling her two dogs and cat. She lives near Waco, TX.